THE GRENLING ABDUCTION

I0557998

Richard Dalglish

THE GRENLING ABDUCTION

DOUBLE DRAGON

A DOUBLE DRAGON PAPERBACK

© Copyright 2017
Richard Dalglish

The right of Richard Dalglish to be identified as author
of this work has been asserted in accordance with the
Copyright, Designs and Patents Act 1988

All Rights Reserved

No reproduction, copy or transmission of the publication
may be made without written permission. No paragraph
of this publication may be reproduced, copied or
transmitted save with the written permission of the
publisher, or in accordance with the provisions of the
Copyright Act 1956 (as amended).

Any person who does any unauthorised act in relation to
this publication may be liable to criminal prosecution
and civil claims for damages.

ISBN 978-1-78695-726-9

Double Dragon
is an imprint of
Fiction4All

Published 2022
Fiction4All
www.fiction4all.com

Cover Art by Deron Douglas

Chapter 1

Although Captain Jarn Theffig had lived in Skunnik for nearly a year, the city still seemed foreign to him. He had learned its streets and alleys and neighborhoods as well as any of the other Vothan Riders who had been assigned constabulary duty there, but when he rode along one of its boulevards or entered one of its peculiar districts, he often had a vague feeling of unease, as he did now. It was early in the morning, and he and a Vothan Rider named Braga were riding south down Zayet Street, one of the wide cobblestone avenues that ran north and south through central Skunnik. They were headed toward a disreputable part of the city known as the Bolt, where a crime had been reported. As they neared their destination, Jarn felt his heart beat a little faster.

He pushed all bothersome thoughts out of his mind and focused on the clip-clop sound of the two horses as they cantered along the cobblestones. The morning was pleasantly cool, and the near-cloudless sky promised a fine day. They turned right at Safflam Street and proceeded for two blocks before turning left onto Trink Street, another of Skunnik's main avenues. As they continued south, the buildings became less grand in style but still looked solid and stable. Jarn approved of plainness of building construction, but the contrast with the grandiose vistas of the northern part of the city was striking. On upper Zayet Street they had passed splendid inns and taverns built of graystone and pinkstone, and their large front doors, often painted blue or red or gold, were set well back from the street proper. Further south

5

the buildings were mostly wood, sometimes brick, and few were taller than three storeys.

They crossed Morsen Street and entered the Bolt, a warren of narrow unpaved streets that sometimes twisted and meandered and often ended abruptly, for no apparent reason that Jarn could see. The neighborhood consisted mostly of small two-storey wooden buildings crowded together like spectators at a hanging, but the Bolt was also home to some of the city's oldest structures. It was also home to most of Skunnik's least respectable denizens, and it seemed to Jarn as if he spent half his time there looking into crimes.

They turned a corner, and Jarn swore. The Yellowshirt named Kurff was standing at the mouth of the alley Jarn was looking for, a block away, as if he were waiting. Jarn slowed his horse to a walk and glanced at Braga.

"I see him," Braga said.

"Kurff," Jarn muttered. "Again."

"Third time in as many weeks."

"Don't remind me," Jarn replied.

They halted at the alley and dismounted. Kurff, who wore the bright yellow uniform of the Acrinite Guardsmen—known to all as "Yellowshirts"—looked up and nodded. Kurff was a half-foot shorter than Jarn but weighed as much or more. His short legs and stout torso reminded Jarn of a barrel set on two sticks. Long, stringy black hair hung in lank twists nearly to his shoulders, and his small, dark eyes stared out from a face that seemed fleshy and gaunt at the same time. Kurff raised a bushy eyebrow and gave Jarn a vague smile. "Saddlemaster Jarn."

"It's Captain Jarn now, Kurff," Jarn replied.

The Yellowshirt shrugged. "You're late to the festivities, Captain Jarn."

"We come when we're called," Jarn said. "We don't have secret sources of information."

Kurff frowned. "Implying that I do?"

"Are you implying that you don't?"

"When an Acrinite finds a dead body or evidence of any other crime, he's likely to come to the Guardsmen first," Kurff said. "You can't expect them to go running to you Voths."

"Why not? We're here to serve."

"Acrinites don't trust you."

"We've played fair with your people, Kurff. Probably better than you deserve."

"Could be I wouldn't argue with you," Kurff said. "But most Acrinites see the Voths—especially you Vothan Riders—as an occupying force."

"We're occupying nothing but our own land—which your Acrinite ancestors stole from us a thousand years ago, through lies and deceit."

Kurff snorted. "If *your* ancestors hadn't been off riding to every part of the known world and beyond, they might have noticed."

"That doesn't excuse theft."

"Leaving a fat coin purse in the middle of the street in a bad part of town doesn't excuse theft, either, it just makes it more likely."

"Never mind," Jarn said. "I want to have a look at the victim's body."

"Right this way, Captain Jarn," Kurff replied before heading into the alley.

"Braga, you stay here with the horses," Jarn said to his companion, and then he turned and followed Kurff

7

down the narrow alley, which ran between a tavern and a saddlery. Jarn entered a small yard behind the tavern and saw the dead man lying on his back. Two Yellowshirts were crouched over him. They looked up when Kurff and Jarn arrived.

"Captain Jarn would like to have a look at our victim," Kurff said to the two Yellowshirts.

The two nodded and moved away. Jarn approached the body and knelt down next to it. The victim wore tan leggings, a dark brown tunic, and black boots. He had short brown hair and a neatly trimmed beard. Dead brown eyes stared up from a face as pale as parchment, and the man's features seemed twisted, as if he had died from a bad fright.

Kurff approached and stood near the victim's feet.

"What have you got so far?" Jarn asked.

"Male, early middle years, looked to be fit before someone stole his life away."

"Any idea who he is?"

"Aye," Kurff replied.

Jarn looked up and glared at him. "Who?"

"Raff Salorian."

Jarn swore. "Reported missing nine days ago."

"Aye."

"Rebels."

"Aye."

"Bastards," Jarn muttered.

"Aye," Kurff said. Jarn stared at him, trying to decide if he was being sarcastic or serious, but the Yellowshirt's stolid face gave away nothing.

It was the usual practice of the major Acrinite rebel group to abduct Acrinites they considered collaborators, hold them for nine days, and then kill them and dump

8

their bodies somewhere in the city. Now and then, they murdered a Voth, but most crimes against the Voths were the work of lone assassins.

"There's a triangle on the sole of his right foot," Kurff said. He knelt down and pulled off the victim's right boot. "Have a look."

Jarn stood up and went to see. He knelt down again and rubbed his thumb over the small black triangle as Kurff held the victim's leg up. The mark seemed to be part of the man's skin, not like ink or dye. If the rebels' recent pattern of abductions and murders held, the victim's body would be drained of blood and missing its heart as well.

Kurff lowered the victim's leg, and Jarn stood up. "I have a litter coming," he said.

Kurff frowned. "Why?"

"To take the body back to headquarters."

"Why? What are you going to do with him?"

Jarn resisted the urge to tell the Yellowshirt it was none of his concern. "We have a mage who claims he can see into dead bodies. Maybe he can learn something about … something."

"Learn what?" Kurff snapped.

"I don't know," Jarn snapped back.

"This man deserves a proper burial, not a game of read my entrails conducted by some petty conjurer."

"He'll get a proper burial," Jarn said.

"Aye, with half his innards missing. I won't have you tampering with the dead, not unless it's your own dead."

"The mage won't tamper with his body," Jarn said, looking uncomfortable as he said it. "He can look … he claims he can look inside a corpse with some kind of second sight."

9

Kurff furrowed his brow and stared at Jarn. "I didn't think you believed in magery."

"Right now, I'm ready to try anything," Jarn said, an expression of unease still clouding his face.

"Do you trust this mage?" Kurff asked.

Jarn shrugged but said nothing.

"I thought not," Kurff said. "Nor do I."

"You don't even know who it is," Jarn said.

"I'll find out soon enough. I want to be present when your mage works his make-believe magic."

Jarn was considering his response when another Vothan Rider, a graybeard named Grion, arrived in the small yard.

"Did you bring the litter?" Jarn asked him.

"Yes, and a message," Grion said. "Line Commander Lahgoh wants you to return to headquarters now. He says it's important."

Jarn nodded. "You and Braga bring the victim on the litter." He turned to Kurff. "I'll let you know when the mage plans to do his … work."

"Thank you," Kurff said. It was the first time Jarn had heard the man utter that phrase.

"No other Yellowshirts or any other Acrinites," Jarn said. "Just you."

Kurff nodded his agreement, and Jarn left the alley.

Chapter 2

The sun had risen above the buildings of eastern Skunnik, but the air still had a bite as Jarn rode north on Trink Street. He was headed toward the Vothan Riders' provincial headquarters, a low, nondescript structure known as the Mang, located in Skunnik's wealthy northern end, the neighborhood called The Basket. The sturdy fortress was two blocks west of the Beldur Palace, the home and headquarters of the Acrinite Guardsman, and three blocks east of the Palace of the High Hext, which had been the home and headquarters of the former Acrinite leader. The Riders could have claimed the Beldur for themselves, but the Yellowshirts had occupied it for a thousand years, and the Riders had no wish to antagonize them further. Besides, occupying such an ostentatious pile of stone and brick would have been out of character for Vothan Riders, who preferred a building that more closely resembled their headquarters back in Rualgar, the capital of Vothan.

Jarn rode through a cross street and saw a shopkeeper in the next block emerge from his shop and begin setting up a stand, piling it with tunics, skirts, and *sashmeens*, the colorful ankle-length garments popular among the Acrinites. He had been meaning to buy one for Sanaja, but he knew he might not see her for months, so he put the thought out of his mind.

When Jarn drew near the shopkeeper, he nodded a greeting, but the man ignored him, which was no surprise. Acrinites bore little love for Vothan Riders. Jarn looked around and saw tavern owners, guildsmen, and other shopkeepers going about their business, some sweeping

11

away dust and debris from low stone porches fronting narrow two-story buildings, others setting up stands and displays. He glanced over his shoulder and then right and left as he passed another cross street. It occurred to him that he had rarely traveled alone in Skunnik. Although no one had officially decreed it, Riders and other Voths with business in the provincial capital, or anywhere else in Acrin, usually traveled in groups.

Jarn didn't think anyone would trouble him during daylight hours. Besides being known for their skill with weapons, the Vothan Riders had a well-deserved reputation for toughness, endurance, and fearlessness. In some quarters, they also had a reputation for violence and brutality, a notion they did little to dispel, even though it was mostly false. Nevertheless, Jarn remained wary. Staying on your guard was how you stayed alive anywhere in the known world.

The Mang finally came within sight, and Jarn turned right, traveling a few blocks before turning left and approaching a building that resembled nothing so much as a plain gray brick topped by a square tower at each corner and a double tower over the main entrance. He passed through a guarded gate in the wall that surrounded the squat fortress and proceeded to the stable, where a groom took his horse. He walked to the main entrance, climbed a stairway to the second floor, and continued to the office of Line Commander Lahgoh.

The door was open, and Jarn stepped into the small front room of Lahgoh's quarters. Sunlight streamed in through three tall, narrow windows arrayed along one wall. The windows extended from a foot above the floor nearly to the ceiling, illuminating the room without need of candles or torches. Lahgoh was sitting at a large oak

12

desk, poring over a map. He wore the familiar leather and brass raiment of a Vothan Rider, and a small insignia on his left shoulder identified his rank as line commander. He had short dark hair with a streak of silver running through it and a dark, neatly trimmed beard. A thin white scar ran from the corner of his left eye down to his beard. He was ten years older than Jarn, but people often took them for brothers.

Lahgoh looked up from the map and gestured for Jarn to take a seat opposite him. Jarn did, and Lahgoh pushed aside the map.

"You'll be wondering why I sent for you," Lahgoh said.

"Aye," Jarn replied. "If it's to give me an assignment away from Acrin, I can be packed and ready to leave in an hour."

Lahgoh gave him a crooked smile and nodded in appreciation of the jape—before shaking his head to reject the notion. "I do have another assignment for you and your men, but it's right here in Skunnik. You're to start immediately."

"I'm supposed to be present when that mage tries to peer inside our latest victim. I told Kurff he could witness it as well."

Lahgoh raised an eyebrow. "You're being kind to Kurff?"

"He raised a stink about giving the victim a proper burial, without defiling his body."

"I'm glad you and Kurff are working well together."

"We're not, and I don't trust him. It wouldn't surprise me if he's a rebel himself, maybe something worse."

Lahgoh shrugged. "The Yellowshirts don't trust us any more than we trust them. Nor do any other Acrinites

13

trust us or like us, excepting those who overcharge us for their weak ale and stale bread."

"Kurff said much the same."

"He isn't wrong. But I didn't summon you to engage in talk of politics—well, perhaps I did."

The light in the room dimmed slightly as a cloud passed across the morning sun. Both men glanced at the windows, as if waiting for the room to brighten again. Lahgoh stood up and went to a side table that held a pitcher of wine and six goblets. He poured wine into two of the goblets, set one on his desk, and handed the other to Jarn. "Vothan strong red," he announced before sitting down again. "None of that sour Acrinite piss."

Jarn nodded his thanks and took a long drink. Then he said, "You were about to tell me why you summoned me."

"We have a delicate situation on our hands," Lahgoh said. "As you know, the Brythyn Realm has long had various treaties and trade agreements with the Acrinites. Now that there is no longer an Acrinite Realm, the Brythyners want a treaty with us."

"I'd take care treating with the Brythyners," Jarn said. "Their pacts with the Acrinites did the Voths little benefit."

"True enough, but now that the Brythyn Realm is on our new border, a peace pact and a trade treaty are in our interest. We'll finally be able to sell Vothan goods to the Brythyners and buy goods from them at fair prices. As for the delicate situation I mentioned, it involves the Brythyn diplomat sent to Skunnik to negotiate the treaty."

"Skunnik? Why not send their man to Rualgar?"

"It's the Brythyners' way of showing their displeasure at the Voths' ascendancy, even as they deign to negotiate with us."

Jarn shook his head. "They're a haughty lot."

"Indeed. And you'll find Lord Grenling among the haughtiest. The Brythyners also want us to make some concessions to the Acrinites. They believe they deserve more self-rule."

"They're lucky we haven't thrown them all out."

"I doubt we could even if we wanted to. The Acrinites outnumber us, and they don't lack for friends."

"All this is for the diplomats to jaw over," Jarn said. "What's it to do with the Riders?"

"I was getting to that," Lahgoh said. "On their way here from Brythyn, somebody snatched Lord Grenling's daughter. She was supposed to marry one of the Acrinite nobility, a lord named Keddro. The marriage had been arranged more than a year ago but was put off because of the war and the other troubles. Lord Grenling is demanding that we find her and punish the culprits responsible for the outrage before he'll sign any treaty with us. Lord Keddro is even more adamant that we find his betrothed. He's let it be known that he thinks the Voths might be responsible."

"Is Lord Keddro a fool then?"

"Aye, and a loud one."

Jarn let out a long breath. "It may have been the rebels."

Lahgoh shook his head. "I don't know that the rebels or their sort would harm an ally of Acrin. I think it's more likely some brigands took the girl for ransom."

"Is Lord Grenling willing to pay a ransom, if it comes to that?" Jarn asked.

Lahgoh hesitated a moment before answering. "Lord Grenling wants us to find her. That's your new assignment."

"Have you sent out search parties?"

"More than a dozen. Both Riders and Yellowshirts are scouring the city and the surrounding countryside, but the search needs to be better organized. I also want suspected rebel locations in the city checked, and I want you to talk to the Grenlings and anyone else who may have information. Lord and Lady Grenling have taken quarters in the Palace of the High Hext. They're expecting you."

Jarn nodded and stood up. "I'll be off then."

"There's one more thing," said Lahgoh. "I may be able to get you some help in locating the girl."

"What kind of help? Not another mage, I hope?"

"You'll remember the woman named Astil."

Jarn stared at his superior officer as if he had grown another arm. "You must be japing."

"She has the very skill we need for this—for your—task."

Jarn sat back down. "She'd never help us, even supposing we could find her in time. And whoever does find her will likely get a bolt in the neck for his troubles."

"We know where she is," Lahgoh said. "A few months after she escaped from the prison in Wyndor City, we picked up her trail. We've been keeping a watch on her ever since. We could have seized her, but we thought it might be more profitable to observe her, see what she does and with whom she deals. Now that we have need of her, we'll bring her in. Luckily, she isn't far."

"She won't work for us."

16

"She might if we agree to grant her a pardon for her former crimes. Especially when she finds out how we tracked her down."

"How did you track her down?"

"We had help from another friend of yours."

Jarn stared at Lahgoh, as if trying to read his thoughts. The answer finally dawned. "Aarla?"

Lahgoh nodded.

"I thought she disappeared into some enchanted forest with her long-lost father."

"Not disappeared. It seems your Saddlemaster Bleuek and young Aarla have become close. She visited him from time to time back in Rualgar, before your company was sent to Skunnik. Young love, you know."

Jarn was stunned. "Did some virrling put me to sleep for a month? Is there anything else I've missed that I should know about?"

"If everything has gone according to plan, Bleuek and Aarla and a squadron of Riders should be bringing in Astil right about now. We'll know soon enough."

Chapter 3

The thief was a half mile in front of her, riding at a slow trot along a trail that wound through the forest southeast of Lake Poltek. Astil suspected he was making for the lake, where he could hide out for a while on one of its islands. Or he might be heading to the Gurgeon, where he could buy protection for a time. She couldn't see him at the distance of a half mile, of course, but she could feel his presence so strongly that she sensed every move he made. Sometimes it seemed as if she even knew the thoughts he was thinking.

The thief and his partner had been servants of a nobleman of the Hirple Realm and had made off with a horde of the nobleman's gold coins. But the thieves had been stupid. As they tied up the outraged nobleman, whose name was Lord Vester, they had discussed their plan in front of him. Each would take half the gold, and they would split up, heading in opposite directions, never to meet again. Lord Vester had hired Astil to find the culprits and retrieve his gold, and she had negotiated with him one of the best deals of her life. She would find one of the thieves— Lord Vester didn't care which—seize the gold he had stolen and return it to the nobleman. Once that part of the plan was complete, Astil was free to find the second thief and keep his half of the gold coins for herself. Lord Vester also expressed a desire that both thieves be killed, preferably slowly, but Astil was interested only in gold.

The first part of the plan had gone exceedingly well. The first thief she tracked, a former groom named Keece, hadn't gone far when she caught up with him. He had hired passage on a barge heading east down the Shaffroth River, intending to go all the way to Rynland. It had been easy to ride ahead of him on horseback and wait for him to come to her. She figured the barge would put in at Ristin to unload goods and pick up other goods, and that's where she confronted young Keece. She had offered him what she thought was a fair arrangement for both parties—he would give her the gold he had stolen, and she would let him live. When he asked if he might keep one gold coin to see him through what might be difficult times, she had refused, telling him to look for work in one of Ristin's stables. She had returned the coins to Lord Vester, who looked both relieved at getting back his gold and surprised that she hadn't kept it for herself. He shouldn't have been surprised. Astil had a reputation to uphold, and she would find little work as a tracker if she didn't live up to her end of the agreements she made. Besides, she had enough enemies and didn't need more. And now she was only a few hours away from getting her reward.

The trail ahead began to climb toward a ridge. She sensed the thief dismount and begin to lead his horse along a series of switchbacks that would take him seven hundred feet up, where he would come to a junction with another trail. Astil rode her horse at a walk. She would wait to see which way the thief headed when he came to the trail junction, but she was betting—and hoping—he would turn right. He did. That meant another mile and a half on the increasingly rugged trail to ascend more than a thousand feet, where the thief would come to another junction. Astil smiled and spurred her horse.

The thief came to the second junction and once again turned right. The trail there headed back down the ridge, through an area of exposed rock and sheer cliffs. When the terrain leveled off again, the trail would take him to another forest. A mile in, the thief would come to a large clearing, where Astil figured he would stop. With its saddlebags filled with so many gold coins, the thief's horse would have to rest soon, even if the thief didn't. Astil smiled. Most people didn't know gold weighed as much as it did. Astil knew exactly how much gold weighed.

Now only a quarter mile away from her quarry, Astil came to the second junction and turned her horse to the right. When she rounded a wide bend in the trail, she spotted the thief for the first time since she had set out to find him. He was still walking his horse, and Astil figured it would take a half hour for him to reach the bottom of the ridge, enter the woods, and come to the clearing. She waited. When the man finally entered the woods and disappeared, she continued on down. At the bottom of the ridge, she spurred her horse and made for the woods. Soon, she could hear the man muttering to himself up ahead.

She sensed him stop. He had reached the clearing. She halted, dismounted, and hobbled her horse. She took her padded jacket from a saddlebag and put it on over her tight black tunic. The front and sides of the jacket were made of thick leather on top of eighteen layers of linen, and its collar was high, to protect her neck. The jacket had stopped more than a few arrows in its time, although Astil doubted that her thief had much skill with weapons, even supposing he had any with him. But she hadn't stayed alive for thirty-two years by taking unnecessary chances. After securing the padded jacket, she loaded her crossbow and then strapped on a special belt of her own design that held spin knives and extra crossbow bolts where she could get to them quickly and easily. A hook on her belt held a length of coiled rope. She also wore her best sword and a fine Vothan dagger.

She crept quietly along the trail until she came within sight of the clearing. The thief was sitting on the ground, pulling off one of his boots. His horse was nearby. Astil stepped into the clearing and raised her crossbow, pointing it at the thief's head.

"You should take those saddlebags off that horse," she said.

The thief jumped as if every muscle in his body had been pricked with a hot needle at the same time. He tripped over his boot, stumbled and fell, and then scrambled up and stared at Astil as if she were a gast risen from the grave. "What, what, what … who are you?" he stammered.

"I'm your misplaced conscience, come back to chastise you."

"What do you … why … I don't …"

"I'm Lady Vengeance, looking for retribution."

"I didn't … I don't …"

"You did, and you do. You stole Lord Vester's gold, and you have it in those saddlebags that you've forced that poor horse to carry these three weeks."

The man swallowed and nearly choked.

"Mouth dry?" Astil asked him. "Nervous? Afraid to die?"

"Don't kill me," the thief said.

Astil glared at him. "You've never heard the word *please*?"

"Please don't kill me."

21

"That's better. The lack of courtesy in the known world sorely troubles me."

"I'm … I'm … I'm sorry."

"Never mind. Now take off your other boot and throw it into the trees. Throw both your boots into the trees."

The thief did as she had instructed.

"The gold coins you stole are in small linen sacks, twenty coins to the sack. Lord Vester told me that you and your friend, Master Neece, stole forty sacks. That means you have twenty. My guess is that you have ten in each saddlebag."

The man shrugged and tried to force a smile. "Gold coins?"

Astil glared at him and aimed her crossbow at his throat. "Take five of the sacks of gold coins from the left saddlebag and place them on the ground. Then we'll walk around to the other side of your horse and you'll do the same."

"You're going to let me keep half the coins?"

"Don't be a fool. I'm going to take all the gold you stole as well as your horse. My horse will carry half the gold, yours will carry the other half."

"What about me? What … what do you mean to do with me?"

She shrugged. "I mean to leave you here. Now, go to the saddlebag and remove half the sacks."

The man let out a long breath and headed toward his horse. As Astil watched, he opened the saddlebag and pulled out a loaded crossbow. He tried to duck and aim at the same time and wound up on the ground next to his horse's left front leg. His bolt flew into the treetops behind Astil.

"Would you like to try that again?" she asked.

The thief flung away his crossbow and shook his head.

"Didn't think so. Get on your feet."

The thief slowly stood up. "Don't kill me. I mean, please don't kill me."

"While I decide whether or not to put a bolt into your thieving heart, you will take five sacks from each saddlebag and place them on the ground, just there," she said, pointing at a spot midway between herself and the thief.

This time, the thief did as he was told. When he was finished with the sacks, she made him kneel on the ground with his hands clasped behind his back. She tied his hands together and then bound his ankles. "I'm going to fetch my horse now," she told him. "Don't go anywhere."

When Astil returned to the clearing, she put half the gold coins into her own saddlebags. She was about to mount up when she heard a noise she didn't like. She looked at the thief, but he was staring silently at the ground.

"Raise your hands high above your head," a voice called out.

Astil was reaching for her crossbow when something or someone struck her back, knocking her to the ground. She reached for her dagger, but a half dozen men fell on her before she could get to it, pinning her to the ground. She could barely breathe. Someone tied a rope around her right hand and pulled it tight. The rope bit into her skin, and she nearly cried out. She felt her ankles being held down and tied together, and she kicked out, striking one of the men trying to secure her. More men fell on her, and a moment later, she was trussed as securely as the thief. With her ankles tied together and her hands bound behind her back, she was hauled to her feet and disarmed. A delicate-looking young woman with straw-colored hair and a vague smile playing on her lips stepped in front of her and looked at her. Astil swore and then muttered the young woman's name: "Aarla."

"Astil," the young woman replied. "So nice to catch up with you again."

"Little bitch," Astil snapped. "Have you come to take me back to that Wyndoran prison?"

Aarla shook her head and glanced to her right. A moment later, a young wispy-bearded man dressed in the leather and brass uniform of the Vothan Riders joined her.

"I'm Saddlemaster Bleuek," the young man said with a slight bow. "I'm here to make you an offer."

Chapter 4

The Palace of the High Hext was even gaudier than the Beldur Palace. The High Hext, also known as Lord Acrin, had been the ruler of the former Acrinite Realm and the head of the religious cult to which most Acrinites bore allegiance, including most of the current rebel groups. The High Hext Lord Acrin had fled with his top advisors when the Voths reclaimed the Acrinite Territory and was thought to be living in the Gurgeon, an underground realm occupied by strange and vile creatures who bore only scant resemblance to men. The High Hext was no doubt dreaming of the day when he and his loyal followers would defeat the hated Voths and regain the land he once ruled.

Jarn had been inside the palace only a few times, and as he and Braga passed through the front gate of the palace grounds, he stared at the massive structure, trying to visualize the interior. Much of it was cavernous, but in some places it was like a maze. The building had been designed to instill awe and a sense of mystery in visitors, who were supposed to feel lost and overwhelmed inside the home of the man who claimed to be His Magnificence the Lord Acrin, High Hext, Defender of the People, and High Exalted Ruler of the Greater Acrinite Realm. Jarn thought it was all a heap of quagwash, and he often wondered how such vain fools as the Acrinites had managed to lord it over the tough and practical Voths for so long.

They crossed the palace grounds, and Jarn glanced up at the main entrance, a huge half-round projection with a curved portico made up of five high and wide arches.

Above the portico, the second level had another circular walkway, with an ornate four-foot-high fence of delicate iron tracery enclosing it. Above that, on the third level, loomed a crown-shaped tower painted in large alternating squares of yellow and red.

"Quite grand, isn't it?" Braga said as they approached the entrance, which was guarded by a pair of Yellowshirts.

"A bit overmuch," Jarn said.

They entered and were greeted by another Yellowshirt, who left them waiting while he fetched someone who would take them to see the Grenlings. The Yellowshirt returned five minutes later with a stern-faced man dressed in the black uniform of a knight of Brythyn, who introduced himself as Sir Tarris.

"Captain Jarn Theffig and Saddlemaster Braga," Jarn said. "Of the Vothan Riders."

"I will take you to Lord and Lady Grenling," Sir Tarris replied, and he turned and began walking down a wide corridor decorated in yellow and blue tiles. Jarn and Braga followed.

The hallway led back outside, to an enormous rectangular courtyard with a wide brick walkway along its perimeter. Stone benches decorated with colorful tiles were located every few yards along the path, and larger-than-life statues of former high hexts looked down from massive pedestals. The three men crossed the courtyard diagonally and reentered the building. Another corridor took them past an enormous, richly decorated ballroom with gold-colored walls, a sky-blue ceiling with an enormous sunburst painted in the center, and a raised platform at one end for minstrels and stage players. It looked to Jarn as if half the singers and lute players in

26

Rualgar could have fit on that stage. They continued to a wide staircase and headed up. The first landing held an array of statues arranged as if they were speaking to one another. They climbed another flight and strode down a hallway decorated with large paintings. It twisted and turned as they passed variously sized rooms, some of them oddly shaped.

Sir Tarris stopped at a closed door, knocked twice, and opened it. He gestured for Jarn and Braga to enter and followed them in. Jarn glanced around. The room was luxurious, but not large. It was conventionally rectangular, and Jarn saw two other doors on the opposite wall. A man who Jarn reckoned to be in his middle years stood up from a cushioned chair, eyeing Jarn. A woman of about the same age, with long straw-colored hair and sad eyes, remained seated. She gave the newcomers a wan smile.

"Lord and Lady Grenling," Sir Tarris announced, and he made the introductions.

Jarn and Braga shook hands with Lord Grenling and nodded to Lady Grenling, who stood up slowly when Sir Tarris crossed the room and opened another door. Jarn and Braga followed Lord and Lady Grenling into a small chamber with a small table and four chairs, two cushioned and two plain wooden ones. The walls were painted white and undecorated, in stark contrast to the rest of the palace. Lord Grenling took the cushioned chair behind the table, and his wife sat in a chair next to it. Jarn and Braga took the two plain chairs facing them. Sir Tarris excused himself, left the room, and shut the door behind him.

"Thank you for agreeing to speak with us on quick notice," Jarn said.

"Whatever we can do to get our daughter back safely we will do," Lord Grenling replied. His wife nodded.

Jarn sized up Grenling. He was nearly as tall as Braga, but not as massively built. Braga was a hulk of a man, with a chest like a brick wall and a face like a block of carved granite. Lord Grenling was tall but lean. He had white hair but otherwise looked to be no more than fifty years old. He had light blue eyes that rarely strayed from whatever they were looking at, hollow cheeks, and thin lips that looked as if they might never have smiled. Those lips had formed the vaguest suggestion of a sneer, as if Lord Grenling was put out by having to deal with two crude and unsophisticated Vothan Riders. No doubt the man still thought of Skunnik and its palaces as part of the Greater Acrinite Realm and wasn't used to Voths holding sway there. Like others throughout the known world, he would have to learn.

Braga reached into a pouch on his belt and removed a small wooden tray and a dozen small sheets of parchment that fit on top of it. He pulled a narrow, pointed implement from a leather sheath on his belt, set the pointed end on the top sheet of parchment, and made some marks. Then he looked up at Jarn and nodded.

"What's he doing?" Lord Grenling asked.

"Braga will be writing down some of the particulars of our conversation," Jarn replied.

Lord Grenling frowned. "Why?"

"Memories can be faulty."

Lord Grenling raised an eyebrow. "I didn't know Voths could write."

"Aye, we can read, too," Jarn said. "To begin, we'd like you to tell us the sequence of events that led to your daughter's abduction."

Lady Grenling stood up. "If you don't mind, I think I would like to rest. Lord Grenling should be able to supply all the ... particulars."

"Of course," Jarn said. "But I would like to speak with you sometime as well. When you're rested."

Lord Grenling frowned. "I hardly think it's necessary to trouble my wife about this matter."

"In an investigation like this, we can't know what's necessary and what isn't until we've solved the puzzle. So we follow every avenue."

"Nevertheless, I don't believe that—"

"I'll be happy to speak with you, Captain Jarn," Lady Grenling said, cutting off her husband. "I'll arrange it for later today, if that suits you."

"It does," Jarn said, and Lady Grenling left the room without looking at Lord Grenling.

"She hasn't been right since Talsie was abducted," Lord Grenling muttered after she left.

"What can you tell us about that?" Jarn asked.

Lord Grenling shot an annoyed glance at Braga, who was staring at his parchment, and then turned to Jarn and began. "We set out a few days ago with a company of knights, four carriages, and a couple of wagons with supplies for the journey. The trip had two aims—to negotiate a treaty with you Voths that we had begun with the Acrinites last year, and to marry our daughter Talsie to Lord Keddro."

"How did Talsie feel about her impending marriage?" Jarn asked.

Lord Grenling furrowed his brow. "I've no idea. What difference does it make?"

"All avenues," Jarn said.

"The marriage was arranged nearly two years ago. I never heard Talsie complain about it."

"How old is your daughter?"

"Nineteen."

"Did she have any suitors back in Brythyn?"

"Only one. The son of a merchant." Lord Grenling's sneer deepened. "He's not even of the lordly class."

"His name?"

"Willim Gilpin."

"How did he feel about Talsie's upcoming marriage to an Acrinite lord?"

Grenling wrinkled his nose and gave Jarn a hard look. "I wouldn't know. The question is entirely irrelevant."

"Not if Master Willim was so troubled by the thought of losing Talsie to someone else that he decided to abduct her to prevent the forthcoming wedding from taking place."

"You must be mad. Willim Gilpin is a skinny, craven wretch. I never could figure out what my daughter saw in him."

"Nevertheless, it would be helpful if we could question the young man. If you would be so good as to summon him to Skunnik."

"Very well," Grenling said, with no attempt to hide his displeasure at the request. "I'll send one of the knights to fetch him as soon as we finish here."

"Thank you. Please continue."

"You may know that the Brythyn capital is not far from Skunnik, only a two-day journey by carriage, one day on horseback."

Jarn nodded. "I've been to your capital."

Lord Grenling looked surprised. "Have you?"

"A number of times," Jarn said.

Lord Grenling looked annoyed.

"I quite enjoyed the food and ale at the Bear Goes Inn," Braga said. "Have you been there, Lord Grenling? It's on Wheat Street, not far from the royal palace."

"I know where it is," Grenling snapped. "And no, I have not been there."

Jarn suppressed a smile. He avoided glancing at Braga, but he was sure the big man was wearing his most innocent expression. "So then, Lord Grenling, you set out from Mystell three days ago and arrived in Skunnik yesterday. Please tell us what took place during the journey."

"We had planned a proper entrance into the city, to be greeted by Acrinite notables as well as Lord Keddro and his family," Lord Grenling said. "We were only a few hours away from Skunnik when Talsie said she felt ill and wasn't up to any sort of ceremony. Typical of her."

"Is your daughter sickly?" Jarn asked.

"Healthy as a pampered lapdog," Grenling replied.

"Yet she said she felt ill."

Lord Grenling let out a long breath. "My daughter is healthy in her body, but less robust in her … thoughts. She's overly shy and tends toward moodiness."

The sound of Braga's writing implement made low scratching sounds, like a child whispering. Lord Grenling glanced at him and seemed about to make a comment, but apparently thought better of it.

"What did you do?" Jarn asked.

"I asked Sir Longboke, one of the knights accompanying us, to take Talsie on horseback to a lesser-used city gate and then to the palace. Somewhere on their way, Talsie vanished."

31

"What happened to Sir Longboke?" Jarn asked. "Did he vanish as well?"

"Oh, no, he's at the Beldur Palace, in a cell down in the Yellowshirts' fine dungeon. He claims that some dark magic knocked him senseless, and by the time he regained his mind, Talsie and her horse were gone."

"Do you believe him?"

"No, but I'll get the truth out of him. First Ulder Peddrin has agreed to lend me a torturer."

Braga's parchment scratching ceased, and he and Jarn exchanged a quick glance.

"Torture is outlawed in Vothan," Jarn said.

"We're in Acrinite Territory."

"The Acrinite Territory is part of Vothan now."

"Ah, yes, so it is. It may take me a while to become accustomed to these recently changed circumstances. It still seems wrong somehow, backwards and strange."

Jarn wanted to tell him that what was wrong had been the Acrinites use of a thousand-year-old deception to rule the Voths in their own territory, and that the wrong had been righted. But he kept those thoughts to himself. "No doubt you'll become accustomed to the changed circumstances soon enough."

"Meanwhile, I'll make use of the First Ulder's torturer," Lord Grenling said, looking Jarn in the eye.

"I won't allow it," Jarn said.

Lord Grenling's blue eyes flashed, momentarily discomposing his calm demeanor. "Very well, Captain. I'll send Sir Longboke back to Brythyn and have him tortured there."

Jarn cursed himself for a fool for giving Grenling a way out. He swallowed and took a breath and waited a beat before continuing, in a voice he tried to make conciliatory, if not soothing. "Lord Grenling, a crime has been committed in Vothan, a crime against your own family. I am bound to investigate it and do all in my power to bring your daughter back to you safely. I will do that according to Vothan law. There will be no torture anywhere in Vothan. In addition, anyone suspected of committing the crime or aiding those who did will be held in Vothan custody. Anyone who may have witnessed the abduction or know anything about it, including Sir Longboke, will remain here in Vothan until the matter is settled."

"A pretty speech," Lord Grenling said. "But how will you stop me from sending Sir Longboke back to Brythyn?"

Jarn looked at Braga. "Go back to headquarters and take a squadron of Riders to the Beldur Palace. Tell the Yellowshirts to release Sir Longboke to you. Take him back to headquarters and put him in a secure room there, well-guarded. Tell Sir Longboke I'll be questioning him shortly."

"Your men will have to get past my knights first," Lord Grenling said.

"I hope not," Jarn replied. "But we'll do what's necessary to uphold our laws."

"Are you threatening me?" Lord Grenling asked.

"Surely not. Your status as a diplomat entitles you to diplomatic courtesy. I'm merely acquainting you with the facts."

"Allow me to acquaint you with some other facts, Captain," Lord Grenling said. "Now that you Voths have taken control of the Acrinite Territory, you've spread yourselves thin. You're far outnumbered by the Acrinites, who still have friends in the neighboring realms north of

33

the Shaffroth. Should the Acrinites ever decide to rebel against your rule—as I hear some are already doing—and if, say, Brythyn were to ally ourselves with them … well, the vaunted Vothan Riders would be no match for such a force."

"Voths don't buckle to threats, Lord Grenling," Jarn said evenly. "And we, too, have allies."

"The Wyndorans?" Lord Grenling snorted. "Schoolmasters and scholars. Hardly a match for trained soldiers and men-at-arms."

"Those schoolmasters and scholars might surprise you," Jarn said. "We've other friends as well."

"Oh? Who?"

"Most of the nearby realms south of the Shaffroth. And Rynland as well."

"Rynland? A bit far flung to be of much use to you if it came to hostilities, eh?"

"Perhaps. But before someone decides to wage war against the Vothan Realm, he ought to have a deep think about what an army of Rynlanders attacking his rear might accomplish."

Lord Grenling looked down at the table in front of him and began to drum his fingers on it. He took a breath and let it out slowly. He nodded once, almost to himself, as if he had come to a decision. Jarn waited. Lord Grenling finally looked up. "Very well, Captain Jarn. We'll do things your way. There will be no torture, and you can take Sir Longboke to your headquarters—for now."

Jarn stood up and Braga followed suit. "I'll keep you apprised of the progress of my investigation, Lord Grenling," Jarn said.

Grenling stood up and eyed Jarn, a look of triumph on his face. "As to that investigation, I want one of my men to be part of it."

"We don't need any help," Jarn said.

"That remains to be seen, but on this I will not be deterred."

Jarn thought fast. He had won the arguments over torture and keeping Sir Longboke in Vothan, but it might be more politically astute to give in on this demand. Besides, he could shunt Grenling's man off to some obscure part of the work. "Very well. Send your man to see Line Commander Lahgoh at Vothan Rider headquarters tomorrow morning."

Lord Grenling smiled for the first time since Jarn and Braga had met him, but the smile held no warmth. "No need. Sir Tarris can accompany you from here."

It suddenly occurred to Jarn that Lord Grenling might have used the threat of torture as a negotiating ploy to gain what he really wanted, one of his own men insinuating himself into Jarn's investigation. Jarn gritted his teeth. Sir Tarris didn't appear to be a man who would allow himself to be shunted off to perform some meaningless task, but it was too late to take back his agreement.

"Perfect," Jarn said, a bit too loudly. "I look forward to working with Sir Tarris."

Chapter 5

"We'll have a meal before we interview Sir Longboke," Jarn said to Sir Tarris as they left the grounds of the Palace of the High Hext through the west gate and headed on foot toward the Mang. It was midday, and a bright sun had turned the day warm.

"Why wait?" Sir Tarris said. "Is your stomach more important than finding Lady Talsie?"

"You seem to have forgotten that Sir Longboke is being transferred from the Beldur Palace," Braga growled. "So we have to wait for him anyway."

Sir Tarris made no immediate response to Braga's remark, but he looked surprised, even shocked. Jarn smiled inwardly but tried not to let it show. Like every other Voth, Braga cared little for kings, lords, or sirs and believed that a man proved his worth by what he did, not by being born with a title. The Brythyners, along with much of the rest of the known world, had much to learn about the Voths.

At the Mang, Jarn commandeered a small room adjacent to his quarters for Sir Tarris to use as an office. He stopped briefly at Lahgoh's quarters to introduce Sir Tarris and explain his presence there. Sir Tarris took the opportunity to complain to Lahgoh about the chamber Jarn had assigned him, protesting that it was "rather small and ill appointed." Lahgoh's response was a look one might give a constantly whining child, an expression that was equal parts penetrating glare, sneering disgust, and a squinting frown that suggested the complainer must be mad or stupid even to consider airing such a worthless, time-wasting grievance. Jarn knew that look. He almost felt sorry for Sir Tarris. Lahgoh was a man whose every aspect of face and form, every mannerism and gesture, every air and expression bespoke a born warrior, a soldier who understood and honored discipline and reviled whining. Yet Lahgoh was not a humorless follower of rigid rules and excessive regulations. He believed in flexibility and initiative, especially among his men, and he also appreciated a good jape. He had even been known to make japes of his own. Every one of his men, including Jarn, would have gladly laid down his life for him.

After a long moment in which Lahgoh's dark eyes seemed to freeze Sir Tarris where he stood, Jarn heard the knight swallow. A moment later, Sir Tarris apologized for complaining and declared that the room would suit him fine. Thus did the Brythyner's ongoing education concerning the Voths take another step forward.

Afterwards, Jarn, Sir Tarris, and Braga took a meal in the Mang's common room. An hour later, they entered the front room of the guarded suite in which Sir Longboke had been installed after his removal from the Beldur Palace dungeon. Jarn and Sir Tarris sat on cushioned chairs facing Sir Longboke, who was slumped on a small couch against the back wall. The room had only one small window, high on the wall, which let in a slanting beam of sunlight. Torches in sconces on the walls cast flickering shadows, and a candle sitting in the middle of a small round table provided token illumination, but the overall aspect of the room matched Sir Longboke's gloomy demeanor.

The two Brythyn knights knew one another, and it was obvious to Jarn that they didn't care for one another. He didn't know either man, so he couldn't glean any insights from their mutual animosity. He felt burdened by having a three-man team for the interview, but he wanted Braga there to make his notations, and he hadn't yet figured out how to rid himself of Sir Tarris.

"Tell us what happened," Jarn said to Sir Longboke. "After you and Lady Talsie left Lord Grenling's train."

Longboke sat up straighter on the couch and cleared his throat. He was about the same height as Jarn, just over six feet, but loose-limbed and gangly. His hair, a dark blond color, hung loosely down past his neck, and his face was drawn and pale, his expression worried. Jarn wondered what concerned him more, that Talsie was missing or the price he might have to pay for failing to protect her.

"We set out on horseback at a fair canter, intending to enter the city through the northeast gate and make our way to the High Hext's Palace before the others arrived," Sir Longboke said in a weary voice.

"It was just the two of you, as I remember," Sir Tarris said.

Jarn glared at him. His mere presence was annoying enough, but meddling in Jarn's questioning was intolerable. He should have spoken to the man before the interview and set down some rules.

"Yes, it was just the two of us," Sir Longboke replied.

"Did it not occur to you or anyone else that leaving the protection of the train could be dangerous?" Jarn asked.

Sir Longboke shook his head. "We'd heard vague rumors about Acrinite rebels harrying the Voths, but we knew of nothing that should be of any concern to us. We had visited the Acrinite Realm countless times before and never had any trouble."

38

"But surely you knew the Voths had conquered the Acrinite Territory," Sir Tarris said. Jarn gritted his teeth. He would have to talk to the man as soon as Sir Longboke's questioning was finished.

"I tell you, we had no reason to expect trouble," Sir Longboke insisted. "And I don't remember you opposing the plan to take Talsie to the city ahead of the train, sir."

Sir Tarris bristled. "I would certainly have opposed it had I known you would lose her, sir."

"I didn't lose her," Sir Longboke said, clearly angry. "Someone took her. Someone put an enchantment on me, and when I woke up, she was gone."

"Did you and Talsie encounter anyone after you left the train?" Jarn asked, trying to regain control of the interview.

Sir Longboke shook his head. "No, no one."

"Tell us about this spell," Jarn said.

Sir Longboke shook his head again, slowly, as if the memory were too painful to bear. "There's little to tell. We were riding side by side and finally caught sight of the city. We stopped at a little clearing to have a dram of wine and a bit of bread and cheese before continuing." He closed his eyes and leaned his head back, as if he were picturing the scene in his mind, despite the pain it brought him. "We were sitting across from each other, Talsie on a downed tree, I on a large boulder, watching the birds and admiring the sky. Talsie was singing to herself. That's the last thing I remember, the blue sky and Talsie singing softly. When I woke up, I was lying on the ground not far from the tree. My horse was where I'd left it. Talsie and her horse were gone. I called her name, but there was no answer. I called her again, called her over and over. I spied a narrow trail and ran up it, screaming her name."

Sir Longboke shuddered as a great sob threatened to overcome him. "I couldn't believe it. I thought she must have ridden to the city without me, though I couldn't understand why. So I headed there as fast as my horse would carry me and hurried to the palace. But she hadn't arrived. No one had seen her. I was frantic. I took a fresh horse and headed back to where we had stopped. I called her name again and again and again, but ..." He shook his head again. "It was as if she had vanished into the air. By the time I got back to the city again, Lord Grenling had arrived. I told him what happened. He swore at me and threatened me and had me thrown into the Beldur Palace dungeon."

"You said you drank some wine," Jarn said. "Did you have a bottle with you?"

"No, I had a skin of strong red."

"Did you both drink from it?"

"Aye."

"Are you sure."

Sir Longboke opened his mouth to speak but hesitated. "I drank, and I believe Lady Talsie did as well, but I can't be sure."

"Think back," Jarn said. "Describe the scene for us, if you please."

"I had brought two small pewter cups. I poured some wine into both and handed one to Talsie."

"And do you remember the lady drinking from hers?"

"I suppose she did. That was the point of pouring it, wasn't it? Yes, she did. I think so. I'm almost sure I remember seeing her drink."

"You suppose, you think so, you're almost sure," Sir Tarris said. "But you aren't really sure, are you?"

Sir Longboke shook his head and looked as if he wanted to cry. "No, I'm not sure. But she didn't refuse the cup, so I assume …"

"Where did the wine come from?" Jarn asked.

"I asked one of the servants in the supply wagon to give me a skin of strong red."

"Do you know the servant's name?"

"It might have been Hanno."

Jarn looked at Braga, who nodded as he wrote down the name.

"Hanno Kanirin," Sir Tarris said, and Braga added the second name to his parchment.

"What became of the wineskin?"

Sir Longboke shook his head. "I don't know."

"What else can you tell us?" Jarn asked.

"I've told you all I can," Sir Longboke said.

Jarn stood up. "We may have more questions for you. Meanwhile, you'll stay here, in Vothan custody. If you think of anything else that may be helpful, tell one of your guards to fetch me or one of my men."

Jarn, Braga, and Sir Tarris left and proceeded to Jarn's quarters. Jarn watched Sir Tarris glance around the front room, waiting for him to make a comment. If he had one in mind, he kept it to himself.

"What do you think?" Sir Tarris asked.

"Someone may have slipped a potion into the wineskin that rendered both Sir Longboke and Talsie unconscious," Jarn replied. "Once they were out, someone lurking nearby could have easily taken Talsie away, possibly tied to her own horse, or even in a wagon or carriage."

"Who?"

Jarn shrugged. "Acrinite rebels. Criminals looking for a ransom. That suitor of hers back in Brythyn, Willim … Willim …"

"Willim Gilpin," Braga said.

"But a sleeping potion in the wine would have required a scheme between the servant and Talsie's abductors," Sir Tarris said. "That's unlikely."

"Quite unlikely," Jarn acknowledged. "It was more likely dark magic, as Sir Longboke claims. Nevertheless, I mean to follow every avenue, which means questioning the servant. I'm assigning that task to you, Sir Tarris. Talk to the servant as soon as you can and report back to me later today. And while you're at the Palace, talk to Lady Grenling about the interview with me that she promised to arrange for today."

"Lord Grenling, too?" Sir Tarris asked.

Jarn shook his head. "No, just the lady."

Chapter 6

Jarn found Lahgoh in a section of the Mang's basement, where he was directing a crew of men who were arranging tables and chairs and cabinets in a large room that Jarn estimated to be twenty-five feet long and eighteen wide. Long, barred windows just above the outside ground level let in plenty of sunlight, giving the room a cheerful aspect despite being in the basement. A large oval table stood in the center of the room, and two smaller square tables had been placed closer to the entrance. An assortment of heavy oak bookshelves, chests, and cabinets were arrayed along the wall to Jarn's right, and carpenters were carrying in long, narrow tables made of unfinished pinewood and arranging them in a row along the wall to Jarn's left. Jarn inhaled the fresh scent of recently sawn pine as the men set down the long tables and placed them according to Lahgoh's instructions. A large, rectangular slab of smooth slate hung on the back wall, and pieces of white chalk sat in a silver bowl on a small table just below it.

"A room fit for a king," Jarn said as he looked around. "Or at least a minor lord. What do you plan to do with it?"

Lahgoh looked up and gave Jarn a satisfied smile. "I'm having an entire suite of rooms down here cleaned up and rearranged for your use during this investigation. This room is for meetings with your extended team. With so many search parties and other helpers, you'll need it. Come with me, and I'll show you the rest."

Lahgoh headed toward an open door at the back of the room, and Jarn followed him into a hallway and then through a door on the left that gave entrance into a small windowless room that contained a square table and four chairs. "This room and another like it across the hall are for questioning people."

They left the small room and peered into its near-twin across the way, and then proceeded to the end of the hall, where they turned left into another short corridor. There was a door halfway down on the right and another door at the end. Lahgoh opened the door on the right, and they entered a large empty chamber. There were two open doors on the opposite side, one straight ahead, the other just to the right. Lahgoh pointed to the one straight ahead. "That's for storing whatever needs to be stored, including documents, confiscated weapons, any clothing or personal items that you might find. That other door leads to your inner chamber."

They entered the inner chamber, which consisted of a main section with a desk, chairs, cabinets, and shelves, and a small alcove with a round table and four chairs, the whole illuminated by sunlight streaming in through long barred windows like the ones in the large meeting room.

"Take some men to help you get whatever you need from your quarters upstairs," Lahgoh said. "I want you to begin organizing the rest of the investigation. Some of the searchers will be returning soon, and they'll report to you here. It might be worthwhile to let the Grenlings see the new headquarters, too, let them know we're taking their daughter's abduction seriously."

Jarn nodded. "I'll need to take some time to watch that mage work his magic with Raff Salorian's body. Kurff is probably there already."

"Do it, but be quick about it. Then come back here, and bring Kurff with you. I want him in on this one,

Captain, and I want you to give him honest work to do. Could be I'll assign him that empty chamber outside your office."

Jarn stared at his commander. "First Astil and now Kurff. Have you anyone else in mind to help me? The High Hext, perhaps? A company of Gurgeonites?"

Lahgoh shrugged. "I'll see what I can do."

Jarn heard footsteps in the outer room and looked toward the door. A man of about sixty years of age, wide-shouldered and sturdy looking, with short, graying hair and a neatly trimmed beard that was also shot with gray, entered and approached.

"Minister Respero," Lahgoh said. "Welcome to our new headquarters. What brings you here today?"

The newcomer, who wore an expensive woolen cloak of dark blue and a pearl-colored silk tunic, looked around and nodded approvingly. "I wanted to see your new constabulary quarters, Line Commander. The place is shaping up nicely."

"Glad you approve," Lahgoh said.

"I also want to talk to you and Captain Jarn about the Talsie Grenling investigation."

Jarn gestured toward the small round table in the adjacent alcove. "Please, Minister, have a seat."

The three sat at the table, and Respero turned to Jarn before beginning. "As you may know, Captain, I'm in charge of negotiating some important treaties with the Brythyn Realm. Lord Grenling, as it happens, is my Brythyn counterpart in the negotiations."

"Commander Lahgoh explained the matter to me," Jarn said. "He called it a delicate situation."

"Indeed it is," Respero said. "The Brythyners, and Lord Grenling in particular, consider themselves to be

45

master negotiators. They have scant regard for Voths—for now—and assume they'll gain a major diplomatic victory at our expense."

"I'm quite sure you'll prove them wrong, Minister," Lahgoh said.

Respero snorted. "Neither Brythyn nor any other realm will take advantage of Vothan as long as I'm minister of treaties and pacts. The other realms, including Brythyn, will learn to respect us, but it may take time. A successful negotiation with Brythyn will go a long way toward persuading the rest of the realms that we're capable of taking our place among them."

"I wish you luck," Jarn said.

"Luck won't solve the problem that is threatening the negotiations," Respero replied. "Talsie Grenling was abducted on what is now Vothan land. Lord Grenling expects us to find her and punish those responsible. I'm hoping you have good news to report."

"Pardon me, Minister, but Captain Jarn has just barely begun," Lahgoh said. "It could be days before we have news."

"But I'm happy to tell you what we've done so far," Jarn said, and he told the minister about his interviews with Sir Longboke and Lord Grenling as well as the addition of Sir Tarris to his team. He wondered if he should mention Astil, but Lahgoh solved that dilemma.

"We'll also have help from someone who specializes in finding people," Lahgoh said.

Respero frowned. "Not that sorceress."

"In fact, it is her," Lahgoh said. "Astil's her name."

"You realize, Commander, that using such a woman could create even more difficulties than I—than we—already face, do you not?"

"I do," Lahgoh replied. "But our goal, mine and Captain Jarn's, is finding Talsie Grenling. If Astil can help in that task, then we would be foolish not to use her."

"I hope you know what you're doing, Commander."

"We're doing all we can and will continue to do so."

Minister Respero stood up. "I'll depend upon it. But be aware that you and Captain Jarn will bear full and total responsibility for the outcome of this situation, whatever it is."

"A responsibility that we are happy to accept," Lahgoh said. "Isn't that right, Captain Jarn?"

"Aye," Jarn said, wishing he were back in Rualgar.

***

An hour later, after dealing with the mage who claimed he could glean information from Raff Salorian's body, Jarn returned to the new basement headquarters with Kurff. He found Line Commander Lahgoh standing at the back of the large meeting room near the doorway, watching people enter. The leaders of some of the search parties had begun to arrive, and Braga and Grion were there as well. Lahgoh glanced quickly at Jarn and then nodded at Kurff. "Senior Patrol Leader Kurff, it's good of you to help us."

"It's my pleasure, Line Commander Lahgoh," Kurff said, bowing slightly.

Jarn nearly rolled his eyes at the exaggerated courtesy both men were showing one another. The last time Lahgoh and Kurff had spoken, they were arguing heatedly over which group should have custody of a Wyndoran youth that Jarn's men had found wandering in Vothan Province. That incident had eventually led to the Voths regaining their rightful possession of the Acrinite Territory.

Lahgoh turned to Jarn. "How did your mage fare?"

"Utterly useless," Jarn said. "I sent him away and turned Raff Salorian's body over to the Guardsmen to be returned to his family."

Lahgoh nodded and turned to Kurff. "We won't give up on finding the criminals responsible for that outrage, but, for now, another crime must take priority."

"Captain Jarn told me about it," Kurff said. "I and my men are honored to help him."

"Excellent," Lahgoh said before turning back to Jarn. "I'll be off. I'll expect daily reports on your progress."

Lahgoh left, and Jarn turned to Kurff. "If I asked you to recommend a Yellowshirt to take general charge of the search parties, who would you choose? Besides yourself, I mean?"

"Patrol Leader Nevvin," Kurff replied without hesitation. "He has a gift for organization and a memory like a well-packed peddler's trunk. He's as tenacious as a razor-toothed hardel and tough as Vothan leather."

Jarn nodded, and Kurff took a seat at the large oval table, which was filling up quickly as more people entered the room. The sound of heavy chairs scraping across the flagstone floor accompanied the subdued murmurings of the assembled group. Sir Tarris arrived, and Jarn gestured for him to sit. Jarn walked to the front of the room and was about to call the meeting to order when Bleuek, the youngest member of Jarn's company, arrived and took a seat. He was smiling. That most likely meant that Astil was in Vothan custody. Whether or not that was good news remained to be seen. Jarn put Astil out of his mind and looked at the group sitting around the large table,

48

which could easily accommodate twenty-five people or more. It was nearly full.

Jarn asked the searchers to report first, but none had found any trace of the missing woman, neither in town nor in the countryside. Jarn, using the notes Braga had taken, reported on his meeting with Lord Grenling and his interview with Sir Longboke. He then asked Sir Tarris to report on his questioning of the servant.

"Here?" Sir Tarris asked, frowning. "In front of everyone?"

"Aye, unless there's good reason not to," Jarn replied.

Sir Tarris made his report, concluding it with his belief that the servant was innocent of any plotting or wrongdoing.

"We need to continue sending out search parties," Jarn said. "I'm putting Patrol Leader Nevvin, of the Acrinite Guardsmen, in overall charge of the search." Nevvin, a skinny man of around forty years, whose yellow uniform hung loosely on his frame, sat up straight and stared at Jarn, as if he couldn't believe what he had just heard. Jarn nodded at him. "I want you to organize the search parties and report to me as often as you can. If you need to hold a meeting, you can do so in this room. Assuming you accept the position."

"I accept," Nevvin said.

"I should tell you that we know of more than a dozen locations in Skunnik that are suspected of harboring rebels," Jarn said. "We need to go in with no warning and question them hard."

"Hang on with that," Kurff said in a loud voice. Everyone turned to him. "According to Vothan law, the

49

people have a right to be safe in their own homes unless there's a clear and compelling need to search."

"You weren't so delicate about unannounced searches when the Acrinites were in charge here," Jarn shot back.

"The Acrinites aren't in charge now, as you never tire of reminding us."

"A young woman has been abducted. I'd say that gives us a clear and compelling need to search."

"You can't just barge into every house in Skunnik because of one crime."

"I don't intend to search every house in Skunnik. Only the places suspected of harboring rebels or criminals."

"You do that then. You won't find anything anyway. You'll just make the people even angrier at you and less likely to help."

Jarn raised an eyebrow. "Oh? And how do you know we won't find anything?"

"Because these rebels are not stupid. The ones operating inside the city won't be leaving evidence on their doorsteps for you to trip over."

"You seem to know a great deal about the rebels."

Kurff rolled his eyes. "Use your brains, Captain. They've been at it for nearly a year, with scant trouble from you and your famous Vothan Riders. Though most of the rebels and their leaders are from the regular army, some of them—perhaps many of them—are led by former Acrinite Guardsmen, it pains me to say. You may have thought the Yellowshirts were no match for the Riders, but we were—we are—every bit as skilled and tough as you. Don't underestimate these rebels."

"I never thought the Guardsmen were an unworthy match for the Riders," Jarn said in a calm voice.

"Then let me and my men visit these suspect houses and ask some questions, although I doubt we'll encounter any actual rebels. But neither the rebels nor their sympathizers are likely to be keen on abducting the daughters of visiting dignitaries, so if someone has heard a rumor, he may be willing to tell me."

Once again, Jarn was suspicious of Kurff's apparent knowledge of the rebels, but he also knew the Yellowshirt had made a fair point. If there was anything to be learned from the Acrinites in Skunnik, it was more likely that the Yellowshirts would discover it. The room had gone quiet, and he felt everyone's eyes on him. Jarn looked at Nevvin. "You're in charge of searching. What do you say?"

"I agree with Senior Patrol Leader Kurff," Nevvin said without hesitation. "And I'd like him to take charge of searching those suspicious places in town that you mentioned."

Jarn looked at Kurff and nodded. "I'll give you the list of suspect houses and other places. You'll organize your own people for the questioning, and you'll report back here each evening, whether or not you find anything. Any questions?"

Nevvin and Kurff both shook their heads.

"Tomorrow I plan to take Sir Longboke back to the site where Lady Talsie disappeared," Jarn said. "He mentioned something about a narrow trail near there, so I'll need another search party to come with us and follow it." He looked at Nevvin, who nodded, and then turned to Sir Tarris. "Have you arranged the interview with Lady Grenling?"

"She said before the dinner hour would suit," Sir Tarris replied.

"Then we should be off," Jarn said.

Braga stood up. "Will you be needing me, Captain?"

Jarn hesitated a moment and then shook his head. "I want to put Lady Grenling at her ease. But I'll want you with me tomorrow." He looked at Bleuek. "I understand you may have some news for me."

Bleuek smiled and nodded.

"Have you brought the extra help Line Commander Lahgoh told me about?"

"I have," Bleuek said. "She's in a locked and guarded suite. Line Commander Lahgoh tried to speak with her, but she just keeps asking about her gold."

Chapter 7

Sir Tarris took Jarn to an apartment in the Palace of the High Hext, where Lady Grenling was waiting in a large sitting room. Tall bookcases and elegant chests and cabinets, all in a fine-grained dark wood, gave the room an imposing character. Bright paintings, each six feet wide and each depicting a single flower, completed a look that was clearly meant to impress. A pair of deep-red cushioned couches and two cushioned chairs in the same blood-red fabric were grouped in a rough square, facing in toward each other. A low table between the couches held a pot of steaming tea and two white cups.

Lady Grenling stood up from one of the couches and tried to smile, but the furrows in her brow betrayed her anxiety. Her eyes were red-rimmed and bloodshot, as if she had been weeping or hadn't slept or, most probably, both.

"Thank you for seeing me," Jarn said to her.

"It's my pleasure, Captain," she replied.

"I'll leave you to it, then," Sir Tarris said, and he left the room. Jarn thought the knight seemed unhappy about leaving Lady Grenling alone with him.

"May I pour you a cup of mallow root tea?" Lady Grenling asked Jarn.

"Yes, thank you."

She poured two cups and handed one to him. She sat on one of the red couches, and he sat on the one facing it. Jarn took a sip of tea and tried to study her without staring. She was a graceful woman, tall and slender, yet not unshapely. Wide-set blue eyes looked out from a face with prominent cheekbones and a jawline so perfect that it

53

might have been the product of a master woodworker. Her lips were small and delicate rather than full, but when she spoke, her mouth seemed to express as much as her words, not with exaggeration, but like an expert stage player clearly speaking her lines for an audience. Neither her figure nor her face seemed to have a scrap of excess flesh, and her light-colored hair was only just beginning to show small signs of gray. Jarn thought she was quite beautiful.

"I'm sorry for your trouble," he said after taking another sip of tea. "I don't want to burden you at such an unhappy time, and I hope you'll forgive any meddlesome questions."

"Ask anything," she replied. "I'm glad to help in any way I can."

"Tell me about the upcoming wedding."

"As Lord Grenling told you, it was first discussed nearly two years ago, before the Gurgeonite War and the Vothan Renewal. It was set to take place here in Skunnik within the month. At least that was the original plan."

"Did something change?"

"The wedding was meant to be a symbol of the renewed friendship between Brythyn and the Acrinite Realm. The newly negotiated treaties held the bones and guts of the new bond, and the marriage was to be its pretty face. As you may know, the High Lord of the Brythyn Realm has no marriageable daughters, so Talsie was selected for the duty."

"But she was not happy about it, I presume."

"No, she was not happy about it. My daughter is fragile, like a delicate flower." At the word *flower*, she glanced up at one of the pictures on the wall opposite her, a pink and gold foxflower painted to look even gaudier than the real thing, and gestured toward it. "Not a flower like these overdone monstrosities, Captain. My Talsie tends to be shy and withdrawn, but those who have become close to her, though they're few in number, love her and care for her deeply."

"Would those who love her and care about her include Willim Gilpin?"

Lady Grenling nodded.

"Tell me about the young man."

"He's also shy and keeps mostly to himself, but he's not as reserved as Talsie. Unlike her, he doesn't always go out of his way to avoid others. He is the kind of person who, when he's with a jolly group, holds back and is barely noticed. But he listens. And he is clever. And when finally he does have something to say, he states it in a clear voice that draws everyone's attention, often to their considerable surprise. He may make only one such statement over the course of hours, but that one statement is often the shrewdest and most memorable."

"Lord Grenling claimed the young man was a skinny, craven wretch."

"My husband is a fool," Lady Grenling replied quickly, in a voice that was probably louder than she intended. She looked down and then gazed at Jarn. "I'm sorry. I should not have said that. I should have said that Lord Grenling doesn't know Willim well enough to have a meaningful opinion. He underestimates the young man. Most do."

"Perhaps Lord Grenling takes an ill view of Willim because he sees him as a possible impediment to the upcoming wedding."

Lady Grenling gave a short, bitter laugh, almost a shout, and clenched her hands into fists. "That wedding was never going to take place."

Jarn frowned. "I don't understand."

"I don't understand it all, either. But after the Voths took control of the Acrinite Territory, the new treaties were to be made with the Vothan Realm. I know that Lord Grenling and Lord Keddro discussed ways to ensure that the treaties would benefit the Acrinites. I believe they also discussed ways to prevent the wedding from taking place."

Jarn's frown deepened. "Why would they do that?"

"My belief is that Lord Keddro, who's older than Lord Grenling, changed his views about marrying Talsie after he learned how strongly she opposed it. Besides, my husband no doubt filled his ears with tales of Talsie's shyness and fragility. I think they both changed their minds about the wedding."

"Why all the scheming? Why not just negotiate the treaties with Vothan and call off the wedding?"

"That would admit to poor judgment. That isn't something lords care to do."

"Did you discuss your suspicions about the wedding with Talsie?"

Lady Grenling shook her head and another tear slipped down her cheek. "To my great regret, I did not."

"So, to all appearances, you were on your way here with Talsie in part to see her married to Lord Keddro."

"That's how it was meant to appear, yes. The truth may be knottier."

Jarn finished his tea and set down his cup on a low table between the two couches. "If I'm to untie the knots, I need to know what they look like."

Lady Grenling shrugged. "Talsie has been abducted. Thus, the wedding will not take place. The problem is solved."

"You're not suggesting that Lord Grenling had anything to do with your daughter's abduction—are you?"

Lady Grenling grimaced, and a tear slipped from her eye. She glanced down and pressed her lips together as if to keep from sobbing, and her hands were clasped together so tightly that the knuckles had gone white. Jarn waited. He could have tried to comfort her with bland words, but he knew better than to fill a silence when talking to a witness. Much better to let her feel the pressure of the silence and hope she would fill it with some useful information. Lady Grenling wiped away the tear, and after a moment, she looked up at Jarn. "I think perhaps you will find my Talsie alive, but you may not find her well."

"Go on," Jarn said, his brows knitted.

"If you do find her … if you do, I won't be surprised …" Her voice trailed off, and she began to weep uncontrollably, her body shuddering with her sobs.

Again, Jarn waited, but as Lady Grenling fought to regain her composure, he had to clench his jaw to stop himself from swearing that he would find her precious daughter and return her safely or die in the effort. He knew he had to focus on the job at hand, and after giving her another moment, he said in a quiet voice, "What is it that won't surprise you?"

She looked up again and Jarn was shocked at the sudden fierceness in her eyes. "I won't be surprised if she's been … if she's been interfered with."

Jarn was stunned, but he immediately understood the awful logic in what she had said. "Are you suggesting that your daughter may have been abducted and then raped, in order to—"

"In order to make her unfit to marry Lord Keddro," Lady Grenling said in a half-strangled voice. "Oh, it wouldn't be a proper subject for the town criers, but it would be known, and no one would blame the lords for the broken marriage pact. The trade treaties and alliance agreements would be signed, Talsie would be quietly shipped back to Brythyn, and Lord Keddro could marry someone else."

"Do you really believe Lord Grenling capable of such a thing?" Jarn asked.

"If I know my husband, he isn't only capable of such a thing, but he probably sold the right to rape my daughter to the highest bidder."

Jarn took a breath. Finally, he asked, "If such a scheme truly took place—and at this point, we have no evidence to suggest that it did—do you also believe Sir Longboke was part of it? Would he be capable of such a crime?"

"I don't know. I have always known him to be honorable, but he is not a man of wealth. It's possible he could be tempted by gold."

"Even if he knew the full extent of the scheme that you suggest might have taken place?"

"He might not have known the full extent."

Jarn wanted to steer the conversation in a different direction. Though Lady Grenling's allegation had shocked him, he knew it was pure supposition, and there were other avenues to explore. "What else can you tell me about your daughter?"

Lady Grenling smiled, and her shoulders relaxed for the first time since Jarn began asking questions. "Talsie's kindness to all marks her most especially," she said. "She treats servants and common folk with the same gentleness and respect she gives to lords and ladies, much to my husband's vexation. She is at all times pleasant and polite, despite her shyness."

"How does she like to occupy herself?"

Lady Grenling's face seemed to light up. "She loves to sing. She has a truly beautiful voice, a magical voice, as if a goddess of song touched her. I hope you may hear her one day."

"I hope so, too," Jarn said.

"She plays as well, lute and lap harp, even the pipe, though she favors instruments that allow her to accompany her voice. She is quite skilled. The music gift came easy to her, though she also had a bit of tutoring in the musical arts."

"Only a bit?"

"Lord Grenling decided how much was sufficient. Enough for her to entertain guests when it suited him, but not enough to coddle her." She spoke evenly this time, but Jarn heard a trace of bitterness in her voice. He decided to change course again.

"Have you any thoughts concerning where we might search for Talsie?"

Lady Grenling shook her head, and Jarn saw her shoulders tense again. "I don't know. She could be right here in Skunnik, locked away in some ..." She sniffed back tears and composed herself. "Please have your men keep searching. They may find her wandering around somewhere, dazed and muddled. Please tell them to treat her gently."

59

"I will," Jarn said.

"And you should talk to Lord Keddro."

"We will. But I'd like to return to Willim Gilpin. Do you believe him capable of abducting Talsie to prevent the marriage? He wouldn't have known of this other scheme to stop it."

"He loves Talsie," Lady Grenling said. "He was distraught about the upcoming wedding. But I don't believe he could commit a crime of violence."

"Forgive me, Lady Grenling, but could your daughter have cooperated with him in such a plan?"

The fierce look that Jarn had seen before clouded Lady Grenling's face for just a moment, and then she shook her head slowly and smiled. "No. You see, while Willim loves Talsie, she does not love him, at least not in the romantic way. They have known one another since they were children, and she still thinks of him as a friend only, not as a possible suitor."

"Are you sure?"

"I'm sure, Captain. Talsie and I are close. She tells me things she tells no one else."

"Willim and Talsie both opposed her upcoming marriage to Lord Keddro," Jarn said. "It's at least possible that they conspired to prevent it."

"Yet she was resigned to the marriage," Lady Grenling replied. "Besides, she would have to come back sometime, so such a scheme would gain them nothing but a few days or weeks at most."

"Are you sure she would have to come back?"

"As I said, Captain, Talsie and I are close. She would not—could not—leave her mother forever."

60

"I see," Jarn said. "I have only one other question before I leave. If you could describe your daughter, please."

"She's beautiful," Lady Grenling said, and a smile lit her face. "She has long yellow hair, quite thick, with a bit of a lazy curl to it, wide blue eyes, and she's about as tall as me and built much the same way." She seemed about to add something, but hesitated, and her expression turned self-conscious.

"Go on," Jarn said.

"I was about to say she looks like me, if you can imagine me thirty years ago, but since I told you she was beautiful, it would sound as if I were boasting."

"Not at all," Jarn said, rising. "It's helpful to know."

Lady Grenling stood up. "I have a small portrait of Talsie that I will give to you before you go." She went to a cabinet and took out a small painting in an oval frame. She came back and handed it to Jarn. "There's my Talsie," she said.

Jarn took the portrait and gazed at it. "She is quite beautiful," he said. "And she does, indeed, look like her mother."

"Thank you," Lady Grenling said.

"Thank you for speaking with me. I may ask to see you again."

"I will be happy to do so, Captain." She walked with him to the door. As he was about to open it, she grasped his hand and said, "Please find my daughter."

"I will," Jarn said, hoping it was true.

Chapter 8

DAY 2

Jarn, Braga, Sir Tarris, Sir Longboke, Nevvin, and a group of fourteen Yellowshirt searchers left Skunnik just before dawn, heading for the place where Lady Talsie Grenling had disappeared. They took the eastern road from Skunnik, riding through the gloom of a cool and cloudy morning, crossing grassy meadows and flat farmland before entering the forest east of the city. Jarn led the way, riding side-by-side with Nevvin. Sir Tarris and Sir Longboke rode just behind. Sir Tarris had insisted that Jarn allow him to keep a close eye on his fellow Brythyner, and Jarn had agreed. He was counting up all such favors to the man, hoping he might make use of them in the future. The fourteen Yellowshirts came next, and Braga brought up the rear. It wasn't lost on Jarn that he and Braga were far outnumbered by their former antagonists, and he wanted his own man in a position to watch the Yellowshirts. The last time Jarn had been in the company of so many Acrinite Guardsmen, he had been a near prisoner, accused of crimes against the Greater Acrinite Realm and threatened constantly. He glanced at Nevvin, but the Yellowshirt seemed intent on the road ahead.

"It won't be far now," Sir Longboke said, interrupting Jarn's thoughts. "Just around that bend up ahead."

Jarn peered ahead through the dim early morning light, looking around at the woods through which they were traveling. Dark clouds still loomed overhead, blotting out the sun and threatening rain. Jarn picked up the pace, and a few minutes later he saw the clearing that Sir Longboke had described. Jarn and Nevvin halted and waited as the others assembled. He noticed that Braga hung back, still keeping an eye on the Acrinite Guardsmen.

"There's the boulder I sat on," Sir Longboke said, pointing at a large rock just off the road. "And the downed tree, where Lady Talsie sat."

Jarn dismounted, and the others followed suit. Jarn turned to Nevvin. "Best if you and your men hang back, if you please. Fewer boot prints to muck up the scene."

Nevvin frowned. "Boot prints?"

Jarn nodded. "Aye. A boot that's stepped in soft mud can sometimes be used to find the real boot after the mud dries."

"A boot's a boot, no?"

"Not always," Jarn said.

Nevvin gave a short laugh. "You Riders are tricksier than I ever thought."

Jarn looked at Sir Longboke. "Show me how you sat on the boulder."

Sir Longboke hesitated a moment and then walked to the boulder and sat down, facing the fallen tree trunk. He pointed. "Lady Talsie sat just there, directly across from me."

Jarn went to the tree trunk and sat. "Like this?"

"Aye," Sir Longboke said.

"Where were your horses?"

Sir Longboke turned his head and pointed. "Just there, hobbled."

Jarn looked at Braga and nodded. The big man led his horse to the spot Sir Longboke had indicated.

"Imagine that's your horse," Jarn said. "There's a skin of wine and two pewter cups in the saddlebag. I'd like you to play out the scene, if you please."

Sir Longboke stared at him. "I don't really think …"

"Do as he says," Sir Tarris snapped.

"Is that how your horse was placed?" Jarn asked.

Sir Longboke nodded and stood up, shooting a hard look at Sir Tarris.

"What about Lady Talsie's horse?" Jarn asked.

"The other side of mine, facing the same way."

"Did she remove anything from her saddlebags?"

"No."

Jarn nodded. "Carry on."

Sir Longboke strode toward Braga's horse. The other members of the company, most of whom had been chatting, went silent and watched him. He opened the saddlebag and took out a wineskin and two small pewter cups. He returned to the boulder, set down the cups on the flattest part of it, and squirted wine from the skin into both. He corked the skin, stood, and picked up one of the cups. He took three steps toward the tree trunk, stopped, and handed the cup to Jarn. Then he returned to his boulder, picked up the other cup, and sat down again.

Jarn raised his cup but didn't drink. "You weren't sure if Lady Talsie drank from her cup. Think back and try to remember. Close your eyes and fix the scene in your mind."

Sir Longboke closed his eyes. "I think … I'm almost certain that she …" He shook his head. "I believe she drank from the cup, but I still can't be sure."

"Bloody hell," Sir Tarris muttered.

"What happened to the wineskin and cups?" Jarn asked.

64

Sir Longboke frowned and looked around the clearing. "I don't know. I left them here when I rode into the city. I've no idea what became of them."

"How much wine did you drink?" Jarn asked.

"I finished a cup."

"How did it taste?"

"Like wine."

"When did Lady Talsie ask that you stop for a rest? How soon before you arrived here?"

"She didn't," Sir Longboke said. "I suggested that we stop here."

"What was her manner?"

"Same as always."

"Nothing to arouse any suspicion?"

Sir Longboke gave Jarn a hard stare. "No, of course not. What are you suggesting?"

"You mentioned bread and cheese," Jarn said, ignoring Longboke's question.

"We never got to them," Sir Longboke said. "The last thing I remember is finishing my wine, and staring at the sky."

"You said there was a narrow trail off the road. Where?"

Sir Longboke stood up and pointed. Jarn went to the spot, followed by Nevvin and Sir Tarris. The trail was narrow and winding, barely wide enough for a horse. Jarn scanned it, looking for hoof prints or boot prints. He began to walk, glancing around as if he were searching for something.

"What are you looking for?" Sir Tarris asked.

Jarn ignored him and kept walking, peering at the ground in front of him and glancing all around. A breeze freshened. The leaves on the tall trees of the forest rustled and whispered. Jarn listened. The sun appeared for a moment as a cloud moved from in front of it, its rays slanting thickly through the trees, illuminating dust motes hanging like mist in the cool air. Ahead, something glowed for an instant before another dark cloud blotted out the sun again. Jarn walked up to a shrub growing under a tall tree. He reached out and plucked a long yellow hair from a thin, gnarled branch. "This may be Lady Talsie's," he announced as Nevvin and Sir Tarris gathered around.

"We'll get started searching," Nevvin said.

The three men returned to the clearing and Nevvin ordered his men to mount up.

"Keep your eyes sharp for more than the young lady," Jarn told Nevvin. "Look for hoof prints, wagon wheel tracks, crumbs, cups, the wineskin, bits of clothing, more strands of hair, dried blood on leaves or branches."

Nevvin nodded and mounted his horse. "If the trail divides, I'll have my men split up as well. We'll follow as many trails as our numbers allow. We'll meet back in Skunnik in a couple of days."

"Report to me as soon as you get back," Jarn said, and then he watched as the fifteen Yellowshirts entered the narrow trail one at a time and gradually disappeared into the dense woods.

***

Kurff entered the Posthole Inn just after midday. As usual, the tiny place at the end of a dead-end alley in the Bolt was dark, dank, and empty of patrons. The proprietor, Maekel Gindee, was behind the bar, wiping the top with a damp cloth. He looked up when the door opened and nodded. "Afternoon, Kurff."

Kurff nodded back and took a seat at a table near the bar. He looked around the small, dimly lit common room, taking note of the barely glowing embers in its hearth, its grimy windows, and bare walls. "No wonder no one comes here. It's dreary. You ought to fix the place up."

"Who says no one comes here? You're here, eh?"

Kurff shrugged. He hadn't come for the tavern's food or mood, and they both knew it. But they would play their little game and see who could score a point. "What's on offer today?"

Maekel hesitated, as if he were not quite sure if the question referred to food or something else, but he recovered himself quickly and replied, "Cold beef and bread, perhaps a bit of bacon."

Kurff didn't reply immediately, staring at Maekel as if to imply that the innkeeper might indeed have given the wrong answer or perhaps answered the wrong question. Kurff let the silence stretch for three more heartbeats and said, "Bring a plate of beef and a tankard of ale, then."

Maekel turned away and lit a few candles in wrought iron sconces along the back wall, adding a slap more brightness to the room, and then disappeared through a door behind the bar. He returned a few minutes later with a pewter trencher piled with sliced beef and a half loaf of dark bread. He set down the food and then went to the bar to fetch a tankard of ale, which he placed next to the trencher. Kurff sprinkled salt from a wooden salt dish onto a slice of beef and took a big bite. He chewed and swallowed and then took a long pull of ale. He belched and finished the slice of beef and then spread salt on another slice. He tore off a chunk of bread and shoved it in his mouth. He felt Maekel's eyes on him. "A bit stale," he said, frowning at the bread.

"Baked this morning," Maekel replied, looking aggrieved.

"Too long in the oven, then."

Maekel sat down opposite Kurff. "You found Raff Salorian." Not a question.

"Aye. The Voths suspect the rebels."

Maekel snorted. "The Voths always suspect the rebels. If it storms today, they'll say it was the rebels' doing."

"He had the black triangle."

"Anyone can ink a triangle."

"Who else would want to kill him? Who else would hold him for nine days beforehand?"

"Aye, so it probably was the rebels." Maekel paused a moment and said, "I heard Raff was ready to make a deal to supply hay and oats to the Vothan Riders." He looked at Kurff as if to gauge his reaction. "You know anything about that?"

"Why would I?"

"You work with them."

"The Vothan Riders don't make me privy to their hay and oats business. But if Raff did a deal with them, it was because he was trying to earn his living."

"You going soft, Kurff? Spending too much time with them Riders?"

"Working with the Vothan Riders is how I get information I might not otherwise get, and don't you forget it. As for going soft, I invite any man in the known world to try me, including you."

Maekel raised his hands in a conciliatory gesture. "Not me, Kurff. I'm no fighting man."

"No. You're just a barkeep who likes to buy information."

"Not buy, Kurff, never buy. I trade information, as you well know."

Kurff shrugged and took a gulp of ale.

"How long has it been since you've been coming in here trying to pry loose some bit of knowledge or another?" Maekel asked sharply, as if he were annoyed. "Half a year or more, eh? Since about the time the rebels started up, eh, Kurff?"

Kurff grunted and shoved another hunk of beef into his mouth.

Maekel frowned and looked even more annoyed. "Got nothing to say, Kurff?"

"I'll have another ale first, if you please."

Maekel, grumbling, stood up and went to fetch it. Kurff watched him. Maekel returned a few moments later with two tankards. He set them down and took his seat again. He seemed less irritated. "So, then, what tidings?"

Kurff looked around the empty dining room and then back at Maekel. "Where is young Hussert today?"

Maekel jerked a thumb over his shoulder. "In the back."

"Probably with his big ear up against the door."

Maekel shrugged. "Never mind. I'm sending him to the market."

"Good. I don't trust him."

Maekel snorted. "He's harmless. His mind is too slow for mischief."

"That sluggish mind will likely bring him to grief one day. You as well, if you're not careful."

Maekel waved away the notion with a backhand gesture. "He's a good lad, for all that."

"I'd keep an eye on that one."

"Bah, he's harmless, I tell you."

The door at the rear of the dining room opened, and a young man carrying two large wicker baskets stepped into the room. He was large, taller than Kurff and heavier as well, his shape reminding Kurff of a pear. He had straw-colored hair, cut short, no beard, small blue eyes, and a wide, flat face as pale as the moon. He grinned, showing large, crooked teeth. "Hoy, Kurff, what's doing?" he said as he approached.

"What's doing, Hussert, is that you're going to the market," Kurff said. "At least that's what Maekel tells me."

"Aye, yes, Maekel tells it true."

"Best get to it, then," Kurff said. "You won't want to be late, else all the best fruit and vegetables will be picked clean. Course, you can always steal what you want from someone else."

Hussert gave a snorting laugh and nodded his big head. "You're a wise one, Kurff. I always say that, don't I Maekel?"

"Aye, that you do," Maekel said. "Now off you go, eh?"

"Hoy, aye, I'm off."

"Aye, you're off all right," Kurff muttered under his breath.

Hussert, a big grin on his face, strode to the front door and left without another word.

When he was gone, Maekel turned to Kurff. "Now then, what's the news?"

"The diplomat sent here from Brythyn to treat with the Voths managed to get his daughter abducted a couple of days ago," Kurff replied. "Lord Grenling's the man's

70

name." Kurff gazed at Maekel, trying to decide if he already knew about the abduction, but the man's face gave away nothing.

"Say on," Maekel said.

"The Voths are in a state over it. Grenling says he won't treat with them until they find his daughter."

"Good for him. What are the mighty Voths doing about it?"

"The usual things the Voths do. Making threats, waving their swords around, giving orders."

"The Yellowshirts helping them?"

Kurff shrugged. "That's our charge now, isn't it?"

"Aye, for those that stayed."

"What, you think I should have joined the rebels or sold my sword to the Gurgeonites?"

"Not for me to tell another man what to do."

"No, but you obviously have an opinion."

Maekel shook his head. "I have as few of those as I can, and what I do have I keep to myself. But if the Acrinites ever rise up and throw off the Voths ..."

"They'll call us collaborators and hang the lot of us, is that what you were going to say?"

"I already told you, I keep my opinions to myself."

"Not all the Yellowshirts who stayed behind are happy about working with the Voths."

"Then why do they do it?" Maekel asked.

"What's their choice? If they flee to the Gurgeon or try to join up with the Yellowshirts who fled last year, they're not likely to be accepted back into the fold."

"There are other choices," Maekel said, his voice pitched low.

Kurff left that hanging in the air, waiting to see if Maekel would do any more with it. He didn't, but Kurff sensed an opening that had not existed before. For the first time in the six months he had been visiting Maekel he felt as if he were getting somewhere.

"About this Brythyner wench—who do your Vothan friends think took her?"

"They're not my friends, and they don't know. Who do you think took her?"

Maekel shrugged. "How would I know? I'd wager you have a thought on the matter, though."

Kurff did have a thought on the matter, one that no one else had, but he wasn't about to share it with Maekel—not yet, anyway. He finished his beef and bread and slid his trencher aside. Outside, a light rain began to fall, pattering against the front windows. In the distance, thunder growled. "I and my men are supposed to be searching suspected rebel locations in the city."

"What suspected rebel locations?" Maekel said, a bit too quickly.

Kurff raised an eyebrow. "There's a list."

"What list?"

"Names scrawled on a piece of parchment—a list."

"That why you're here?"

"I'm here for the beef and ale."

"Bugger you, Kurff," Maekel snapped.

Kurff grinned at him. He knew what Maekel wanted to know—if the Posthole Inn was on the list of suspected rebel locations. But he wanted the man to work for the information.

"Who's on the damnable list?" Maekel asked sharply.

"I'm not free to divulge official information."

"Blast you all to hell, Kurff, is the Posthole on it or not?"

Kurff took a long pull of ale and belched. "The smugglers and cutpurses you deal with—any of them do the bidding of the rebels?"

"I don't know any smugglers and cutpurses."

"No, no, of course not. But do any of them aid the rebels?"

"How would I know?"

Kurff shrugged. "Maybe while you weren't knowing any cutpurses or smugglers, you also weren't knowing any rebels."

"You're spouting quagwash now, Kurff."

"I saw the list of suspected rebel houses," Kurff said. "The Posthole isn't on it."

Maekel looked relieved, though he also looked as if he didn't want to show it. "No reason it should be," he said. "Not that a man's innocence would matter to the Voths."

"What've you got for me?" Kurff asked.

Maekel shot Kurff a bright smile. "Another ale?"

Kurff ignored the jape. "Some Voths think the rebels snatched the Brythyner lass."

"Hah, the rebels again. The Voths must think of nothing else." Maekel squinted at Kurff, giving him a hard stare. "You seem to be more than a bit interested in them as well, Kurff. You really going to help the Riders catch rebels?"

Kurff shrugged. "There could be more than one reason I might be interested in the rebels."

Maekel eyed him intently, and then nodded. "Yes, I suppose there could be after all."

Chapter 9

Astil was sitting at a square table in a small, windowless room in the basement of the building known as the Mang, in northern Skunnik. The waif Aarla sat opposite, gazing at her intently, as if trying to hear her thoughts. The young Vothan Rider named Bleuek sat to her left, his gaze alternating between her and Aarla. An armed Rider stood guard near the door, and Astil knew that two more Riders were standing watch just outside.

"Who are we waiting for?" Astil asked.

"Captain Jarn," Bleuek replied.

"Jarn Theffig?"

"Aye. You remember him, eh?"

Astil frowned and gave a little nod. She did remember Jarn Theffig, though he had been a saddlemaster when she last encountered him. "What does he want with me?"

"Wants to make you an offer."

"The same offer everyone else has been making, no doubt."

"Aye. You should take it."

Astil shook her head and then looked at Aarla. "What's your role in this mummers' farce? I thought you had taken up with some old virrling in a hidden fold of some secret forest. What was his name? Yellow? Yelling?"

"Yellig," Aarla replied. "My father."

Astil raised an eyebrow and gave Aarla a grudging nod. "That would explain your annoying powers."

Aarla gave her a vague smile and nodded back. "Aye, such gifts as you and I possess usually pass through family lines."

"What of your mother?"

"A mortal woman who died birthing me."

"That would explain the meagerness of your powers."

"And how did you come by your mighty powers?" Bleuek asked.

Astil shrugged. "I don't know. I'm an orphan. I assume my father was a virrling or at least a powerful mage."

"Powerful goblin, more likely," Bleuek said.

Astil shot him an icy smile. "Mind yourself, Saddlemaster. You don't want to make an enemy of me."

"How do you find people?" Aarla asked.

Astil shook her head. "I don't quite know. It helps to have one of my quarry's possessions." She tapped the side of her head with a finger. "I see my prey in here, as clear as Telnan crystal. I see where he goes, see the path he's following, sometimes even before he does." She narrowed her eyes at Aarla. "How do you do whatever it is that you do?"

Aarla shrugged. "Like you, I don't entirely understand it. Sometimes I know things, of a sudden like. The knowledge comes unbidden into my mind, but when it happens, it's never wrong."

"My misfortune," Astil said, frowning. "Tell me, will you always be able to know where I am?"

"I can sense you," Aarla said. "As you sense your quarry."

"You didn't answer the question," Astil said.

At that moment, the door opened and the Vothan Rider Jarn Theffig stepped into the room, carrying a small leather case.

Aarla stood up. "I've enjoyed talking to you," she said, giving Astil one of those annoyingly vague smiles that sometimes crossed her face, as if she possessed some secret knowledge that no one else had. Astil was torn between an urge to slap the waif's face and a desire to ask her what she knew. But Aarla turned and left the room, and Captain Jarn took the chair she had been sitting in and set the leather case on the floor. Saddlemaster Bleuek pulled his chair around and sat next to the captain.

"I hope you're enjoying your stay with us," Captain Jarn said to her.

Astil was decidedly not enjoying her stay with the Vothan Riders. She had spent a sleepless night in a locked and guarded room, plagued by nightmares about her gold, which the Riders had taken from her. "I want the gold you stole from me."

"Not stole. Your gold is in safekeeping until you can reclaim it."

"Your saddlemaster told me about your offer. My answer is no."

"Then we've no choice but to send you back to Wyndor," Captain Jarn replied. "To serve out the remainder of your sentence."

"Do that," Astil replied. "I'll enjoy escaping again."

The captain shrugged. "We'll enjoy finding you again."

"Not if I murder your little bitch hound first."

"You're a criminal, but I don't believe you're a murderer."

"I can learn."

"Aarla can go to a place where even you can't find her."

"Ah, yes, her father's famous enchanted forest. But this prattling grows tiresome. When do we leave for Wyndor? I'm beginning to miss their fine jail. Not that I'll be there for long."

"Do you really suppose the Wyndorans will let you escape again? You'll be an old wrinkled crone by the time you get out." Captain Jarn gave her an appraising glance. "A shame to waste such beauty as you possess on rats and night bugs."

"I don't succumb to flattery, Captain. Especially flattery from Voths, rare though it is."

"You're not stupid, so perhaps you'll succumb to sense," the captain said. "If you agree to help us, you might spend a week, maybe two, probably no more than three, searching for Lady Talsinora Grenling. Once you find her, you'll be free, with a full pardon for your past crimes, which the Wyndorans have already agreed to. Of course, you'll have to promise not to commit any crimes in the future."

"Of course. But why should I trust you?"

"As I said, you're not stupid. You must know that we Voths are as good as our word."

Astil did know, but she wasn't about to admit it. Besides, there was another matter of greater importance, one that might just sway her to the Voths' cause. "What about my gold? I earned it honestly."

"So you did," Captain Jarn said. "Right now, it's still yours. We have it in safekeeping for you. Of course, if you don't receive a pardon, you will forfeit any riches, honestly gained or no."

77

"Let me make sure I understand you, Captain. If I were to help you find this Brythyner princess, or whatever she is, the Wyndorans will grant me a full pardon, and you'll return my gold to me. All of my gold. And I'll be free to go on my way."

The captain nodded.

"Not that I'll ever help you, of course, but let's suppose, just for a moment, that I did agree to do so—how do you propose to proceed?"

"I believe that Talsie isn't far away. It's even possible that her abductors are holding her here in Skunnik. Once you located her, you would tell us where she is, and we would devise a plan to rescue her."

"What if she isn't nearby?"

"If you determine that she's at some distance, then you would lead me and a group of my men to the location."

Astil laughed. "You expect me to join a squadron of Vothan Riders?"

"No, not join, simply lead us to Talsie."

"I work alone," Astil said. "If I were to agree to help you—I won't, but if I did—I would never consent to be accompanied by Vothan Riders."

"Then you would have to get word to us somehow."

Astil shrugged. "Not necessarily."

Jarn narrowed his eyes at her. "I won't have you putting Talsie at risk just so you can demonstrate your boldness and add another blood-soaked adventure to your long list of feats."

Astil shook her head and laughed again. "Blood-soaked adventures, eh? You've just described the Vothan Riders, not me."

78

"Contrary to what you might have heard, the Riders try to avoid bloodshed whenever possible."

"You've made a good job of fooling the known world."

"Much to our advantage."

"Ah, a bit of Vothan deception, then," Astil said.

Jarn shrugged, but she saw the ghost of a smile cross his face.

"If you help us, you can work alone. As long as you agree to act in Talsie's best interest."

"And I wouldn't want anyone following me—like your little witch."

"Agreed," Jarn said.

"I would want the agreement in writing."

Captain Jarn picked up the leather satchel, placed it on the table in front of him, and opened it. He pulled a parchment from it and slid it across the table. Astil raised her manacled hands from the table, and Bleuek unlocked and removed them from her wrists. Astil picked up the parchment and read it, and then she read it again. It was signed by High Lord Graef Haffindel, the leader of Wyndor, and Semsen Torgmar, the leader of Vothan. She read it a third time. It seemed solid.

Another question occurred to Astil, more out of curiosity than self-interest. "Why should you trust me?"

"I don't, but I'm told that once you make an agreement, you live up to it," Captain Jarn replied. "There's apparently some honor in you, of a sort."

"You've flattered me twice now, of a sort," she said with a half-smile. She couldn't help but notice that the captain's rugged-looking face was not unhandsome, and, like most Voths, especially Vothan Riders, he was exceedingly fit. She began to wonder what he looked like under all that leather and brass.

"Well, what's it to be?" the captain asked, interrupting her musings.

"Do you have ink and a quill?" she asked.

Bleuek stood up and went to a small cabinet in a corner of the room. He opened a drawer and took out an inkpot and a fine goose quill. He handed the quill to Astil and set the inkpot in front of her.

"I want all my gold," Astil murmured as she signed the parchment.

"You'll get all your gold," Captain Jarn said. "After you help us find Talsie Grenling."

**

After his successful negotiation with Astil, Jarn sent a message to Sir Tarris to arrange another meeting with Lord and Lady Grenling, for that day, if possible. He planned to take Astil to the meeting and then send her off immediately after. He was eager for the sorceress to begin her mission. Every hour that passed made it less likely they would find Talsie Grenling alive.

While he was waiting in the basement headquarters to hear from Sir Tarris, he sent a messenger to fetch Grion, for whom he had a special assignment in mind. When Grion arrived, Jarn took him to his inner office in the Mang's basement headquarters, which the men involved in the investigation had begun calling the "Rats Nest." Jarn sat behind his desk, and Grion sat in a chair facing him.

"Lady Grenling thinks her husband may be responsible for Talsie's abduction," Jarn told the graybeard. "She believes that he and Lord Keddro want to back out of the marriage arrangement without having to admit they used poor judgment in negotiating it in the first place."

Grion gave Jarn a skeptical look. "Does the lady have any evidence of such an outrage?"

Jarn shook his head. "None that she gave me, though she seems to honestly believe it."

"How would Grenling have accomplished such a deed?"

"We can only speculate. He claims Talsie complained of feeling ill during the trip to Skunnik, but it may be that he told her to enter the city separately from the train. If so, he could have hired brigands before they left Brythyn to abduct her on the way."

"What of Sir Longboke?"

"He might have been part of the scheme or a victim of it—if there was such a scheme."

"If he was a victim, how did the schemers render him unconscious without revealing themselves?"

Jarn shrugged. "A spell, a potion, a knock on the head from behind. Right now, we know little to naught, but I aim to follow every possible avenue. I want you and a team of spies to keep a close watch on Lord Grenling while he's in the Palace of the High Hext. Choose men who know something about carpentry or masonry, or at least sweeping and cleaning, and feign some repairs."

"What about the Yellowshirt company that guards the palace?"

"I'll talk to Kurff and have him inform their captain that you're coming."

Grion arched an eyebrow. "You trust Kurff?"

"No, but for now I need him."

Grion nodded. "I'll pull together a team. Let me know when we can go in."

"Get yourselves some tools and leather aprons," Jarn said. "Or some brooms and mops."

"Brushes and paint," Grion said, rising. "I've noticed a few worn spots here and there in the Hext's House. We surely don't want such a grand palace to plunge into shabbiness."

"Surely not," Jarn said.

Grion left, and not long after, Sir Tarris arrived.

"Lady Grenling will see you now," the Brythyner said.

"Not Lord Grenling as well?"

"He says he's occupied with other concerns."

"No matter. Wait here, and I'll fetch Astil."

"That woman sends a cold chill down my spine, I don't mind confessing," Sir Tarris said.

Jarn laughed. "It's one of her gifts, as she would be only too happy to explain."

"I want to be present when you and she meet with Lady Grenling."

"Becoming keen on chills down the spine, Sir Tarris?"

"I'm keen on protecting Lady Grenling. And I must insist that the witch not be armed during the interview."

"She won't be," Jarn said. "Not until she leaves on her mission."

***

Jarn, Sir Tarris, and Astil rode to the Palace of the High Hex and entered the grounds through the main gate.

They left their horses with a pair of grooms and headed on foot toward the palace's grand front entrance.

"We'll meet with Lady Grenling in the Red Room again," Sir Tarris said.

"I know the Red Room," Astil said. She veered left and headed toward a side entrance guarded by a pair of Yellowshirts. "This way is shorter."

Sir Tarris stopped and glared at her, but when she kept walking and Jarn followed, he ran to catch up, muttering under his breath.

"I see you know your way around the palace," Jarn said, amused at Sir Tarris's discomfiture. "I suppose I shouldn't be surprised."

"No, you shouldn't," Astil said. "I've been here often enough."

She took them directly to the suite of rooms where Jarn had met with Lady Grenling before, and Sir Tarris knocked on the door to the outer chamber. A servant opened it and took them to the inner room, where Lady Grenling was waiting. She stood up and gave Jarn a warm smile.

"Lady Grenling, this is Astil," Jarn said, gesturing toward the sorceress. "She has a gift for finding people, and she's agreed to help us look for Talsie."

Lady Grenling nodded at Astil. "Please, sit."

The servant left, and Jarn and Astil sat on the red couch across from Lady Grenling. Sir Tarris remained standing, his eyes on Astil and his hand never far from his sword.

"I need something that belongs to your daughter," Astil said. "To help me find her."

"Tell me what you require," Lady Grenling replied.

"An item of clothing, a brooch or necklace, a comb, a brush, a favorite cup. Anything of hers."

Lady Grenling thought for a moment and then stood up. "Her ring. She brought a ring with her."

She left through a door at the back of the chamber and returned a few minutes later with a ring in her hand. Astil stood up, and Lady Grenling handed the ring to her. The sorceress examined it for a few moments and then nodded to Lady Grenling. "A polished saffite stone in a fine gold band. A costly piece. Your daughter has good taste. Did she wear this often?"

Lady Grenling frowned and shook her head. "No, not often. Mostly at fests and tournaments and the like. Will it not suffice for your purposes?"

"It will suffice," Astil said.

"I showed Astil the portrait of Talsie you gave me," Jarn said to Lady Grenling. "And I had one of my Riders, a man skilled in picture making, sketch some likenesses from the portrait."

Lady Grenling looked at Astil. "She's a delicate creature, Talsie is. You'll take care with her if … when you find her, will you not?"

"Of course," Astil replied, a bit too quickly. She turned away from Lady Grenling and looked at Jarn. "Have you seen to the provisions I asked for?"

Jarn nodded. "I have."

"And you'll return my weapons to me?"

"They're waiting for you, along with your horse. I should also tell you that a few of my men have volunteered to accompany you, if you like."

"As I told you before, Captain, I prefer to work alone, thank you. Unless you yourself would like to accompany me." She gave Jarn a smile that might almost have been seductive, and he saw her shoot a quick glance toward Lady Grenling, as if to gauge her reaction. When she turned back to him, she put a hand on his shoulder. "You can at least take me to the trail you found, Captain, if you're not afraid of traveling alone with me."

"Then we'll take our leave," Jarn said to Lady Grenling. Astil was already headed toward the door.

Chapter 10

Jarn and Astil returned to the Mang. The sorceress went to her rooms to prepare for the next day, which would see her begin her search for Talsie Grenling, or so Jarn hoped. He went to the large meeting room in the Rats Nest, waiting for whoever might show up. He didn't expect to see Nevvin yet, but Kurff and the city searchers should have something to report. As he waited for Vothan Riders and Yellowshirt search-team leaders to arrive, he thought about Astil. She had briefly flirted with him in front of Lady Grenling, as if she thought she could make the other woman jealous. A foolish notion, except that Jarn, too, had an inkling that Lady Grenling might be treating him perhaps a bit more warmly than might be warranted, given the circumstances of their acquaintance. Perhaps her clearly troubled marriage had something to do with her manner toward him. None of that explained why Astil would want to make her jealous, other than Astil's natural penchant for causing trouble.

He waited a few more minutes as the last few Vothan Riders and Yellowshirt searchers entered the large meeting room. Grion came in, looking pleased with himself, and nodded at Jarn. That meant he had assembled his team of spies and was ready to begin surveillance of Lord Grenling at the Palace of the High Hext. Bleuek entered, also looking pleased, whether because of his recent success in leading the team that captured Astil or because Aarla was nearby Jarn didn't know, but the young man had proven himself competent and resourceful. Jarn would have to give him another assignment worthy of his talents. Kurff arrived soon after, which was fortunate, since Jarn needed him to arrange for Grion and his group of spies to go to the palace without arousing suspicion.

There were about twenty men in the room when Jarn asked someone to close the door and then sat down at the head of the large oval table and called the meeting to order. "First, I have news. We've engaged an expert tracker to help us find Talsie Grenling. She has a special gift for finding people, and we believe she might succeed even when more-traditional efforts fall short."

"What tracker?" Kurff asked, his dark eyes narrowed nearly to slits.

"Astil," Jarn replied. "Any questions?"

"Just one," Kurff responded. "When did you and Commander Lahgoh lose your minds?"

"Astil has the skills we need to find Talsie Grenling," Jarn said, echoing the same argument Lahgoh had made to him.

"She has the skills to slip a blade between your ribs or put a bolt into your throat," Kurff said. "The woman is as dangerous as a wounded quagbeest and quite possibly mad. And won't your Wyndoran friends be angry when they hear you're employing a criminal who escaped from their jail?"

"The Wyndorans granted her a full pardon in exchange for her helping us."

"More fools them. What makes you think you'll ever see her again?"

"We're holding a load of gold that belongs to her."

"Ah," Kurff said, nodding. "I see."

"I'll have your report about your searches inside the city now, if you please."

Kurff stood and unrolled a parchment on which he had written some notes. "My men checked all sixteen of the sites you suspect of harboring rebels or rebel sympathizers. They turned up nothing."

"Did they ask questions?"

"Of course they asked questions. They even searched a few of the places—with the owners' permission, of course—but there was naught amiss."

"Did any of your men get a sense of anything? What do their instincts tell them?"

"Their instincts tell them you're dropping your bucket down a dry well."

"What's your sense?"

Kurff shrugged. "I agree with the men. The Grenling girl is not in the city. You had better hope the witch finds her and is as good as her word, or that Nevvin does. That's not to say that either of them will find her alive."

"We still don't know if she was taken by rebels or by brigands who want to ransom her."

"She was snatched the day before yesterday," Kurff said. "If it's brigands wanting ransom, Lord Grenling should hear something soon."

"What if it turns out to be rebels wanting ransom money?" Braga asked.

Kurff frowned and shook his head. "Not the rebels' usual practice."

"Doesn't mean they can't change," said Braga. "It would earn them some gold and put the frighteners into any former allies of Acrin that might be considering treaties with the Voths."

"Until we get a demand from the abductors, it's all guesswork," Jarn said. "Meanwhile, Lord Grenling has summoned a young man from Brythyn who is close friends with Talsie. I plan to talk to him the moment he arrives."

"Why?" Kurff asked.

"The young man may have been distraught over Talsie's impending marriage to Lord Keddro. He may have abducted her to prevent the wedding."

"You're suggesting that a lovesick young man overcame a knight of Brythyn and made off with the victim?"

"I'm exploring all avenues, Kurff."

Kurff shrugged. "Fair enough. But if you really think the love-crazed whelp is your chief suspect, then you ought to let me help you interview him. I have some notions about—"

"I know you have some notions," Jarn said, interrupting. "Those notions are devious and possibly illegal."

"Hog's breath," Kurff shot back. "Abducting young women is devious and most certainly illegal. Finding the culprit who did it is fitting and proper."

"It isn't fitting and proper when you lie to the people you want information from."

Kurff glared at Jarn and pointed a stubby finger at him. "Says you. If you had the brains you were born with, you'd use every arrow in your quiver. You wouldn't be so damned delicate about how you treat lawbreakers. You'd follow every avenue, if I may borrow a phrase."

Jarn heard some of the Yellowshirts snickering, and he gritted his teeth, forcing himself to pause before speaking. "We're talking about a suspected lawbreaker, Kurff. We don't know yet if the young man is guilty."

Kurff gave a low growl and shook his head disgustedly, looking as if he wanted to spit. "I realize we don't know yet if the young rogue is guilty," he said in a half-strangled voice, as if he were speaking through clenched teeth. "That's the aim of hard questioning, to get at the truth."

"Torturing people doesn't get at the truth," Braga said.

Kurff fixed him with an icy stare. "I'm not talking about torture, Braga. I've never tortured anyone." He turned back to Jarn. "Let me ask you a question, Captain. What's worse, a lie that might get at the truth or a dead young woman?"

"I take your point," Jarn replied. "But for now, we'll do it my way."

***

After the meeting, Jarn went to see Lahgoh in his quarters. As he approached the door, which was partly open, he heard Lahgoh speaking. He poked his head in, intending only to let his commander know he wanted to speak with him whenever he was finished, but Lahgoh looked up and gestured for him to enter. When he did, he was startled to see a woman he knew but had not seen in years sitting across from Lahgoh. She wore the leather and brass uniform of a Vothan Rider and the insignia of a captain on her shoulder.

"Liora," Jarn said.

"Captain," she responded.

"I sent for Liora to help us in the Talsie Grenling matter," Lahgoh said.

Why, Jarn wanted to ask, but he held his tongue. Instead, he said, "I'm sure she'll be a great help. Did you have anything particular in mind?"

Lahgoh shook his head. "I'll leave that to you."

"Very well," Jarn said.

There was a momentary silence, which, thankfully, Lahgoh finally filled. "I've been bringing Liora up to date on the investigation, and she'll no doubt have some valuable ideas about it."

Liora smiled, and Jarn remembered why he had been so attracted to her all those years ago. "I'm sure Captain Jarn has his own ideas," she said to Lahgoh, and then she looked at Jarn and her smile vanished. "You may need some time to decide what to do with me."

Jarn nodded. "I'll think it over and let you know tomorrow."

Liora turned back to Lahgoh. "I'll take my leave now. It's good to see you again, Line Commander." She stood up and left the room without even a glance at Jarn.

Jarn took the chair Liora had been sitting in. It was warm, and he felt a brief shiver run down his spine. He shook his head and tried to clear his mind.

"You all right, Jarn?" Lahgoh asked, knitting his brow.

"Fine," Jarn said. "But suddenly, there are a lot of women involved in this case."

Lahgoh frowned. "I thought Liora might be of service."

"No doubt she will, but …"

"Go on."

"Liora and I were once, uh …"

"I see. How long ago?"

"Nine years," Jarn said. "We were both barely out of training."

"Will her presence here cause you difficulty?"

Jarn shook his head. "No. Seeing her surprised me, that's all. It's been a long while."

Lahgoh drummed his fingers on his desk. "Do you have any tasks she might do? She's an accomplished spy, among her many other talents."

"I'll find something," Jarn said.

"What of your investigation?"

"I asked Grion to gather a team of spies to keep an eye on Lord Grenling, just in case Lady Grenling's suspicions have merit."

"Lord Grenling is pompous and arrogant, but it's difficult to believe he would have his own daughter abducted."

"I agree," Jarn replied. "But there is something amiss with that man. There may be advantage in watching him without his knowing."

"What of Lord Keddro?" Lahgoh asked.

"I plan to speak to him tomorrow. I'll ask Sir Tarris to arrange it."

"Have Tarris accompany you to the interview."

Jarn nodded. "I will. I hope to talk to Willim Gilpin tomorrow as well."

"Perhaps Sir Tarris should help you there, too."

"Perhaps so. Kurff asked to sit in, but I told him no. I don't like his manner of questioning."

"Nor do I, but he has gotten results."

"Aye, but he's also persuaded innocent men to admit to guilt."

"Don't reject his help entirely," Lahgoh said. "I don't need to remind you how important this matter is."

"No," Jarn said.

Chapter 11

DAY 3

Jarn and Astil headed out before dawn the next day, riding to the clearing where Talsie Grenling had been abducted. The sun was up by the time they got there, and Jarn pointed to the trail where he had found the strand of hair. "We think whoever took her went that way. A Yellowshirt named Nevvin and fourteen of his men set out along the trail yesterday. You may run into them."

"Perhaps they'll already have found the girl," Astil said.

"Perhaps so," said Jarn.

"But you'll still return my gold."

"Of course."

Astil smiled. "Then I hope to see you again soon, Captain. Perhaps I'll stand you to an ale or two at one of Skunnik's finer taverns."

Before Jarn could think of a reply, she wheeled around and disappeared up the trail. Jarn shrugged, turned his horse around, and headed back to Skunnik.

***

Twenty yards in, Astil stopped, listening hard to the sound of Jarn's horse cantering away. Soon she could no longer hear it, but she waited a few minutes more before turning around and riding back to the clearing. She stopped and pulled the sketch of Talsie Grenling from a saddlebag. She studied it, then put it away and took out Talsie's ring, which she had put on a fine silver chain. She clasped the ring in her left hand and closed her eyes, concentrating. The image of Talsie appeared in her mind, the image from the sketch. She squeezed the ring and concentrated harder. She opened her eyes and took a deep breath. She put the chain around her neck and placed the ring under her tunic, against her skin. She closed her eyes again and tried to clear her mind. Instead of concentrating, she let her thoughts wander, watching them as if from a distance as they scurried and pranced, wheeled and turned and veered off, twisted back on themselves, mingled, mixed, and merged. She opened her eyes and frowned. A moment later, she spurred her horse and set off at a canter.

***

Aarla woke up at dawn. She had slept in the woods, in a clearing just off the road that ran between Brythyn and Skunnik, close to a gurgling stream that had lulled her to sleep the night before. She threw off her wool blanket, got up and stretched, watching the early morning sun paint the eastern sky pink. She talked to her horse, Cutter, and stroked his head and neck. Then she walked along a narrow path that sloped downward from the clearing to the stream, at a spot where it widened into a pond just before tumbling over some large boulders. She listened to the sound of the small waterfall for a moment and then removed her clothes and plunged into the pond.

The cold water was like a blow to the body and it made her head hurt, but she ducked under the surface and opened her eyes, hoping she might catch a fish for her breakfast. She surfaced and swam around, ducked under again, but didn't see any fish large enough for a meal. She swam to the edge of the pond, heaved herself out, and stood shivering on the muddy bank. She squeezed the water out of her long yellow hair and headed back to the clearing. She waited until the rising sun had dried her off enough to get dressed again and then headed away from the path and into the woods to search for something to eat.

She spotted a thicket of weeds and approached it, listening to the twittering of birds in the canopy above and blinking against the slanting rays of sunlight slipping in between the tall trees. She stooped down and grabbed a weed, yanked it out of the ground, and sniffed it. "Boarweed," she murmured. She tore off some leaves, put them in her mouth, and chewed. She pulled up a dozen more weeds and took them to the pond to rinse off the dirt. She ate the leaves and some of the stems and washed it down with pond water before searching for something else. She found a patch of dragonweed just off the path, near the road, and smiled. It was one of her favorites. She found a slim but sturdy branch that had fallen from a tree and used it to dig up one of the dragonweed plants. She took it to the pond, thoroughly rinsed the dirt from the entire plant, and then ate the tender part of the roots before eating the leaves and flowers.

Aarla found some mareweed for Cutter, and when he had eaten his fill, she took him to the pond to drink. The sun had been up for two hours when she saddled the horse, mounted up, and headed up the path toward the road that would take her to Skunnik.

Just shy of the road, she stopped and listened. She heard the sound of a horse cantering. She closed her eyes and let her mind settle. Sometimes she knew things. She didn't know how she knew them, but whenever she knew something, she knew it for sure; her mysterious knowledge, when it came, was never wrong. She knew

95

that a young man on horseback was heading her way, and she knew there was something about him that she needed to discover, something amiss.

She dismounted and led Cutter back into the woods, far enough in that she would not be seen from the road. She waited, listening to the other horse. Finally, it passed. Still she waited. She left Cutter and headed toward the road. When she reached it, she looked toward Skunnik and saw the horse and rider in the distance. She waited until he was out of sight and then went back to Cutter, mounted up, and headed toward the city.

***

After taking Astil to the site of Talsie Grenling's abduction, Jarn returned to Skunnik and went to the Mang's dining hall for breakfast. The huge room projected out from the east side of the otherwise rectangular building like an open desk drawer, allowing windows on three sides. A twenty-foot-high ceiling gave the room a cavernous aspect that was relieved by the abundant sunlight streaming in through the windows on bright days. At night, torches set in high sconces along the walls provided illumination.

The dining room was not crowded at that hour, and Jarn sat by himself at a table near a window, where he took his time eating boiled eggs, a slab of bacon, honey-covered flauns, and strong tea. As he ate, the eastern sky slowly went from black to gray and then gradually turned to a soft rose color. Jarn gazed through the window and watched the silent spectacle of another daybreak. He felt the air move and turned to see Liora Vaningo standing next to his table, gazing at him. She was tall and lean, but not unshapely, and her dark shoulder-length hair was as curly as he remembered. Her features were fine, almost delicate, but he detected a grim seriousness in her expression that had not been there nine years earlier.

"Liora," he said. "Good morning. Sit."

She hesitated a moment and then sat down across from him. "Have you sorted out how I might aid your investigation?"

Jarn shook his head. "Not yet. I have some interviews coming up, but they're already arranged."

"Perhaps it was a mistake for Lahgoh to send for me. Perhaps I should return to Rualgar."

"Now that you're here, you may as well stay, for a few days, anyway, until we see how things progress."

She nodded. "A few days, then."

"Have you any thoughts about the Grenling case?"

She shook her head. "It seems as if it's all down to your search parties."

"You may be right. If the searchers don't find Talsie, I'm not sure what else we can do."

Liora gave him a long look. "You're troubled," she said at length.

Jarn nodded. "There is something odd about this case, something I'm missing."

"Who have you spoken to so far?"

"The victim's parents, Lord and Lady Grenling, and Sir Longboke, the knight who was escorting Talsie when she was abducted."

"Who among them do you believe?"

Jarn gave a short laugh. "I don't know yet."

"Then it's best to believe none of them."

"You've become cynical, Liora."

"So I have," she said, standing up. "Let me know when you have something useful for me to do." She turned and walked out of the dining room, just as Bleuek entered.

"Who was that?" Bleuek asked after he joined Jarn.

"Liora Vaningo, a captain in the Riders."

"I've not met many Vothan Riders who are women," Bleuek said.

"We don't have many, but Liora is among the best. Lahgoh summoned her from Rualgar to help in the Talsie Grenling matter."

"The Talsie Grenling matter is why I'm here. We just got word from the Palace that the knights who went to Brythyn to fetch Willim Gilpin couldn't find him. He wasn't at home, and his friends say they don't know where he took himself off to. Sir Tarris said the knights will keep searching, but when they find him, they'll keep him in Brythyn. That's by Lord Grenling's order."

"Damn this case," Jarn muttered. "I'll need to persuade Lord Grenling to let me take part in Gilpin's questioning. Which means a trip to Mystell."

"If they find him."

"Aye, if they find him.

"Perhaps we should send some scouts to Brythyn," Bleuek said. "We might find him first."

Jarn shook his head. "If any Vothan spies were discovered in Brythyn, we'd have a wagonload of diplomatic unpleasantness on our hands."

Bleuek shrugged. "Then the trick is not to be discovered. Which is the point of spying—I mean scouting—is it not?"

Jarn glanced out the window again before turning back to Bleuek. "Is Aarla still in town?" he asked.

"She's nearby, but most likely not in town. At this hour, she's probably in a tree with a family of squirrels or sharing breakfast with a pack of wolves. She doesn't care much for cities."

"But you'll be seeing her again?"

"Aye, I hope to anyway."

"Do you think she'd fancy a trip to Mystell to have a look around?"

Bleuek grinned. "I think she might. As long as I can go with her."

"Be ready, but don't leave until I say so," Jarn said. "This matter needs a bit more consideration."

***

After breakfast, Jarn went to his private office in the Rats Nest to plan the day's activities. The suite of rooms was a bit grand for Jarn's taste, and despite the row of windows on the east side of his inner chamber, the location at the back of the Rats Nest, away from the main meeting chamber, made him feel isolated. Although he was a well-respected leader and not a man to be trifled with, he had always associated with his men and didn't care much for fancy trappings of authority.

Jarn left the office and walked down the short hallway to the large meeting room at the front of the Rats Nest. He sent a guard to fetch wine and then sat at the head of the oval table that dominated the room. The guard returned with a pitcher of mild red, and Jarn poured some into a tankard, took a gulp, and then turned his chair around and looked at the slab of slate mounted on the wall. It was blank. Jarn got up and took a piece of chalk from the silver bowl on the small table below the slate. He wrote the name *Talsie Grenling* at the top of the slate and drew a line under it. Below the name and just to the right of it, he wrote three names, one below the other to form a column, *Lord Grenling*, *Lady Grenling*, and *Sir Longboke*, each of whom Jarn had interviewed. To the left of that column, he wrote the names *Willim Gilpin* and *Lord Keddro*, two men yet to be questioned. On another part of the slate he wrote *Nevvin* and to the right of that, *Astil*. He drew lines under both names.

He stepped back and looked at the two names on the left. Jarn had never met Lord Keddro, but he was reputed to be arrogant, constantly dissatisfied, and not very clever. Jarn figured he would more likely respond to courtesy and deference than to threats and demands. One way or another, he was determined to learn Lord Keddro's honest views about Talsie Grenling and their planned wedding.

Jarn heard footsteps and turned around to see that Sir Tarris had entered the room. The knight nodded and then shifted his gaze to the slate, before looking back at Jarn.

Jarn poured another tankard of wine from the silver pitcher the guard had brought and handed it to Sir Tarris. "Sit and enjoy some Vothan mild red."

Both men sat and Sir Tarris took a gulp of wine. "Quite good," he said, before gesturing toward the slate and shooting Jarn a sly grin. "I see that Braga isn't the only Voth who knows how to write."

"Sometimes writing things down helps me think about a problem that needs to be solved," Jarn said, aware that Sir Tarris might have just given Lord Grenling a slight jab.

"And have you solved the problem?" Sir Tarris asked, all seriousness again.

Jarn shook his head. "No. But we still have Willim Gilpin and Lord Keddro to interview. I would like you to go to Lord Keddro's house and arrange a meeting for later today. I understand that you know the man."

Sir Tarris nodded. "We've met, but I don't know him well."

"What can you tell me about him?"

Sir Tarris hesitated a moment before replying. "He is not what most would call pleasant or gracious. Truth be told, he can be haughty and overbearing."

Jarn thought the same description applied to Lord Grenling, but he kept that thought to himself. He wondered what Sir Tarris would say about his lordship if he could speak honestly. "I want you present at Lord Keddro's interview," Jarn said. "He may be less haughty speaking to a knight of Brythyn than to a Vothan Rider."

"What if Lord Keddro says he can't talk to us today?"

"Explain to him that the more time that passes, the less likely it is that we'll find his betrothed."

"What if he says it has naught to do with him and he shouldn't be bothered about it, as I suspect he might?"

"Tell him that in this kind of investigation, sometimes a seemingly insignificant scrap of information can make the difference between success and failure, sometimes between life and death. We'll want to see any letters he received from Lord Grenling, or from Talsie."

"He won't like that."

"No, I suppose not. Don't mention any details that might trouble him, but do what you can to set the meeting for today."

They finished their wine, and Sir Tarris left. Jarn copied the names he had written on the slate onto a sheet of parchment and went back to his office, taking his tankard and the pitcher of wine with him. He sat at his desk, staring at the names, trying to solve a puzzle that

101

didn't want to be solved. Jarn was still staring, still thinking, when Grion arrived with news.

"Lord Grenling has left Skunnik," Grion said. "He's gone back to Brythyn. We never got a chance to spy on him."

"Did he take Lady Grenling with him?" Jarn asked the graybeard.

"I don't know," Grion said. "Kurff gave me the news, but he didn't say anything about the wife."

Jarn got up and went to the sideboard where he had set the pitcher of wine, refilled his tankard, and poured another, which he handed to Grion before sitting down again.

"Thanks," Grion said with a grateful nod. "How do you like the quarters here in the Rats Nest?"

"More than suitable," Jarn said. "Though I'd sooner be back in Rualgar, or anywhere in Vothan Province."

"Aye, wouldn't we all. Just the same, though, the work here needs to be done, and you're the man to do it."

"This case has me feeling otherwise, Grion. I learned this morning that Willim Gilpin has gone missing, and now Lord Grenling has run off back to Brythyn. It has me wondering what else will go wrong."

Jarn heard footsteps in the outer chamber and looked up. Sir Tarris appeared at the door to the inner room looking unhappy.

"I need to speak with you, Captain," the knight said.

Jarn gestured for him to enter and take a chair next to Grion. "A problem with Lord Keddro?"

Sir Tarris nodded. "He's left town and gone back to his castle. If we're to question him, it will have to be there. It's about fifteen miles east of the city."

Jarn exchanged a glance with Grion and then stood up. "Then we had better get started," he said, wondering if the parade of ill tidings would ever run its course.

Chapter 12

Jarn spotted the castle of Lord Keddro looming in the distance just beyond the village of Brinnik, where Jarn, Braga, and Sir Tarris had stopped briefly to rest their horses and quench their thirst with a round of ales. They had set out a couple of hours earlier in hopes that Lord Keddro would receive them and answer a few questions. At the very least, Jarn hoped to meet the man and size him up. He had heard plenty about him, but he believed that rumor and gossip were no substitute for taking the measure of a man face to face.

As they approached the castle's gatehouse at a walk, Jarn saw that the fortress was small but sturdy and of an older style, with a tall stone keep behind an inner wall. The outer curtain wall was thirty feet high and fronted by a narrow moat, fed by a branch of the Porro River, a tributary of the Shaffroth. When they had approached within shouting distance of the men standing guard on the twin towers flanking the gate, they stopped. Jarn had asked Sir Tarris, a member of the noble class of Brythyn, to take the lead, at least until they got inside and met with Lord Keddro. He glanced at him now and gave a slight nod.

Sir Tarris nodded back and then turned his attention to the guards. "Greetings, good sirs," he said. "We've come to discuss a matter of importance with Lord Keddro." He gestured toward Jarn. "This is Captain Jarn Theffig, who is investigating the abduction of Lord Keddro's betrothed, Talsinora Grenling, a young lady of Brythyn. Please tell his lordship we are here and would see him, if you please."

Without a word of acknowledgement, one of the guards disappeared. The three visitors waited. The guard returned a few minutes later with Lord Keddro's answer. "His lordship says you should go away and leave him in peace, to grieve over his loss. He has nothing to say to you."

"We wouldn't stay long," Sir Tarris said. "Just a few questions only. Surely he can spare a moment or two."

The guard atop the tower raised a crossbow and aimed it at Sir Tarris. "You'll be lucky if I spare your life. Go on now, leave at once, or I'll put a bolt through your eye."

"No need to make threats," Sir Tarris said. "I'll have you know I'm a knight of Brythyn."

"I don't care if you're the king of the faeries," the guard said. "Be gone or be shot."

"Insolent wretch," Sir Tarris muttered, glaring at the guard.

"You there," Jarn called to the guard. "We're leaving now, so you can put away your weapon and hold your ill-mannered tongue. Tell his lordship that since he won't meet with us here, I expect to see him tomorrow morning at my headquarters in the Mang. I'll send a company of Vothan Riders here to escort him."

"You had better send two companies," the guard growled.

"Perhaps I will. Or three. The Vothan Riders have companies enough."

"Do you plan to storm this castle, Sir Vothan Rider?"

"If need be," Jarn said, and then he turned to Braga and Sir Tarris. "Let's not waste any more time here."

They wheeled about and headed back to Skunnik.

When Jarn returned to his office, he found Bleuek and Aarla waiting for him in the outer chamber. Bleuek stood up when Jarn entered. "I have good news," he said, his eyes bright.

"Say on," Jarn replied.

"Aarla found Willim Gilpin. She told me, and so we seized him. I have him in one of those little rooms you're supposed to use for questioning people."

Jarn stared at Aarla. "You're a wonder. How did you do it?"

"Mere good fortune," Aarla replied. "I was about to head into Skunnik this morning from the forest where I took my rest last night when I felt something odd."

"One of your little inklings or suspicions?"

Aarla nodded. "It's hard to explain. It's like feeling a tiny stone inside your boot, only it's inside my head. I was just ready to leave the woods and come here, when I sensed something nearby that was not quite right. Then I heard a horse approaching on the road. I knew right away that something was awry with whoever was coming, so I waited for him to pass and then followed at a distance. He slipped into the Bolt and went to a shabby-looking inn, where I figured he meant to get a meal. I went to find Bleuek, and we went back to the inn."

"He was sitting by himself in the dining room when we got there," Bleuek said. "I asked him if he was Willim Gilpin, and he turned as white as new snow. He said his name was Perrin Whimby or some such nonsense, and I drew my sword and told him I was taking him to the Mang for questioning in the matter of the abduction of Talsie Grenling."

"Good work, Bleuek, and you, too, Aarla. I am much obliged—again—for your help."

Aarla gave Jarn one of the vague, fleeting smiles that sometimes crossed her face, and then she nodded slightly and said, "You're welcome."

"You find civilized folk endlessly intriguing, do you not?" Jarn said.

"I do," Aarla said. "I can see why the virrlings of old were so fascinated by you—and why they eventually left you to make your own way."

"No doubt your father has told you stories."

"He has. I've stories of my own as well, though not so many."

Jarn imagined Aarla and Yellig sitting in the old virrling's cottage somewhere inside his enchanted forest, drinking tea or mead and making merry over the follies of mortal men. "Well, we do the best we can," he said. "Some of us, anyway."

Aarla gave him another fleeting grin. "I know."

"You said you knew right away that something was amiss with Willim Gilpin. Do you believe he's guilty of abduction?"

"I don't know," Aarla replied. "Something is surely off with him, but whether or not he abducted Talsie Grenling or committed any other crime, I can't say."

"You want me to help you interview him?" Bleuek asked Jarn.

Jarn hesitated a moment as a thought occurred, and then he shook his head. "I mean no offense, Bleuek, but I have someone else in mind. Go to the Beldur Palace and tell Kurff that I need him at the Mang as soon as he can get here."

Jarn ate a quick meal in the dining hall with Bleuek and Aarla and then went back to his office to wait for Kurff. The Yellowshirt finally arrived, and they went over their plan for questioning Willim Gilpin. Jarn expected Kurff to make a cutting comment about him changing his mind, but he didn't bring up the subject. Jarn was still dubious about Kurff's techniques for questioning suspects, but he told himself he had to be open to anything that might help him find Talsie Grenling.

It was early evening when Jarn and Kurff entered the interview room. The air felt cool, as if they had descended into a cave. Walls of rough-cut gray stone added to the chamber's cave-like character. A sconce was set into each wall, but only one torch had been lit, the one above the door. It shed scant light and cast flickering, misshapen shadows.

Willim Gilpin was sitting at a square table, facing the door. He was slender and of average height. Jarn thought that he somewhat resembled Bleuek, though he looked much more solemn than the young Rider, who usually wore a smile. Willim had large brown eyes and long eyelashes, short brown hair that looked as if it was already getting sparse, thin lips, and hollow cheeks. He reminded Jarn of a too-serious poet or perhaps a love-struck troubadour, though he had to admit that the overall effect might not be unpleasant to young women who preferred men of a sensitive nature.

Jarn and Kurff sat down across from the young man. "Have you had a meal?" Jarn asked, knowing that he had.

"Aye," Willim said. "What's this all about, then? Why did your man seize me?"

"Your friend Talsie Grenling was abducted on the way here from Brythyn," Jarn told him, studying his face. "We're talking to her friends to try to find out what happened to her. You are a friend of Talsie's, are you not?"

"I am," Willim said.

"Does she have many friends?"

Willim shook his head.

"How long have you known her?"

"Since we were children. Longer than I can remember."

"Good friends, then, eh?"

The young man nodded, but his face showed no expression, no emotion. Kurff was eyeing him intently but had yet to speak.

"Who do you think might have done such a thing?"

"I don't know. It's monstrous."

"Aye, it is that. We'll find the bastards who did it, make no mistake."

"Good," Willim said.

"We've already talked to a large number of people, including a few who claim they saw the abduction," Kurff said, speaking for the first time.

Willim stared at him and swallowed. "Have you?"

"Aye," said Kurff, narrowing his eyes at Willim. "They described the culprits. One of the descriptions could fit you. Any reason that might be so?"

"No reason at all," Willim said.

"Do you have a twin brother?"

"No."

"Twin sister?"

"No."

109

"Can you think of any reason these villains, whoever they be, would have taken the lass?"

Willim shook his head. "No. No reason whatsoever."

"No?" Jarn said. "The Grenlings are wealthy. Surely it will have occurred to you that some brigands might have abducted Talsie to ransom her."

A tiny muscle in the young man's cheek, just below his right eye, twitched. He rubbed it with the tips of his fingers. "I suppose it's possible."

"Yet you just said you could think of no reason—no reason whatsoever—for the girl's abduction," Kurff said.

"Well, I, I …"

"Do you know who was accompanying Talsie when she was taken?" Jarn asked.

"I, uh, let me see. No, I, I don't know."

"Sir Longboke," Jarn said. "Do you know the man?"

"I … I … I'm acquainted with him, yes. I know him slightly."

"Lord Grenling believes Sir Longboke did the deed. Do you believe that's a possibility?"

Willim gave a slight shrug. "Perhaps it is. Yes, I suppose so, a possibility."

Kurff leaned toward Willim and frowned. "A possibility. Thus a reason. But a moment ago you lacked the wit to even think of a reason."

Willim leaned back a fraction of an inch, and Jarn saw a sheen of perspiration on the young man's forehead reflecting the torchlight. "But I, I didn't know Sir Longboke was with Talsie when she … when it happened. So, no … no, I wouldn't have known it was a possibility, until I knew, until you told me he was the one who accompanied her. You see?"

Kurff, still glaring at Willim, began tapping his fingernails on the table. After a long moment, Jarn stood up. Kurff followed suit, and the two headed toward the door.

"Are we finished, then?" Willim asked, wiping his brow with his hand. "May I go?"

"No," Jarn said. He and Kurff left the room and went to Jarn's office, where Jarn picked up a sheaf of parchments with writing on them.

Kurff looked around the office and gave Jarn a puzzled look. "A bit grand for a Vothan Rider, no?"

"I'm trying not to let it spoil me," Jarn replied. "What do you make of Willim Gilpin?"

"He's lying."

"I agree. But is he guilty?"

"Why else would he lie?"

"A fair question, but I'm getting the sense that there's some new knot to be added to the tangle. Not unlike this entire damned case."

"If he is guilty, we'll break him. If we don't break him tonight, we can try again tomorrow."

"I've another idea in mind," Jarn said. "If he doesn't confess tonight, I plan to turn him loose and have someone follow him."

Kurff nodded and gave Jarn a conspiratorial smile. "Who do you have in mind for the job?"

"A Rider named Liora Vaningo. Lahgoh summoned her from Rualgar, and she's eager for an assignment."

Kurff laughed. "I had forgotten that some of the Vothan Riders are women. You Voths have some strange customs."

Jarn shrugged. "They're not strange to us."

111

"No, only to the rest of the known world. Is it true you vote for your leaders?"

"It's true."

Kurff shook his head. "Strange customs, indeed."

"Let's go back," Jarn said.

A minute later, they reentered the interview room. Kurff took his seat across from Willim, but Jarn remained standing and began to page through the sheets of parchment he had picked up. He kept an eye on Willim, looking for any telltales on his face as Kurff resumed the questioning.

"The captain has the results of our work," Kurff said to Willim. "Statements signed by the witnesses, testimony from Lord and Lady Grenling, and a sworn account from Sir Longboke, who was felled by dark magic as he and Talsie rode toward Skunnik. We also have expert judgments from mages skilled in the kind of spells that could cut down a knight from a distance. We don't yet know how you did it, but you'll tell us, and then we'll see what we can do to let you make amends."

Willim stood up so quickly he knocked his chair over, and his body went rigid when it clattered to the stone floor. "You're mad. I didn't do anything."

"Lawbreakers always say that," Kurff said. "Now sit down and we'll sort it all out."

"But I didn't—"

"Silence!" Kurff shouted. "I told you to sit down."

"I'm a subject of the Brythyn Realm. You can't bully me."

Kurff laughed. "Can't we?"

"You're not in Brythyn," Jarn said in an even voice. "Now do as Senior Patrol Leader Kurff says and sit down, and we three will set things to rights."

112

Willim hesitated a moment and then picked up his chair and sat.

"All three of us know the real crime here," Jarn said, nodding slowly. "The real crime is Lord Grenling trying to marry off his sweet young daughter to that fat and pompous Lord Keddro. If I was in love with a beautiful young woman and her father arranged a marriage with an old, overbearing swine, I'd have a long hard think about rescuing her as well."

Willim looked as if he might jump up again. "But," he began. He didn't finish.

"But what?" Kurff asked.

"Nothing. Never mind."

Jarn glanced around the room, as if he were looking for someone hiding in the walls, and then turned back to Willim. "What Kurff and I say in this room remains in this room—the Grenlings don't need to be privy to our conversations. Do you understand?"

Willim nodded quickly.

"It wouldn't surprise me if Talsie asked you to rescue her," Kurff said. "Is that what happened?"

"No," Willim replied. "No, she didn't."

"It's a noble thing, your wanting to protect her," Jarn said. "But telling it true won't put her in disgrace, I promise you that. But we need to know everything."

"I ... no, it wasn't about protecting her," Willim said.

"What was it, then?" Kurff asked. "Why did you abduct the lass?"

"I didn't."

"You said it wasn't about protecting her—what was it about?"

"I just meant that she didn't ask me to do anything."

"So you abducted her all on your own, without her asking to be rescued," Jarn said. "Very gallant of you."

"I didn't abduct her."

"No, no, of course not, we know you didn't do it yourself, you hired people to do the deed."

"I didn't hire anyone," Willim said.

"Ah, some friends, then, willing to do you a good turn," Jarn said.

"No. No one did me a good turn."

"You did it yourself, then," Kurff said.

"No, no, no, I already told you, I did nothing."

Willim's eyes were darting around the room as if they were trying to follow the antics of a group of dancing faeries. Jarn almost felt sorry for him. "Did Longboke help you?" Jarn asked.

"No!" Willim shouted, his voice nearly breaking. He cleared his throat and began again, but there was no mistaking the quaver in his voice. "No one helped me, because I didn't do anything that needed help. I did not abduct Talsie Grenling."

Jarn and Kurff looked at one another briefly and then back at Willim. Jarn heaved a deep sigh that would have done a stage player proud and said, "Let's start again at the beginning, shall we?"

Chapter 13

Before she reached Skunnik, Astil left the road and skirted around the city to the west, riding across fields and farmland, heading for a small wooded area a mile north of town. The air was clear and cool, and the fine morning held the promise of a pleasant day. She reached the woods without running into anyone else and dismounted, picking her way slowly through the trees until she came to a small clearing. After tying her horse to a tree, she sat on the ground and leaned back against another tree, listening to birds singing and twittering among the treetops. She thought about her gold, languishing in a Vothan vault somewhere inside the Mang. Talsie Grenling also came to mind, and Lady Grenling as well. Astil removed the silver chain from around her neck and looked at the saffite ring Lady Grenling had given her—Talsie's ring. She stared at it and then squeezed her fingers around it, nearly tight enough to bend the gold shank. She eased her grip. It wouldn't do to damage a lovely ring made of fine gold. She stretched her legs out on the grass, closed her eyes, and fell asleep, her crossbow by her side.

At dusk, Astil emerged from the woods and headed for the road that would take her south to Skunnik. She rode at a slow canter, passing few others along the way, and entered the city through the north gate without challenge. There were people about when she turned onto Baddler Street, but she looked straight ahead and didn't catch anyone's eye. Among the crowd were tradesmen heading home, young sons of wealthy lords looking for a likely tavern in which to while away the night, and servants hauling carts laden with loaves of bread and casks of wine to take to the great houses of the northern ward, where prosperous Acrinites continued their grand traditions, despite the Vothan Renewal. The voices of these denizens of the night mingled with the clip-clop of horses and the creak of wagon wheels slowly rolling along the street.

Astil turned into Nopping Lane, a narrow street that was little more than an alley. She glanced to her right at the Rook's Inn and considered stopping. The Trickle Inn, farther down the lane, was smaller and usually less crowded, and she decided to head there. When she reached it, she dismounted, proceeded to the courtyard behind the inn, and handed her horse to a stable boy before going inside. When the proprietor greeted her, she told him she wanted a room for the night and would pay him for it now, as she meant to leave well before dawn. He showed her the room and then went to tell the stable boy to bring up her saddlebags. As soon as the bags arrived, she went downstairs to the dining room.

After a meal of leek and barley soup, dark bread, and a tankard of wine, Astil returned to her room to rest.

An hour past midnight, she left the inn and proceeded on foot to the vicinity of the Palace of the High Hext. She pulled her hood over her head and wrapped a dark purple scarf around her neck, arranged so that she could pull it up over the lower part of her face. She had left her padded jacket behind. The ability to move freely, she had decided, outweighed the risk from knives and arrows. Trying to appear casual, she strolled along the city blocks adjacent to the palace grounds, keeping to the side of the street opposite the palace, until she had made a couple of slow circuits around the huge structure. The four main

116

gates to the palace were guarded by Yellowshirts, but that was to be expected and mattered not.

Astil waited in the shadows on the other side of Fish Street from the palace's back gate, standing just inside the mouth of an alley. During her circuits around the grounds, she had seen that the block in which she now stood had an inn, a tavern, a tannery, a leather shop, a cloth shop, a bakery, and a chandlery. The shops and businesses were closed at that hour, and the modest inn and small tavern, though still open, were quiet.

When she was sure no one else was about, she walked west on Fish Street until she was across the street from the palace greensward and gardens, which had a ten-foot-high wall surrounding them. Without stopping, she turned around to look behind her, walking backwards for a few steps. She turned around again and kept walking until she was near the middle of the north wall of the gardens. A moment later, she removed a grappling hook from her belt. It was attached to a coil of thin but strong rope. Holding the end of the rope with her left hand, she heaved the hook over the wall with her right hand. She tested it. The hook held. She used the rope to scramble up the wall, took a quick look around, and then dropped down on the other side. She was inside the outer palace grounds, but the wall around the inner grounds was higher and better guarded.

She walked quickly to the crescent-shaped pond in the middle of the green and ducked into a small garden situated in the curved area between the two points of the crescent. She leaned back against the dogsbark tree that stood in the center of the garden and took some deep breaths, waiting for her heart to slow. When she felt calm, she closed her eyes and listened to the night. She heard in the distance the usual sounds of a large and prosperous city that wasn't quite ready to turn in for the evening—voices, music, horses at a walk or a slow canter—but closer by, all was silence.

Astil stepped out from the garden and glanced at the pond. Still as death, it reflected a half moon and hundreds of bright stars in a perfect mirror image of the sky. Astil felt as if she could stare at it all night. A soft breeze, barely a whisper, rose up, rippling the pond and fluttering the reflected stars and moon.

Astil turned her gaze from the pond to the palace. She had been inside on more occasions than she could count and knew its plan well. It was four hundred feet long, three-hundred and thirty feet wide, and seventy-five feet high. It had eight hundred rooms, including sixty suites for ulders and other official members of the High Hext's inner circle, forty suites for guests, and two hundred bedrooms for priests and various functionaries. It had dining rooms, drawing rooms, galleries, and music rooms, and Astil knew nearly all of them. She understood the workings of the palace's illusions, which the builders had fashioned with the help of a group of mages. She also knew most of the palace's secret passages, hidden staircases, and concealed chambers, and she could guess at the rest. She had even sneaked in once before, and back out again, just to see if she could do it. The risk had not been as great then, since she was supposed to be there anyway and could easily have talked her way out of trouble. She had also explored the place late at night, poking around wherever she could, wherever there was an unlocked door or, come to that, a locked door that gave way to the special tools she had designed to defeat locks. She had explored storerooms, armories, and dungeons, had strolled through servant's quarters, closets, wine cellars, and wardrobes.

Until yesterday's meeting with Lady Grenling, the last time she had been inside the palace was a year before, when she had met with the sorcerer Grune Grohar, First Ulder Leedrus, and the Yellowshirt named Kurff. She shook her head at the memory. Grohar and Leedrus were dead—Leedrus by her own hand—and Kurff was now working with the Vothan Riders. Stranger still, so was she. A year ago, no one would have imagined that both she and Kurff would be helping the Voths, or that the Voths would rule the Acrinite Territory.

She put thoughts of the past out of her mind and focused again on the palace, recalling its plan and design, picturing in her mind the best path to the Red Room. Once inside the building, she would feel somewhat more at ease, but first she would have to scale the inner palace wall without being seen and then enter the palace itself. She pulled the purple scarf up around her face, leaving only her eyes exposed, and walked at a brisk pace from the pond to a small clump of bushes thirty yards away. There was no cover between the bushes and the inner palace wall, but she hadn't come this far in her thirty-two years by playing the craven.

She took a breath and began walking toward the wall, turning her head left and right as she went. She saw no one. When she neared the wall, she broke into a slow run. Moments later, she was leaning against the wall's western section, catching her breath. She put her ear against the rock but heard nothing. She stared at it, willing herself to see through it, but her skills did not include the ability to gaze through rock and rubble. Once again, she reminded herself that taking chances was how she made her way in the world.

The inner curtain wall was thirty feet high and at least ten feet thick. It was patrolled by a pair of two-man teams of Yellowshirts who paced along the wall-walk in the same direction and tried to stay directly opposite one another. When the High Hext resided there, it was considered a great honor to be assigned guard duty, and four pairs of guards patrolled the wall back then.

Astil squatted down and leaned back against the wall, waiting for the first pair of Yellowshirts to show up on the wall-walk above. Once they arrived, she would have four or five minutes until the second pair came, and less time than that before the second group turned the corner and faced in her general direction. But she couldn't make her move until the first group had nearly reached the southwest corner of the wall. Meanwhile, there would be guards on the towers of the palace itself, ready to sound the alarm if they saw something amiss.

She heard low voices and pressed herself tight against the wall. The first pair of guards was approaching. She held her breath. The voices became louder. Thirty feet above, the guards passed her position, still murmuring. She began to count, listening as their voices faded. When the time was right, she heaved her grappling hook over the wall, hoping it would catch on the first attempt. It didn't. The sound it made as it scraped the graystone wall sent an unpleasant chill down her spine, but she caught the hook before it hit the ground and immediately tossed it again. This time it held, and she climbed quickly, reaching the top of the wall within seconds. She crouched down on the wall-walk, listening. She raised her head and spotted the second pair of guards, walking along the north wall, approaching the northwest corner. There was no time to retrieve her rope, but she had to get rid of the grappling hook, lest the guards spot it. She reached up and grabbed it, and then tossed it back over the wall.

Stooped over in a low crouch, she headed south along the wall-walk until she came to a set of steps leading down to the ground. She went halfway down and then pressed herself against the wall until the second pair of guards strode past. That meant the first pair were directly opposite her position but far enough away that they most likely would not spot her. By now her heart was pounding and she could feel a light sheen of perspiration under her tunic. Staying close to the wall, she descended the rest of the way down the stone steps.

She took a moment to catch her breath. The first pair of guards had nearly reached the northeast corner, which meant the second pair would be approaching the southwest corner, their backs to her. She took off across the lawn, heading for the northwest corner of the palace, where a square addition had been built to house servants' quarters. Another, smaller, addition extended south from it, forming a small space that was protected from view on three sides.

Astil reached the space and huddled against the corner formed by the square addition and the west wall of the palace proper. Her breathing slowed. Her heart calmed. She listened to the night. It was quiet. There was an outside door to the servants' quarters, but it was on the opposite side. The door was below ground level, down a short flight of steps. If she reached it without being seen, she would have good cover. She crept forward and peered out, watching for a pair of guards to show up on the wall-walk. They arrived two minutes later, and she waited until they were three-quarters of the way along the west wall. She stepped out from her hiding place and walked quickly to the other side of the addition and then down the steps that led to the door. The servants' residence was one of the few areas of the palace that was unfamiliar to her, but logic suggested that the door would open to a hallway and should be empty of people that time of night. In the rooms off the hallway, she supposed, the occupants would be asleep. Once inside, she could access a service hallway that ran the length of the west side of the palace.

She tried the door. It was locked. She retrieved her special tools and went to work, as quietly as possible. Ten minutes later, she was covered with perspiration, but the door was still closed. She wanted to kick it. She worked her picklock for five more minutes and then abandoned the attempt to unlock the door. She would have to slip into the servants' quarters through a window and hope all the servants were sound sleepers.

Chapter 14

As usual, Kurff couldn't sleep. He had been staring at the slice of moonlight decorating the wall opposite his bed, wondering if he might detect its slow movement, hoping the attempt might lull him to sleep at last. It didn't.

He quietly slipped out of bed, dressed himself in civilian clothing, and left his rooms in the Beldur Palace. A few minutes later, he was stepping out into the cool late-night air, heading for the palace's main gate. After passing through, he headed south down Sonto Street to begin a long, late-night trek through Skunnik. He walked at a fair pace, neither ambling nor rushing, peering into the night, occasionally glancing from side to side, ready for trouble but expecting none. Skunnik was his city and always would be, and the Vothan takeover be damned.

That takeover marked the beginning of the fretful dreams that plagued Kurff's sleep. Although the frequency of those dreams had gradually diminished, his memories of last year's troubles remained vivid. Soon after the thousand-year-old Acrinite Deception was revealed, the Voths marched on the Acrinite Territory. Despite superior numbers, the regular Acrinite army had crumbled before the feared Vothan Riders, and the High Hext and his upper echelon of leaders—along with nearly half of the Acrinite Guardsmen—had fled as soon as it became clear the Voths would not withdraw. That left the remaining Yellowshirts to give battle and eventually negotiate the terms of surrender. Under normal circumstances, the Acrinites could have counted on allies rallying to their aid, but once their ancient deception became known, they had no allies.

Kurff was still of two minds about the disaster. That the Voths, barely one step up from barbarians, should rule the refined and civilized Acrinites was the height of absurdity. On the other hand, a race of people who had deceived the known world for a thousand years and tried to subjugate another race of people under false pretenses probably deserved their fate. Kurff still hadn't reconciled the two conflicting views.

He had played a key role in the drama, from beginning to end. He had seized the Wyndoran youth whose father had discovered the first clues to the Acrinite Deception, setting events in motion. Kurff had then lost the Wyndoran through Vothan trickery, before helping the sorceress Astil recapture him.

The thought of Astil sent a shiver down his spine, despite the pleasant late-night air and the warmth he felt from his own exertions trekking through the city. Now Astil was back, and helping the Vothan Riders. Kurff shook his head at the thought of it. Line Commander Lahgoh was mad to think the woman would keep her word, although the horde of gold the Voths were holding might persuade even such as she to stay true to her promise—unless she could retrieve her gold through guile or treachery. It would be fascinating to observe, especially if Astil, who also had been involved in the sequence of events that led to the Vothan Renewal, wound up playing a part in the Voths' downfall. The irony would be exquisite. Having dealt with Astil in the past, however, Kurff would try to observe from a safe distance.

Kurff reached Laekkish Street and turned right. He was headed in the general direction of the Bolt, the seedy neighborhood in the southwest quadrant of the city where whores and gamblers and cutpurses mingled with cooks, scullions, and barkeeps, and where young farm boys out for a night of adventure often got more excitement than they had reckoned on.

He walked a block and turned right again on Zayet Street, heading north again. That part of the city was quiet this time of night, but the Bolt wasn't far off now, and anyone who wanted a tankard of ale or a game of dice or an hour with a whore could easily find what he sought. The Vothan Riders had mostly left the Bolt alone, except when the odd dead body showed up or someone reported a robbery or a rape. The Riders didn't have the numbers to patrol every inch of the city, even with a contingent of Yellowshirts helping them. The rebels' activities, which seemed to be on the rise, spread them even thinner. No wonder Jarn Theffig had agreed to let that sham mage try to look inside Raff Salorian's corpse.

Kurff felt satisfaction in demanding and receiving permission from Jarn to attend the mage's ministrations, useless though they were. He also felt a small sense of triumph at his challenge to Jarn during the big meeting in the basement of the Mang, when he had defended his fellow Guardsmen. He recalled Jarn's reply—*I never thought the Guardsmen were an unworthy match for the Riders*—and wondered if he had meant it. Even more surprising was that Jarn had asked for Kurff's help in questioning the Brythyner Willim Gilpin. It seemed as if Captain Jarn Theffig might finally be wising up. Perhaps living in Skunnik among Acrinites was improving the man's outlook.

Kurff wondered what Jarn and Lahgoh and the other Vothan Riders thought of the Yellowshirts who had fled.

Strutting braggarts that they were, the vaunted Riders would loudly demean any who fled before them, but the truth would be thornier. Many Acrinites suspected, and some hoped, that the absent Yellowshirts—sometimes called "Lemonbacks"—would return in strength one day to wrest control of the Acrinite Territory back from the Voths, reinstate the High Hext as leader, and put the barbarians in their proper place. That possibility raised a question, one that few Acrinites discussed openly but that Kurff thought about often. If the Lemonbacks returned to wage war against the Voths, would the Yellowshirts who hadn't fled—and who were now under the command of the Vothan Riders—join them?

Kurff put the thought out of his mind and turned left at Lannix Street. He went on for a block and stopped, closing his eyes for a moment and listening, but the night remained calm and quiet. He walked another block on Lannix, another block closer to the Bolt, where he stopped again. He had come to Trink Street. The eastern edge of Horsan Park was across the street, and just beyond the two-block-wide park was the Bolt. He saw lights across the way and thought he heard voices in the distance, though they were still too far away to be distinct. He looked north up Trink and then at the park again. He crossed the street and entered the park.

The park's tall trees blocked the moonlight, and Kurff had no torch, but he knew the park as well as he knew his own rooms in the Beldur Palace. He had grown up in the Bolt and played in the park nearly every day, him and his brother and their band, defending what they considered their corner of the park against other groups of young rogues and roisterers. The park was where he learned to fight, where he learned to take a beating

126

without shedding a tear, and where he learned how to be with a woman.

He crossed the wooden footbridge over the Spellent Creek and continued down the wide main path that traversed the park diagonally. He veered right at the intersection with a narrower path and continued north before turning west and picking up an even narrower trail that few others knew about. That trail gradually descended to below street level, ending at a small clearing. Kurff picked his way through the trees beyond the far edge of the clearing until he came to an untidy pile of dead branches that looked as if they might have been kicked into a small heap with little regard for neatness. When he grabbed the topmost branch to pick it up, the entire pile came with it, the branches and twigs having been hollowed out and then glued together. He set it aside and picked up the green rug that lay below it, which resembled a patch of grass. He set that aside as well, and then raised the round wooden door that seemed to be set into the ground but that was really the entrance to a large room made of stone and heavy timbers. He sat down and dropped his legs into the hole before descending the stone steps that led down to the room.

At the bottom of the steps, he felt for the flint and candle that lay on a shelf carved into the side of the steps. He lit the candle, held the flickering flame out in front of him, and peered into the dim light that it cast. He took a few paces toward the table that was set against the wall opposite the steps. An empty wine bottle stood in the middle of the table, a rolled-up parchment sticking out of its mouth. Kurff went to the table and pulled the parchment out of the bottle. He read the words on the parchment by the light of his candle and then set the flame to it, burning it to ash. Then he ascended the steps and reentered the park. He closed the wooden door, placed the green rug over it, and set the glued-together pile of branches on top of the rug.

He made his way back to a regular path and exited the park on Hunter Street, which at that point formed the northern border of the Bolt. He turned right and walked to Trink Street, where he turned left and began the long walk back to the Beldur Palace.

Chapter 15

Jarn sat at the large table in the Rats Nest meeting room, gazing at the slab of slate hanging on the back wall. The Talsie Grenling case had roiled his mind ever since the unsuccessful questioning of Willim Gilpin. He and Kurff had been unable to break him, despite their hard questioning, and Jarn finally let the young man go. He had set Liora Vaningo on Willim's trail but didn't expect much to come of the surveillance. On the more hopeful side, Liora had been happy to get an assignment, and Jarn was glad he could give her one. Perhaps the hard looks she had been casting his way would soften.

As for finding Talsie, Jarn had little hope beyond Astil, a state of affairs that was maddening to contemplate. No one in the known world possessed more tracking ability than Astil, but she had always used her rare gift to enrich herself, often skirting laws and sometimes breaking them. Jarn shook his head and nearly laughed out loud. The Vothan Riders had dealt with unsavory types before—sneak thieves, touts, cutpurses—but never anyone as dangerous as Astil. And yet he knew that if Talsie was still alive, Astil was more likely than not to find her, if she wanted to. Although Jarn would not have admitted it to anyone, he actually thought Astil would keep her word. But he was also thankful that the Vothan Riders were holding some of her gold hostage.

Jarn looked at the names chalked on the slate. At the top, with a line drawn under it, *Talsie Grenling*. Below that and to the right, a list: *Lord Grenling*, *Lady Grenling*, *Sir Longboke*. To the left, two more names, *Willim Gilpin* and *Lord Keddro*.

Jarn rose from his chair and picked up a wool cloth from the table that held the bowl of chalks. He wiped away the name *Willim Gilpin*. Then he picked up a piece of chalk and added the young man's name to the right-hand column. *Lord Grenling*, *Lady Grenling*, *Sir Longboke*, *Willim Gilpin*. Four people interviewed. Questions asked and answered, suspicions aroused, guilt denied. He looked at the name that remained on the left—*Lord Keddro*, yet to submit to questioning. Then he gazed again at the longer list.

Lord Grenling. The Brythyner had made a hostage of Brythyn's impending treaty with Vothan, claiming he wouldn't relent until the Voths found Talsie. Did he have authority from the High Lord of Brythyn to hold up the treaty? And even if so, why would he do it? What was to be gained? Meanwhile, Lord Grenling had been accused—by his own wife—of arranging the very crime he said he wanted solved. Even supposing he was guilty, how would he have accomplished it? Easily enough, Jarn thought. A lord could hire mercenaries to do his bidding or rely on his own loyal knights. As for opportunity, a young woman riding on a less-traveled road with only a single knight to protect her offered opportunity aplenty to would-be abductors, especially if the knight was temporarily disabled by a spell or a potion.

Lady Grenling. She had been the accuser, claiming her husband had arranged the abduction to prevent Talsie's marriage to Lord Keddro without having to admit to poor judgment. This seemed unlikely, but perhaps not to Lady Grenling. Perhaps she genuinely believed Lord Grenling was guilty. If not, then what game was she playing? Was she using the abduction to be rid of her husband, whom she clearly did not care for, by casting suspicion his way? Or had she herself arranged the crime with a plan to sow suspicion elsewhere? A lady could hire mercenaries nearly as easily as could a lord.

Sir Longboke. The man seemed genuinely distressed over Talsie's abduction, but Jarn had known other scoundrels who could lie convincingly. Lady Grenling had said he was not a wealthy man. Could he be in league with Lord Grenling—or Lady Grenling, come to that—in exchange for gold? Traveling with the young woman, Sir Longboke would have had opportunity. But what had he done with Talsie before riding to Skunnik? Murdered her and buried her? Handed her over to accomplices? Jarn heaved a sigh and shook his head. He found it difficult to believe the knight had harmed the young woman, especially since he could not fathom a purpose, beyond gold, for such an act.

Willim Gilpin. The young man had not broken under hard questioning by Jarn and Kurff. Did that mean he was innocent? Jarn still believed that a young man in love might persuade himself to commit a crime to prevent his loved one from marrying another. But could he have felled Sir Longboke? Possibly, with help from friends, but by all accounts, he had few. Did he have aid from a mage or a spellcaster? Had he enough coin to afford such aid? What of Talsie? Would she not have fought to protect herself? Finally, how would Willim have known that Talsie would leave the train and present an opportunity? He wouldn't—unless Talsie had told him she planned to do so.

Jarn looked away from the slate and closed his eyes. His mind felt like a whirlpool spinning bits of chaff. He stood up again and wrote the word *Rebels* on the slate. He stared at it a moment and then circled it.

131

The rebels had mostly targeted Acrinites they considered collaborators, although they also murdered Voths and attacked Wyndorans and Telnans and others who dealt with Voths. The murders were bad enough, but the abductions were gruesome, designed to instill fear and terror. A victim's dead and bloodless body appeared nine days after he was seized, an interval that sparked the rumor—no doubt promoted by the rebels themselves—that victims died from a nine-day-long, drop-by-drop bloodletting. Yet Jarn doubted that the rebels had abducted Talsie Grenling. Of course, he couldn't rule it out—he couldn't rule anything out—but he thought that avenue would prove the least fruitful.

Also in the realm of the less fruitful was the notion that common criminals had abducted Talsie and were holding her for ransom. She had been taken three days ago—four days ago, now that it was near to daybreak of another morning—and there had been no ransom demand.

Jarn stared at the final name on the slate. *Lord Keddro.* Jarn had never met the man, but he was reputed to be arrogant, constantly dissatisfied, and aggressively unpleasant. So far, he had lived up to his reputation, but his refusal to meet with Jarn to answer questions would not stand, even if it required a show of force to persuade him. But Jarn was hoping Lord Keddro might respond better to courtesy and deference than to threats and demands, and he was willing to try such an approach. Tomorrow would tell.

Jarn's eyes seemed to be frosting over from staring at the slate, and he needed air. Or perhaps he needed a tankard of strong red wine. No, air would be best. He had been drinking more than enough strong red of late.

He left the Rats Nest through the front entrance, climbed the stairs to the ground floor of the Mang, and went outside into the cool night air. He inhaled deeply, hoping to clear his mind or at least set it on a less taxing course, and started walking toward the front gate. He nodded to the guards as he passed through, and then left the Mang's grounds and headed south on Zayet Street.

Halfway down Zayet he turned left on Clood Street and came to Sonto. He walked another block to Meera Street, the easternmost of Skunnik's four main avenues, and turned right. After three blocks, he came to Barrel Street, which ran southeast on the diagonal from the central city grid. Lower Barrel Street served as the main boulevard of the neighborhood known as the Shield, which lay inside a shield-shaped loop of the Santeris River. The area was home to the city's docks and marketplace as well as a wide, grassy expanse that served as the city's fairgrounds. It was also the place where troubadours, street magicians, storytellers, and other performers staged their nightly entertainments.

Tonight, like most nights, the fairground was lit by a large bonfire, and three groups of performers had staked positions around it, each with a basket on the ground for collecting coins. Jarn veered to his right and entered the grounds, heading for a pair of jugglers, the performers closest to the river. They were tossing knives, clubs, and what appeared to be small war hammers back and forth between them, drawing applause, laughter, and more than a few gasps from the small but admiring crowd they had drawn.

Jarn slowed his pace, keeping an eye on the jugglers but staying behind the crowd. He glanced toward the river, which was murmuring softly inside its banks, and saw stars reflected on its placid surface. A cheer rose up, drawing Jarn's attention. He turned away from the river and watched the jugglers for a while, dropping a coin into their basket before moving on to the next performer, a street mage who was also something of a storyteller.

The mage was dressed in a long black robe festooned with five-pointed white stars and crescent moons, and he wore a black skullcap sprinkled with tiny white dots. Jarn didn't know if the costume was meant to mark him as a sage or signify that he was more jester than mystic. The man kept up a near-constant patter, telling far-fetched tales and delivering amusing asides that drew laughter from the crowd. Jarn suspected the stories were mainly intended to distract the crowd's attention from what the mage was doing with his hands, like a feint an army makes to divert attention from the real target, or false evidence planted by a criminal to lead investigators astray. A tall young woman in a white dress served as the mage's helper and foil, and Jarn thought about Aarla. She had traveled for a time with a street magician after fleeing a cruel foster family.

Jarn watched the mage intently, but he couldn't help but laugh along with the rest of the crowd at the man's daft stories and silly japes. He tried to determine how he managed his clever tricks, but the mage's hands outwitted Jarn's eyes, and he gave up the attempt and decided just to enjoy the man's harmless deceptions. After a while, he dropped a coin into his basket and moved to the final group, a foursome of singers and musicians.

The troupe, two men and two women, stood further from the bonfire than the other performers, probably so the crackling fire wouldn't interfere with their music. One of the men played a lute, and the other played a kind of horn, occasionally switching to a pipe. The two women sang. Both had long golden hair and looked as if they might be sisters. Jarn stopped and listened, captivated by the music, the finest he had heard since leaving the Vothan Territory. The musicians were as skilled as any in Rualgar, and the women's voices harmonized in a way that made Jarn suddenly sure they were sisters. The crowd here was silent, enchanted by the seemingly effortless playing and the thrilling beauty of the women's singing. Jarn thought he had never heard such perfect voices, pure, clear, and strong but also warm and graceful.

After they played their last song, the audience clapped for a long time. The two musicians bowed solemnly, and the singers curtsied and smiled, soaking up the crowd's appreciation. Soon the sound of coins— including Jarn's—clinking in their basket accompanied the cheers and claps. The crowd eventually thinned out, and soon the bonfire died to embers. Jarn saw that the other performers had gone, but he decided to stay a while longer, thinking he might stroll along the river walk. As the men put their instruments in their leather cases and the singers took their ease, Jarn told them he enjoyed their performance.

"Thank you," the lute player replied.

"I noticed you expressed your appreciation with a few coins," one of the singers said, flashing a smile. "Thank you."

Jarn smiled back and shrugged. "Not enough to reward your fine offerings, but I'd be happy to stand you all to a round of ales or wine or whatever suits."

"Not for me," the lute player said. "A soft bed calls. But thanks just the same."

"Nor I," said the piper, shaking his head. "Thank you for the kind offer."

"Another time, perhaps," Jarn replied. "I may come back again tomorrow night, or the next."

The piper shrugged. "You may catch us then, but we leave for the Gliffring Festival soon."

"Let's be off, then," said the other woman.

"I maybe could enjoy some wine," the woman who had first spoken said to Jarn.

Since her three companions had declined his invitation, Jarn wasn't sure how to respond. As he thought about it, the woman reached into a cloth satchel and pulled out a wineskin. She held it up for Jarn's inspection and raised a questioning eyebrow. "I figure you won't mind if we don't have goblets."

"I, uh …"

"You meant to repair to a tavern and treat us, but it's a pleasant night, and I know a spot where we can sit and watch the river and quench our thirst, and you can tell me again how much you enjoyed our music."

Jarn laughed. She was as bold as any Vothan woman, and he knew he would enjoy her company. "Lead on," he said, and she handed him the wineskin, took his arm, and headed toward the river.

"There," she said, pointing at a huge drumble tree as they approached the riverbank. Enormous exposed roots extended more than ten feet from the bottom of its trunk toward the river. "Those big roots are like a giant's lap, and you can lean back against the trunk and watch the river roll by."

They sat down next to each other on the big roots and Jarn uncorked the wineskin and handed it to her. "Jarn Theffig," he announced.

"Maiya Enderill," she said and took the skin. She squirted some into her mouth and handed it back to Jarn, who did likewise.

"Telnan summer wine," he said. "Delicious but costly."

She nodded. "One of the minor lords of Telna gave us a dozen bottles. To show his appreciation."

"It should have been two dozen, at least. You sing beautifully. You and your sister."

She looked at him and raised an eyebrow. "You're a good observer. You'd make an excellent constable."

Jarn laughed. "As it happens, I have constabulary duties here in Skunnik, though lately I've been questioning my excellence at the job."

"Tell me about it, if you like. Or we can just watch the river."

Jarn decided to opt for river watching. The Santeris ran gently here as it curved toward the bottom of the Shield, burbling just loudly enough to be heard above the sound of the drumble tree's leaves as a light breeze stirred them. Jarn tilted his head back to take another mouthful of wine and gazed at the stars glowing against the black sky, like a handful of salt thrown onto a mage's cape. He turned to Maiya and handed her the wineskin. "Do you visit Skunnik often?"

"Yes, and I always come here. This tree is one of my favorite places in the known world."

"I'll wager you've seen a deal of it—the known world, I mean."

Maiya nodded. "I've been to every realm this side of the Great Ocean. What about you? You look like a man who's seen a bit of the world."

137

Jarn nodded. "Every realm, same as you. Though it appears I'll be spending most of the rest of my time here in the Acrinite Territory."

"For your constabulary duties."

"Right."

"Which at the moment are troubling you."

"Right again."

"But which you can't talk about, at least not to a stranger."

Jarn smiled. "Somehow, I don't consider you a stranger."

"Well then."

"There are political considerations."

"I see." She leaned back against the tree. "Some years ago, my brother Reivick—he's the lute player—was passing the time in an alehouse in Mence, a village in the Hirple Realm. He had one ale too many—or mayhap it was more than one too many—and began to hold forth about some dispute between Hirple and Sloken. The Hirps didn't take kindly to my brother's argument, right though it was, and would have given him a proper thrashing if my cousin Zelmer hadn't shown up and dragged him away."

"The perils of politics," Jarn said. "Or perhaps the perils of too much ale."

Maiya laughed, a high, clear sound nearly as pretty as her singing. "I'll wager you're investigating the disappearance of that diplomat's daughter. No wonder you're worried about politics."

Jarn wanted to tell her he was more worried about the diplomat's daughter, but he decided it was time to steer the conversation in a different direction. "Your cousin Zelmer, is he the piper?"

Maiya nodded.

"A talented family," Jarn said.

"Yes, the music gift seems to have been passed down from parents to children going back at least to my great-grandmother."

"I hope you've brought your talents to the Vothan Territory."

"Aye, we have. Quite popular we are in your land, I don't mind saying."

"Voths appreciate beautiful music." He gave her a glance. *And beautiful women*, he wanted to say but didn't. The way she glanced back at him, with a hint of a smile, made him think she might have heard his thought anyway.

"You Voths also have a fondness for wanderers."

"Aye, we do. Because of our history."

"Descended from the Vos, the Horse People, one of the Three First Tribes."

"You know your ancient legends."

"After the Vos were cheated out of their rightful homeland, they went wandering for hundreds of years, eventually coming back to where they began and settling in the Vothan Territory, which by then was under the rule of the Acrinites."

"Until last year," Jarn said.

Maiya nodded. "When the ancient deception was finally revealed, the Vothan Renewal took place. And now here you are, keeping the peace in Skunnik, the same city from which the Acrinites once ruled the Voths."

"I hope to return to Rualgar one of these days. Perhaps the next time I see you, it will be there."

"Mayhap. Though my sister is eager for marriage, which could put an end to our little troupe."

139

"Surely not. You've enough singing talent to carry on, no affront to your sister."

"We'll see," Maiya said.

"Does your sister have marriage prospects?"

Maiya laughed. "Aye, in every town. But we hail from Rynland, and Kaila won't plant deep roots anywhere but there."

"No doubt you've prospects of your own."

"Aye, but I like the wandering life, though I might agree to us becoming the house musicians of a high lord, if there are any worthy ones left."

"It almost makes me regret we have no high lords in Vothan," Jarn said. "I'd put in a word."

She rewarded him with a smile that outshone the light from the moon. "Perhaps you're better off without lords, after all. As for us, we'll continue to follow the Trail."

"The Trail?"

"The Minstrel's Trail. The circuit most of us follow. It runs between Rynland and Wyndor."

"By river or road?" Jarn asked.

"Both. East on the Shaffroth, by barge or river cog, then west from Rynland on the old King's Road or the Alder Road. I prefer the river."

Jarn smiled. "I thought maybe you did."

"I like rivers," Maiya said. "See how this one makes five quick loops in this part of the city, as if it can't make up its mind."

"That's why we build bridges," Jarn said.

"Yes, but bridges are boring."

"Yet useful, if one has need of haste."

"Haste has its place, but leisureliness has its own rewards."

140

"Yet too much meandering can make a journey longer than it needs to be."

Maiya shrugged. "Sometimes the journey itself is the purpose of the journey."

To that, Jarn made no reply. They finished the wine, and he walked Maiya to the Shieldstone Inn, where she and her three companions were staying. Maiya promised to send word to the Mang next time they were in Skunnik, and they shared a friendly kiss before Jarn headed back to headquarters.

As he approached the Palace of the High Hext, he wondered what Lady Grenling was doing. He would have to question her again, and Lord Grenling as well. When he passed the main palace gate, he thought he saw some movement, a quick flash of reflected moonlight or a shadow or night bird along the palace wall. He was peering into the darkness, trying to find whatever he had seen on the wall, when a loud voice startled him.

"Captain Jarn, is it?"

Jarn turned quickly, his hand going to his sword. Kurff, wearing civilian clothes, was standing there smiling at him. Jarn relaxed and nodded. "I hardly recognize you, Kurff. I've never seen you not in your uniform."

The Yellowshirt glanced down at his dark gray tunic and then back at Jarn. "I hardly know myself. But as I'm not on duty this fine night, I thought I'd go about as just another Skunniker."

"A bit late to be going about."

Kurff nodded. "I was about to say the same to you."

"I couldn't sleep."

"A common malady," Kurff said. He gestured toward the Palace of the High Hext. "Something interesting in the palace?"

Jarn shrugged. "Something caught my eye, or so I thought. An owl, perhaps, or a bat. Or a trick of the eye."

Kurff looked at the palace. "Nothing there now."

"No."

"You fancy a closer look?"

Jarn shook his head. "I fancy an hour or two of sleep before the sun comes up."

"Very wise," Kurff said. He paused a moment and then added, "Thanks for inviting me to the Gilpin party. We worked well together."

"It's an interesting technique you have for questioning people," Jarn said.

"Aye. A shame we couldn't break the little bastard. You were wise to have someone follow him. You did have someone follow him, eh? A woman Rider?"

"Liora Vaningo. A captain, like me. I don't expect much to come of it."

Kurff shrugged. "Nevertheless, all avenues."

Jarn nodded. "I'll be off then."

They parted, and Jarn headed back to the Mang, wondering what Kurff was doing wandering around the city in the small hours of the night without his uniform.

142

Chapter 16

Astil peered up the steps from the door to the servants' quarters, watching for the guards on the wall-walk. A few minutes later, one of the two pairs of them passed her position, and she quickly climbed the steps back to ground level. She knew she was taking too many chances, but anger and annoyance were driving her now, seasoned by frustration. Anger and enmity had always been fine spurs to action, as long as she maintained control and paid close attention to the task at hand. It was a fine balance, and Astil had always kept it, had never done anything foolish. Let the dull and witless make stupid mistakes, not her. But now she felt herself treading that fine line. On the other hand, she was not about to turn back. There was no other choice but to forge ahead.

The nearest window, at eye level, was unglazed but shuttered from the inside. She took a breath and pushed gently on the wooden shutters. She heard a squeak as they moved on their hinges. She pushed them open, peered into the gloom inside, and then hoisted herself up and thrust her head and upper body through the window. She brought her arms through, lowered herself to the floor, and pulled her legs inside before rolling forward on her shoulders and rising to a wary crouch in the darkness.

Astil drew her dagger and listened. She heard nothing. The short hallway was dimly lit by a lone candle in a sconce near the opposite end, where it met another hallway. She walked to the end, turned left into a wider hallway that paralleled the north wall of the palace, and then immediately turned right into another main hallway, which ran south. Candles on the wall at regular intervals

143

gave modest illumination. She came to a spiral staircase and heard voices murmuring somewhere above. Still as a stone, she waited. The voices faded. Holding her dagger, she began to climb, peering up as she went. At the first landing, she paused briefly and looked around, then continued up to the next floor, the one she wanted.

Another hallway, this one decorated with paintings and tapestries and busts in alcoves. She made her way to the Red Suite, stood outside the door. She tried the door handle. It was locked. She found her picklock. Men's voices sounded from around a corner, heading her way along another corridor. *Damn.*

She knocked on the door, loud enough to be heard inside, but, she hoped, not so loud as to draw the attention of the approaching men. The door opened a few inches, and a man dressed in the black uniform of the Brythyn Realm peered out and squinted at her.

"Sir Tarris sent for me," she said, forcing herself not to glance in the direction of the voices.

"Sir Tarris isn't here," the Brythyner said, frowning. "This is Lord and Lady Grenling's suite."

"I know, but he's accompanying them, and I have something important to tell him. It's about Talsie." She removed the silver chain from around her neck and held the saffite ring toward him. "This is hers." The ring slipped from her hand and fell, and the guard dropped his eyes. At the same moment, Astil kicked open the door and threw herself at him, slamming her head into his gut and tackling him to the floor. She scrambled up and put a knee into his groin and then slipped her dagger from its sheath. "Not a sound, or your blood will be marring this fine carpet," she whispered as she held the blade against his throat. The man gasped, trying to get back his breath. She slipped his sword and dagger from their sheaths and slid them across the floor before getting up to retrieve the ring and close the door.

The man, still gasping, drew himself up to a sitting position and glared at her.

"Never mind," she said. "You're not the first man I've bested. Consider it an honor to meet me."

"What do you want?" he rasped.

"To talk to the lady."

The door to the private chamber opened and Astil turned toward it, ready to hurl her dagger. Lady Grenling stood there in a long blue robe, her eyes going wide when she saw Astil. "You," she said. "You're supposed to be looking for Talsie."

"We need to talk," Astil said.

"I'm sorry, my lady," the guard said, slowly getting to his feet. "Please return to your bedchamber."

Lady Grenling ignored him and stared at Astil. "Talk about what?"

Astil held up the saffite ring

Lady Grenling stared at it a moment and then looked at the guard. "Go into the small bedchamber and wait. This woman and I will talk here."

The guard frowned. "My lady?"

"Do as I say," Lady Grenling ordered. "Leave your weapons. I'll knock when we're finished."

The guard nodded, strode to the door that opened to the suite's small bedchamber, and went inside, closing the door behind him.

Lady Grenling narrowed her eyes at Astil. "If you wished to speak with me, you could have told Captain Jarn. You could have come here with him, during the day, like a normal person instead of a thief."

"I have my own way of doing things, so save your bluster," Astil said. "Why did you lie about the ring?"

"I didn't lie."

"I know you played me false, because when I tried to picture Talsie in my mind, I couldn't. That never happened before. I thought I was losing my touch."

"Perhaps you are," Lady Grenling said.

"No. I did see someone in my mind, but it wasn't your daughter, Lady Grenling. It was you." She held up the ring again. "This is yours. I want to know why you gave it to me, why you tricked me."

Lady Grenling glanced at the door behind her and then back at Astil. "Not so loud, if you please."

"Then tell me why you lied."

"I didn't. The ring is Talsie's. It was mine, yes, but I gave it to her."

"You're lying. You don't want me to find your daughter."

"Of course I do. But I don't … I wasn't sure I could trust you. I've heard about you, you see, and I didn't—"

"Your precious Captain Jarn trusts me, why shouldn't you?"

Lady Grenling's blue eyes flashed. "You break in here, attack my guard, threaten me, and then ask why I don't trust you?"

"This conversation grows tiresome," Astil said. She pointed to the door to the smaller bedchamber. "Is that where Talsie was to sleep?"

Lady Grenling nodded.

"Then there will be a chest of clothing in there. Tell your man to bring it out."

Lady Grenling knocked on the door to the small bedchamber, and the guard opened it.

"Bring Talsie's chest out here, if you please," she told him. "And then return to the room until I knock again."

He did as she asked, once again closing the door behind him.

"Open the chest," Astil said.

Lady Grenling went to the chest and raised the lid. Astil stepped close to it and peered inside.

"That scarf," Astil said, pointing at a colorful silk scarf. "Take it out and give it to me."

Lady Grenling took the scarf and handed it to Astil. Astil put it close to her face and inhaled. She detected the slightest scent of perfume, different from Lady Grenling's.

"I'll be going now," Astil said. She glanced at the window, saw that the sky had lightened. The sun would be up soon.

Lady Grenling held out her hand, palm up. "My ring, if you please."

Astil gave her a cold smile and said, "I'll keep the ring." She left the room and made her way through the palace, nodding and smiling at everyone she passed, and left through the front doors. By the time she got outside, the sun had risen, daubing the eastern sky with soft pink smudges.

Chapter 17

DAY 4

Jarn was awakened by someone pounding on the door to his quarters and shouting his name. He swore under his breath, slipped out of bed, and opened the door. Bleuek was standing there, breathing hard, as if he had run up the stairs.

"The sorceress is here to see you, Captain. She says it's important."

"Astil? Astil is here?"

"Aye, she is."

Jarn couldn't believe it. He had expected Astil to be well along in her quest to find Talsie Grenling, not loitering around Skunnik, disturbing people's sleep. "What does she want? And why isn't she on the trail?"

"She wouldn't tell me anything," Bleuek said. "Just demanded to see you and told me to be quick about it. I put her in one of the interview rooms."

"How long has the sun been up?"

"Not an hour."

"Go back and tell her I'll be there shortly."

Jarn dressed quickly and went down to the Rats Nest, where he found Astil and Bleuek in the same room in which he and Kurff had questioned Willim Gilpin. "Why are you not out tracking Talsie Grenling?" Jarn asked before sitting down opposite her.

Astil gave him a cold smile and held up the saffite ring Lady Grenling had given her two days before. "Because the lady played us false. This ring she gave me doesn't belong to her daughter."

148

Jarn glared at her. "What are you saying?"

"The ring is Lady Grenling's, not Talsie Grenling's. It led me to her, not her daughter."

Jarn leaned back in his chair and closed his eyes. "We need to speak with Lady Grenling, find out what she has to say about this," he said after a moment's pause.

"I already talked to the woman. She admitted her deceit."

"Why would she deceive you?"

"She said she didn't trust me."

Jarn's mind was reeling. He was counting on Astil more than he had admitted to himself, and now, whether because Lady Grenling had played them false or because Astil was playing some devious game of her own, that avenue was closed.

"It makes no matter, I'll find her," Astil said, as if she had heard his thoughts. "I have a scarf that belongs to the girl." She set the saffite ring on the table and stood up. "When you return that to the lady, you might ask her what she's playing at. In the meantime, I'm off to find her daughter. I'll expect you to take good care of my gold."

Jarn was about to tell her he would send one of his men to go with her, but he knew she would refuse. She left the room without another word.

"Shall I have Aarla follow her?" Bleuek asked.

Jarn shook his head. "Best not. If she found out, that would be the end of our agreement."

"What about Lady Grenling?"

"Time to pay her another visit," Jarn said.

***

149

Jarn sent Bleuek to fetch Sir Tarris and went to the Rats Nest meeting room to wait. He stared at the slate with the chalked names and drew a circle around *Lady Grenling*. When Sir Tarris arrived, they went to the Mang's dining room for breakfast, and Jarn told him what had happened. Bleuek and Braga joined them, and they made their plans for the day.

When they returned to the Rats Nest, Grion was waiting with a message—Lord Keddro had arrived, as requested, to speak with Jarn.

"Bring him to my private chamber," Jarn said. He glanced at Sir Tarris. "I didn't expect he would come here."

"Nor did I," Sir Tarris said, a puzzled look on his face.

Jarn sent Bleuek to report the latest news to Lahgoh and asked Braga to be ready to accompany him and Sir Tarris to the Palace of the High Hext to talk to Lady Grenling, as soon as they had completed their business with Lord Keddro. Then he and Sir Tarris went to Jarn's suite of rooms in the rear of the Rats Nest and waited in the outer chamber.

"You need not participate in the questioning," Jarn said to Sir Tarris. "As you're a Brythyner, it may be ill-judged for you to do so."

Sir Tarris nodded. He seemed relieved.

Grion arrived with Lord Keddro and two of his knights, surly-looking men with wary eyes and perpetual frowns. Lord Keddro, however, smiled warmly as he introduced himself. "A pleasure to meet you, Captain Jarn," he said. "So sorry about yesterday. Bit of a misunderstanding, I'm afraid, all my fault, but I hope to set it all aright."

"I appreciate your coming, Lord Keddro," Jarn said, returning the lord's smile and giving him a quick appraisal. He wore a luxurious gray woolen cloak over a yellow silk tunic whose fine cut could not quite obscure his bulging figure. His long, dark hair was shot with gray, and his beardless face had seen little sun.

"It's my pleasure," Lord Keddro replied, still smiling.

"I gather you know Sir Tarris," Jarn said.

"Aye, we've met."

"Lord Grenling assigned him to help in the investigation."

Lord Keddro nodded. "Glad to hear it."

"I join Captain Jarn in thanking you for coming," Sir Tarris said. "He assures me we won't keep you long."

Lord Keddro waved away any concerns. "No matter. Truth is, now I'm here, I find myself eager to try some fine Vothan wine, if the captain cares to indulge an old man."

Jarn turned to Grion. "Fetch us a bottle of strong red, if you please, Grion."

Grion nodded and left the room.

Jarn gestured toward his private chamber. "We'll talk in there."

Lord Keddro told his knights to remain in the outer chamber, and then he and Sir Tarris entered the inner office. Jarn followed, closing the door behind him, and gestured toward the alcove, which held a round table and chairs. "Please, sit."

They took seats at the table, and Jarn turned to Lord Keddro. "As you know, I and my men, ably aided by Sir Tarris, are investigating the disappearance of Talsie Grenling."

Lord Keddro furrowed his brow, and his face became solemn. "A crime and a shame," he said, shaking his head. "That poor young woman."

"A young woman who is betrothed you, your lordship," Jarn said.

Lord Keddro nodded. "Arranged near two years ago, before the ... before you Voths came into your own."

"Has something changed since then?"

"Not sure what you mean, Captain."

"There's a rumor that you or Lord Grenling—or perhaps both of you—desire to break the marital arrangement."

"Who might be the source of such a rumor?"

"As I'm sure you will appreciate, Lord Keddro, during an investigation like this, I'm not free to divulge such information."

Grion entered with a bottle of wine and three goblets. He poured and handed a goblet each to Jarn, Sir Tarris, and Lord Keddro.

Lord Keddro took a swallow and nodded appreciatively. "Quite good," he said.

"Is there any truth to the rumor I mentioned?" Jarn asked.

"Yes," Lord Keddro replied.

Jarn raised an eyebrow. "Go on."

"The marriage was to seal the new treaty between the Acrinite Realm and Brythyn. But the Acrinite Realm is no more. Now the Voths are responsible for negotiating treaties and agreements. The marriage no longer signifies."

"Yet Talsie accompanied Lord and Lady Grenling to Skunnik."

152

"So as not to arouse rumors or gossip," Lord Keddro said. "These diplomatic maneuvers must be handled delicately."

"Forgive my bluntness, Lord Keddro, but I gather that there was no actual love or affection between you and Talsie Grenling, is that right?"

Lord Keddro nodded. "None whatsoever, though I do hope you find her."

Jarn remembered Lahgoh telling him that Lord Keddro had implied that the Voths might be responsible for Talsie's abduction. He either had changed his view or was engaging in some maneuver of his own. "Any notions about where we might look?"

"None at all."

"Did you and Talsie exchange letters?"

"A few. Mostly formal."

"Did she ever write anything that hinted at trouble?"

"What kind of trouble?"

Jarn shrugged. "A suggestion that she might refuse to go through with the marriage."

"No, nothing like that."

"Perhaps a mention of another suitor, someone else she might hold dear to her heart."

"I doubt there was anyone else. Her mother sheltered her from the world."

"Interesting you should say that," Jarn replied. "Lady Grenling told me that a young man named Willim Gilpin was quite fond of Talsie."

A vague smile lit Lord Keddro's face. "Did she? Perhaps you should talk to the young man."

"We have done."

"And what did he say?"

"Once again, Lord Keddro—"

"You are not free to divulge such information. I quite understand."

"When we find Talsie Grenling, how will you and Lord Grenling go about canceling the marriage, now that, as you say, it no longer signifies?"

Lord Keddro smiled. "As I'm sure you will appreciate, Captain Jarn, with complicated diplomacy such as this, I'm not free to divulge such information."

"Of course," Jarn said. "I wonder if I might have a look at the letters Talsie sent you."

Lord Keddro shrugged. "I see no reason why not. I'll have one of my men deliver them to you here."

"You need not trouble yourself," Jarn said. "I'll send one of my Riders to your castle to fetch them."

Lord Keddro frowned but quickly resumed his genial humor. "But I insist, Captain. It's no bother, and my men frequently ride into Skunnik."

"Very well," Jarn said. It was time to change the subject. "By the way, my lord, how long have you known the Grenlings?"

Lord Keddro furrowed his brow and glanced at the ceiling. Jarn wondered if he was casting his mind back to his first meeting with Lord Grenling or trying to work out why Jarn had asked the question. "Oh, I suppose it's been ten years or more," he said at length.

"Would you describe yourself as a friend of his lordship?"

"I would describe myself as his sometime partner in conducting trade and other business."

"Friendly partners?"

Lord Keddro shrugged and then gave a nod. "I would say so, yes."

"And when you two conduct your trade and other business, do you represent your realms or yourselves?"

"Sometimes one, sometimes the other, sometimes both."

"I assume the business you've conducted with Lord Grenling has been mutually satisfactory."

"Always. He is shrewd and reliable. You Voths would do well to finish negotiating your treaty with him."

"Of course, any treaty would be an arrangement between Vothan and Brythyn, rather than between individuals," Jarn said.

"Of course," Lord Keddro replied. "Have you any other questions, Captain?"

"I think not," Jarn said, standing up. Lord Keddro and Sir Tarris stood up as well. "I won't keep you any longer."

The three men went into the outer room, where Lord Keddro's men were waiting.

"We'll see ourselves out, Captain," Lord Keddro said. "I hope you'll keep me apprised of the progress of your investigation. And if you need more help with your searches, I will be happy to have my knights lend a hand. Just say the word."

"I appreciate that," Jarn said. "Will I find you in your castle or at your house here in Skunnik."

"Impossible to say," Lord Keddro replied. "Best to check the house first. If I'm not there, have someone fetch me."

They left, and Jarn and Sir Tarris returned to the alcove and took seats across from one another at the round table. Jarn refilled their goblets and handed one to Sir Tarris. "What do you make of Lord Keddro?"

"I'm surprised he was willing to come here and even more surprised he was so pleasant."

"Why do you suppose that was?"

Sir Tarris shrugged. "Perhaps he wants to help improve relations between the Acrinites and the Voths."

"Perhaps. But there may be other reasons for Lord Keddro's seeming cooperation and good humor."

"Such as?"

"If Lord Keddro comes to us, then there is no reason for us to go to him. Thus, we need not enter his castle."

"You think he has something to hide?"

Jarn nodded.

"What?"

Jarn said nothing but stared at Sir Tarris as if he was challenging him to provide his own answer.

Sir Tarris's eyes went wide. "Talsie? You think he's hiding Talsie in his castle?"

"I don't know, but we can't rule it out."

"But why? Why would Lord Keddro have Talsie abducted and then hide her there?"

Jarn considered telling Sir Tarris about Lady Grenling's fears that her husband and Lord Keddro had conspired to abduct Talsie to put a halt to the wedding. But the Brythyn knight might feel compelled to share that information with Lord Grenling, which would further muddle an already troubled investigation. No, Jarn would keep that piece of intelligence to himself and his own people, at least for now. "I don't know why Lord Keddro might have had Talsie abducted," he said. "But we must consider the possibility and leave no avenue untrod." Left unsaid was the possibility that Talsie's body was buried on the grounds of Lord Keddro's castle.

"Do you plan to go to the castle and demand entrance?" Sir Tarris asked.

Jarn shook his head. "No, at least not yet."

"What's our next move?"

"Since Lady Grenling seems to have deliberately misled Astil, we need to question her again. It may not be a pleasant encounter."

"Then, if you don't mind, I won't accompany you."

"I don't mind," Jarn said. "Actually, I prefer it. I want you to talk to Grion and devise a plan to keep a watch on the road from Lord Keddro's castle to Skunnik. It passes through the village of Brinnik, which is not far from the castle, so you can keep an eye on the road from there. Take a third man if you need to, but begin the surveillance today. I'll want daily reports on any movement or activity, beginning tomorrow."

Sir Tarris nodded and stood up. "I'll get on with it, then. I'll see you tomorrow with the first report."

Chapter 18

Jarn went to the Palace of the High Hext to confront Lady Grenling. When he arrived, a Yellowshirt guard took him to the suite of rooms where he had first questioned Lord Grenling. The guard told him to wait in the outer chamber, and then disappeared. A few minutes later, Lord Grenling arrived.

"Ah, Lord Grenling," Jarn said, surprised to see him. "I thought you had returned to Brythyn."

"So I did, and now I've returned," Lord Grenling replied, a hint of annoyance in his voice. He remained standing and did not invite Jarn to take a seat. "What brings you here again, Captain? Do you have news of Talsie?"

"I'm afraid not," Jarn said. "We're here to speak with Lady Grenling."

Lord Grenling frowned. "I thought you had already done so."

"So I did, and now I've returned," Jarn replied. "There is an important matter I need to discuss with her."

Lord Grenling's frown deepened into a glare. "She isn't here. She's gone back to Brythyn."

Jarn felt the muscles in his jaw tighten. He also noted a flicker in Lord Grenling's eyes that made him suspect the man was lying. "When will she return?" he asked.

"I don't see how my wife's travel schedule could possibly be any of your concern."

"Perhaps I didn't make myself clear—I need to speak with your wife about an important matter that concerns your daughter's disappearance."

"Then speak to me about it."

158

"Very well," Jarn said. "The tracker I hired to help us search for Talsie accompanied me to a meeting with Lady Grenling. This tracker, a sorceress named Astil, asked for a small item that belongs to your daughter. Lady Grenling gave her a gold ring set with a polished saffite. The ring is not Talsie's. It belongs to your wife."

"Are you calling my wife a liar?"

"The ring led Astil back to Lady Grenling, not to your daughter."

"And you trust this sorceress, do you?" Lord Grenling said, a sneer beginning to twist his face.

"I would not have hired her otherwise," Jarn said, trying not to choke on his words.

"I know something about this Astil of yours," Lord Grenling said. "I know what she is, and I know what she has done. She's a criminal and a thief, skilled with the dagger and the crossbow and the gods know what other weapons. She has blood on her hands. The Wyndorans put her in prison, but she outsmarted them and escaped. This is the woman you hired to find my daughter. You should be out there looking for Talsie yourself, Captain, not hiring murderers to do the job."

"Why would Lady Grenling have deliberately misled her?" Jarn asked in an even voice, ignoring Lord Grenling's words, which, to Jarn's great regret, were mostly true.

"She didn't!" Lord Grenling shouted. "But if she did, she had good reason. Most likely to protect Talsie from your murderous hired blade."

"If Lady Grenling returns to Skunnik, please have her send for me so I can ask her myself."

"My wife won't be returning to Skunnik, so stop wasting my time and go find my daughter. Because I tell

159

you now, Captain, that the treaty being negotiated between Brythyn and Vothan is in jeopardy unless you do."

"Treaties are not my domain," Jarn said. "You'll have to issue your threats to Minister Respero."

"I will, Captain, you can depend on it."

"I'll make one final point before I leave," Jarn said. "Treaty or no treaty, I will follow every possible avenue of investigation and do everything I can to find your daughter, return her to you, and seize those responsible, whoever they might be."

Before Lord Grenling could reply, Jarn turned and headed for the door.

***

When Jarn returned to the Rats Nest, Braga told him a boy had come with a message for him, which was written on a piece of parchment waiting on his desk. Braga said the boy told him that a woman had paid him a falcon, a small silver coin, to deliver it and that she wanted him to wait there for a reply.

Jarn thanked Braga and went into his chamber to read the message, which was folded and sealed inside another sheet of parchment. The message was from Lady Grenling. Jarn sat down to read it.

My dear Captain Jarn. I must see you at once, but I am in fear for my life and have gone into hiding. I am staying in the Stone Bridge Inn, on lower Zayet Street. I'm using the name Esmae Lingren. Please come, but come alone and tell no one else of this. The inn has a small alcove off the dining room where we can meet. Send a message with the boy. Come soon. I need you.

160

Jarn read it again, and then set it on his desk and read it again, staring at it as if he could will it to explain itself.

Five minutes later he was in Lahgoh's chamber, sitting on the other side of the line commander's desk and watching him read the note. Lahgoh looked up, frowning. "A strange turn of events."

"It gets stranger," Jarn said. "Not an hour ago, Lord Grenling told me she had returned to Brythyn. I believe he was lying, and I also believe he does not know her actual whereabouts."

"Why would the lady go into hiding?"

"She told me she suspects her husband of being involved in Talsie's abduction. If he learned of her suspicions, she may be in danger from him."

"She may have been lying about her husband's involvement."

"True, but if Lord Grenling found out she told such a lie, his rage might be all the hotter."

"This case is becoming ever more tangled," Lahgoh said. "I suppose you'll go to the lady."

Jarn nodded.

There was a knock on Lahgoh's door. "Enter," he said.

The door opened and Liora Vaningo entered the chamber.

"I thought you were trailing Willim Gilpin," Lahgoh said.

"I was, but I have news to report," Liora replied. She looked at Jarn. "Braga said I'd find you here."

"Sit and tell us your news," Lahgoh said.

Liora fetched another chair and sat next to Jarn. "After you and Kurff turned Willim loose, he went directly to a small, out-of-the-way inn and took a room. He seemed to know exactly where he was going."

"Did he?" Jarn said. "And which of Skunnik's fine establishments did the young man go to?"

"The Stone Bridge Inn, on lower Zayet Street."

Jarn and Lahgoh glanced quickly at one another and then turned back to Liora.

"Go on," Lahgoh said in a quiet voice.

"The inn is near the stone bridge that crosses Tennie Creek. I hired a room there as well, to stay close. This morning, as I was finishing breakfast, a woman of around fifty years came to the inn and took a room. She appeared anxious and kept looking around, so I followed at a discreet distance after she went upstairs, and took note of which room was hers. I went to my own room and left the door slightly ajar, so I would know if Willim came out of his room. Soon after, I heard a light rapping sound and peered out. The woman was tapping on Willim's door. When he opened it, they embraced and kissed like lovers."

Jarn closed his eyes. "Was this woman tall and slender with long yellow hair, blue eyes, and fine features?"

Liora raised an eyebrow and gazed at him. "Aye, she was. Can you read thoughts, then?"

Jarn shook his head. "She's Lady Grenling, mother of the victim. I've just received a message from the lady asking me to come to the Stone Bridge Inn to meet with her. She says she's in fear for her life."

Liora's eyes went wide, and she peered at Jarn as if he had just sprouted wings. "Lady Grenling, you say?"

Jarn nodded.

Liora shook her head and let out a long breath. "Two days ago you told me you believed there was something odd about this case. It appears you were right."

"And you told me to believe no one," Jarn said. "It appears you were right as well."

"Bring Lady Grenling back here," Lahgoh said to Jarn. "Her husband may enjoy diplomatic courtesy, but if she fled his household, then she does not. Fetch the Gilpin lad, too, but take them separately and don't let either know the other is in custody. Inform me when you get back. I want to meet your Lady Grenling, and her young swain as well."

***

Jarn wrote a message to Lady Grenling letting her know he would meet her at the Stone Bridge Inn. A half hour after giving the message to the boy to deliver, he sent Braga, Bleuek, and Liora to the inn ahead of him, with instructions for one of them to stand by in the common room while he spoke with Lady Grenling and the other two to confront Willim Gilpin. Soon after they left, Jarn set out for the inn.

When he entered the inn's small common room, he spotted Braga, Bleuek, and Liora, who were sitting at a table near the door, tankards of ale in front of them. Braga nodded, signaling that they had seen Lady Grenling come downstairs and enter the small alcove at the rear of the room, near the right corner. Jarn nodded back and headed that way. He passed a table at which sat four well-dressed men, prosperous merchants by the look of them, who were eating a midday meal of venison stew and arguing about the price of wheat. A couple of graybeards at another table glanced at Jarn as he strode by, took note of his uniform, and quickly turned back to their goblets of wine.

Jarn, who had never been inside the Stone Bridge Inn, liked the look of it. Large front windows let in plenty of sunlight, and a sturdy wooden chandelier suspended from the central rafter added the light of two dozen candles. The tabletops were clean and the flagstone floor looked to have been recently swept. He felt the eyes of the barkeep on him as he stepped into the alcove and wondered if the man was also the proprietor.

Lady Grenling was sitting at one of four small tables in the alcove, which was otherwise empty. A pair of high windows let in slanting afternoon sunlight, and a single large candle on each table provided additional illumination. Lady Grenling looked pale, whether because of the bright sunlight or because she was worried, Jarn could only guess. She wore a plain black dress and sat facing the alcove's entrance, which meant Jarn's back would be to it. He was glad one of his own was in the outer room to watch out for mischief. Two wine goblets were on the table, each half full of red.

Lady Grenling stood up and extended a hand. "Captain Jarn, thank you for coming."

Jarn took her hand, which was warm and dry. She kept her grip on his hand a second longer than necessary and gave him a smile before sitting down.

"Your note said you are in fear for your life," Jarn said. "From whom?"

"My husband."

Jarn raised an eyebrow. "How so?"

"He found out that I suspect his involvement in Talsie's abduction."

164

"How did he find out?"

"I … I found a letter from Lord Keddro to Lord Grenling implicating both men, and he … my husband … saw me with it. I pretended I was looking for something else, but he knows I know."

"When did this take place?"

"Yesterday. I left the palace early this morning and came here."

"Does anyone else know? Your maid, a lady-in-waiting, anybody?"

"No, no one else knows. But you'll protect me, Captain, won't you?"

"Yes, of course. You're to be taken to the Mang, the safest place in the city. You'll stay there under protection of the Vothan Riders until this business is sorted out."

"Oh, thank you, Captain, but I … I had another thought in mind."

"Say on."

Lady Grenling took a sip from her goblet, looking up at Jarn as she drank. Jarn, wary of possible mischief and mindful of Sir Longboke's troubles, decided he would not drink from his goblet.

"I need to go to Rynland," Lady Grenling said. "I … I know some people there. I can begin a new life. You'll take me, won't you, Captain. Please?"

"What about your daughter?"

"When you find her, you must send her to me there," she said, her voice barely above a whisper. "Without telling anyone else."

Jarn frowned. "Rynland is far. You ask much of me."

"I know," she replied, nodding slowly. She looked as if she might cry. "I … I'm not without substantial means

165

of my own. I will pay you for your troubles. Please say you'll help me."

"First we must get you to the Mang. Once you're there, we can discuss our options."

"Yes, thank you, Captain, but I want to set out for Rynland at once, today if possible, tomorrow at the latest. If it's to be tomorrow, I prefer to stay here."

"You're very brave," Jarn said, trying to sound sincere. "But I must insist on taking you to the Mang. You'll be safer there."

She swallowed and looked toward the entrance, her eyes quickly flitting back and forth, as if she might be looking for someone. Jarn resisted the urge to turn around and see for himself. By now, two of his people should be having a nice chat with Willim Gilpin up in his room.

"Very well," Lady Grenling said at length. "But can we leave for Rynland tomorrow?"

Jarn stood up. "We'll have plenty of time to discuss options."

Lady Grenling finished her wine and stood up. "I have a trunk in my room, and a small bag."

"I'll have someone fetch it to the Mang," Jarn said.

They left the alcove, and Jarn saw Braga, still sitting at the same table, watching the alcove. He heard Lady Grenling give a little gasp when she recognized him. She hesitated, but Jarn took her arm and led her forward.

"Braga, you'll remember Lady Grenling," Jarn said. "Please take her to headquarters and see that she gets our finest suite. Inform Line Commander Lahgoh as soon as you arrive."

Lady Grenling stopped and stared at Jarn. "I thought you would take me."

166

"I have other business to attend to. I'll be coming around to see you a bit later."

"But—"

"Come along now, my lady," Braga said. "Your horse is already saddled and ready to go."

Lady Grenling nodded and, without looking at Jarn, planted a tight smile on her face and left with Braga through the front door.

In the dining room, the four merchants had continued their animated conversation without paying heed to anything else, and the two graybeards had studiously avoided everything but their wine goblets. The barkeep, however, was eyeing Jarn suspiciously. Jarn met his gaze and went to him.

"I'm investigating the abduction of the daughter of a visiting diplomat, Lord Grenling, of the Brythyn Realm," Jarn said. "The woman who just left is Lady Grenling. I have some questions to ask you. I suggest we go to the alcove to talk."

"We can talk right here," the barkeep said.

Jarn shrugged. "As you please. Do you own the inn?"

"I do," the man replied.

"Your name?"

"Nerrod Pennemon."

"When did Lady Grenling arrive?"

"This morning. Early."

"By herself?"

"Aye."

"Did she have any baggage?"

"One small bag."

"She mentioned a trunk."

Nerrod shook his head. "She came on horseback. She had no trunk."

167

"I'll just go have a look in her room," Jarn said. "Which is it?"

"Second floor, last room on the right. Mind you don't take anything."

"If there's a trunk, one of my men will be along to fetch it. The lady will be staying elsewhere."

Nerrod shrugged. "It makes no matter to me. I've already been paid for ten days' lodging."

Jarn stared at him. "The lady told you she planned to stay for ten days?"

Nerrod shook his head. "I was paid seven or eight days ago, for two rooms, ten days each. I was to leave them empty till the lodgers showed up, and that's what I did."

"When did the lodgers show up?"

"One yesterday, the lady this morning."

"And the lady said her name was Esmae Lingren?"

"Aye."

"What of the other lodger? When did he arrive?"

Nerrod frowned. "I don't feel right talking about my patrons this way."

"A young woman's life is at risk," Jarn said. "Was the other lodger a young man with short brown hair, brown eyes, and a bit of a starved look about him?"

Nerrod hesitated a moment, then gave Jarn a slight nod.

"Which one paid for the rooms seven or eight days ago?"

"Neither. A man came by and made the arrangements."

"What man?"

"Never said his name."

"Describe him," Jarn said.

"About as tall as you, long-limbed and lanky, with long darkish-yellow hair nearly down to his shoulders."

"Was he dressed like a knight?"

"No, he was dressed plain-like, but he had a knight's bearing, if you know what I mean."

"I know just what you mean," Jarn said. "I'll go and see the room now."

Jarn went upstairs and headed for the last room on the right. As he passed a door on the left, he heard Bleuek's voice and smiled. The questioning of Willim Gilpin had begun.

Jarn entered the room Lady Grenling had occupied and spotted a travel trunk in one corner. A leather travel bag lay on the bed. He quickly searched the room but found nothing else of interest. He left and knocked on the door of Willim Gilpin's room and then opened it. Bleuek, Liora, and Willim Gilpin looked up at him.

"Captain Jarn," Bleuek said. "Like to join our little get-together?"

Jarn nodded. "At the Mang, if you please."

Chapter 19

When Jarn returned to the Mang, the Yellowshirt Nevvin, who Jarn had put in charge of the search parties looking for Talsie Grenling, was waiting for him in the Rats Nest meeting room, looking worried. When Jarn entered the room, Nevvin stood up and told him he had some important information to share.

Braga was there, too, and he informed Jarn that Lady Grenling was safely ensconced in a comfortable suite, with two guards outside her door. Jarn told Braga that Bleuek and Liora would be arriving soon with Willim Gilpin and reminded him that Willim and Lady Grenling should be kept apart from one another and apart from Sir Longboke and that none of the three should be told of the others' whereabouts.

That done, Jarn turned to Nevvin, hoping for some good news concerning the search for Talsie Grenling. "We'll talk in my office," he said and picked up one of the candles from the large oval table. He and Nevvin left through the back door of the meeting room and walked down the short hallway that ran between the two interview rooms, turned left into another short hallway, and then right into the outer room of Jarn's private suite.

Nevvin glanced around the large outer chamber as he followed Jarn into his inner office. "Fine quarters," he said.

"A bit too fine for my taste," Jarn replied, embarrassed that an Acrinite was admiring a Voth's accommodations.

"Ah, yes, you Voths like to keep things spare and simple, eh?"

"It's what we're used to."

Jarn lit candles in sconces on the wall and then took a seat behind his desk. He gestured for Nevvin to take one of the plain wooden chairs facing it.

"This is more the Vothan custom," Nevvin said, nodding. "Mine as well, truth be told."

"Tell me your tidings," Jarn said.

"Two days ago—it was the day we left—I divided my men into two groups. I took one group west, toward Wyndor, the other group headed north toward Brythyn. On the way, we stopped in the villages to ask at the inns about any young women or suspicious travelers anyone might have seen, but no one admitted to seeing or knowing anything. Late yesterday, we ran across a large party of armed and mounted men, more than twenty of them. I met with their leader to ask if they had seen anyone who looked like Talsie Grenling, and I recognized him as a knight of Brythyn, though he was dressed plain, not in the uniform of the Brythyn Realm."

Jarn stared at him. "Are you sure?"

"Aye, Sir Givrill is the man's name, one of Lord Grenling's men. I remember seeing him before, in Skunnik, back before the late war with you Voths. I was about to acknowledge that I knew him, but then I thought better of it, though I can't say why."

"Did he recognize you?"

Nevvin shook his head. "I'm sure he did not. No haughty Brythyn knight is likely to have paid any heed to a Yellowshirt." He grinned as he said it, betraying no sense of affront.

"Did you find out what they were doing in Acrinite territory?"

171

"I figured they were searching for Talsie Grenling, same as us, but they claimed to be a hunting party from Drinnik, a town not far from the border with Wyndor. They didn't look to me like hunters. They looked to me like knights, and they had that Brythyner air of arrogance about them."

"But they weren't dressed as knights."

"No, they were not. It didn't smell right to me, so I decided to follow them, at a distance, figuring maybe I could find out why twenty Brythyn knights were skulking about the Acrinite Realm—excuse me, Captain, I meant the Acrinite Province—disguised as hunters."

"What did you learn?"

"The lot of them made for Lord Keddro's castle, which is where I left them. Then I came straight here."

Jarn closed his eyes and rubbed his brow. His head was beginning to ache, and he felt like downing a flagon of strong red wine. He opened his eyes and looked at Nevvin. "You've done well."

Nevvin shrugged. "We've seen no sign of the young lady, so I can't fairly accept praise for having done well."

"You showed initiative. You used your brains. You discovered some useful information."

Nevvin grinned. "Aye, we Yellowshirts are like that. Almost Voth-like, if I may be so bold. But what do you make of what I told you? If you don't mind my asking, I mean."

Jarn wasn't sure he should divulge his suspicions about Lord Keddro, but Nevvin had proved himself loyal, and there was no reason not to share information. "Lord Keddro was here yesterday, all smiles, friendly and cooperative. But I believe the reason he came here was to prevent anyone from entering his castle. I believe he is hiding something."

Nevvin frowned. "What? Not the young lady?"

"We don't know," Jarn said. "But it might well be that he's holding Talsie captive there—or worse."

***

Soon after Jarn's meeting with Nevvin, Bleuek and Liora arrived at the Mang with Willim Gilpin. Jarn told them to put Willim in the same interview room he had been in the day before, when Jarn and Kurff had questioned him. Then he sent a meal to Lady Grenling in her suite. After that, he told the men standing guard outside Sir Longboke's room to take the knight to the second interview room and guard him there. He repeated to everyone the instructions that the three detainees should not be allowed see one another or learn that the others were also in custody. Next, he reported to Lahgoh. Finally, Jarn, Braga, Bleuek, and Liora took a leisurely evening meal in the Mang's dining room. Jarn was in no hurry. He wanted to give Lady Grenling, Sir Longboke, and Willim Gilpin plenty of time to worry, and, despite his lack of sleep, he would question them all night and into the small hours if necessary.

Jarn planned to question Willim Gilpin first, then Sir Longboke, and Lady Grenling last, although he expected to conduct more than one interview for each. How many more depended on what he learned. He hoped to use information gleaned from one as a means to gain information from the others. That was why it was critical that they be kept apart and not know that their fellow schemers were also in custody. He and Bleuek would interview Willim Gilpin, and he would include Braga in the questioning of Sir Longboke. He would question Lady Grenling by himself, at least for the first interview, and talk to her in her suite. It figured to be a long night, but Jarn was looking forward to the evening and wondered who would break first.

After their meal, Jarn told Braga and Liora to get some rest, and he and Bleuek proceeded to the interview room where Willim Gilpin was being held.

Jarn sat down opposite Willim. Bleuek stood in a corner, watching.

"Nice to see you again, Willim," Jarn began. "Anything new to tell me?"

"I've nothing to tell you," the young man said. "Why have you seized me?"

Jarn gestured toward Bleuek. "This young man is Bleuek, who you've met before. He's a saddlemaster with the Vothan Riders, and he'll be assisting me." Jarn turned to Bleuek. "Saddlemaster Bleuek, say hello again to Willim Gilpin, of Brythyn, a friend of Talsie Grenling's. Explain to Willim why we have seized him."

Bleuek nodded and flashed Willim a wide grin. "We think you're guilty," he said.

Willim glared at Bleuek, but made no reply.

"Why did you travel from Brythyn to Skunnik yesterday?" Jarn asked.

"When I heard Talsie had gone missing, I wanted to come here, see if I could help."

"You didn't mention that yesterday when you were here."

"You didn't ask."

"Tell me about the Stone Bridge Inn."

"It's an inn. What's to tell?"

174

"Why did you stay at that particular inn?"

Willim shrugged. "It's an inn. It had a room."

"When you left here last night, you went straight to the Stone Bridge Inn and hired a room, is that right?"

"Aye."

"How much did the innkeeper say it would cost you?"

"I don't remember."

"Are you wealthy, then, that you need not worry about how much a thing costs?"

"I'm not wealthy."

"You will be if you marry Talsie Grenling."

"I won't be marrying Talsie Grenling."

"No, I suppose not," Jarn said. "It's another Grenling woman that you're interested in."

Willim's pale face twitched and his eyes went wide for an instant, but he quickly regained his composure. "I don't know what you mean."

"I think perhaps you do."

"I'll say nothing more to you," Willim said.

"It makes no matter," Jarn said. "We know Sir Longboke hired the rooms you and Lady Grenling occupied at the Stone Bridge Inn, and we know he hired them eight days ago. We also know that you and Lady Grenling are more than friends. I plan to give the evidence to Lord Grenling. Then I'll turn you over to him. I don't know what he'll do with you, but as long as he's on Vothan soil, he has diplomatic protection, so he can do what he pleases. Think about that while you're thinking about whether or not to start telling me the truth about what happened to Talsie Grenling."

Jarn stood up and nodded at Bleuek, and the two left the interview room.

***

Jarn sent for Braga, and the two entered the other interview room, where Sir Longboke was sitting in a chair, slumped over the table, his elbows resting on the table top and his chin resting on his hands. His face was drawn and wan, and the long twists of his yellow hair looked like a dirty mop. He looked as if he might have been weeping.

Jarn took the chair opposite Sir Longboke, and Braga sat off to the side, where he fixed a baleful look on the knight.

Sir Longboke was the first to speak. He looked at Jarn and asked in a hoarse whisper, "Have you any news of Talsie?"

"I'll ask the questions," Jarn replied.

"But …"

"You said you were felled by sorcery, dark magic."

Longboke nodded. "Aye."

"Why do you believe that?"

"I told you. One moment I was awake and gazing at the sky, and the next I remember is awakening hours later."

"Anything like that ever happen to you before?"

"No, never."

"Think it through, Sir Longboke. Did this unknown sorcerer put a spell on you right then, as you and Talsie drank your wine, or do you believe some villain enchanted you earlier, without your knowledge, and was somehow able to start the spell at just the right moment?"

"How would I know such a thing?"

176

"Did you feel strange or odd in any way as you and Talsie left the train and rode off by yourselves?"

"What do you mean?"

Jarn shrugged. "As if you were in the grip of some kind of ensorcellment."

"No, nothing like that."

"And yet you, Sir Longboke, a fair-sized man and an armed knight, you were felled by some unknown, unseen enchanter even as you came within sight of the city."

"Yes."

"Why did you hire two rooms at the Stone Bridge Inn eight days ago, for ten days each?" Jarn asked, changing the subject to put the knight off his guard.

Sir Longboke gave a little gasp, and his face paled. He swallowed and said, "I don't know what you mean."

"Of course, you know what I mean," Jarn said. "You just don't yet know if you should come clean and tell the truth." He stood up. "We'll let you think about it for a while, but we'll be back. Think about it long and hard. Make sure you make the right decision."

Chapter 20

Astil came to the village of Winnik as the sun neared the western horizon, turning the sky a deep pink streaked with bands of flame orange. She proceeded along Winnik's main street at a walk and stopped at the first inn she came to, the Dragon's Tooth. Only a few people were on the street, a few guildsmen closing their shops for the night and farmers ready to head home. A pair of painted women stood in the shadows on the other side of the street opposite the Dragon's Tooth, eyeing the few men standing nearby. The men paid them no mind.

Astil dismounted and tied her horse to the rail in front of the inn. She entered and approached the barman, who told her three rooms were available, two on the second floor and one on the third, and she could have her pick. She told him she would take the third-floor room and pay him now for one night, as she meant to leave long before dawn. He showed her to the room, and then went to tell the groom to stable her horse and fetch her saddlebags. A half hour later, she went down to the inn's common room for a meal.

The small room had nine tables, two occupied. A man and woman sat near a back corner, quietly conversing in the dim candlelight, and three men—nobles or prosperous merchants by the look of them—sat at a table toward the front, chattering and laughing over their roasted beef and tankards of ale. Astil took the table near the other back corner, and when the serving maid arrived, she ordered a plate of roasted beef, a bowl of leek soup, and a goblet of red wine. The inn didn't have Vothan strong red, so she settled for the Acrinite spiced. She would have to mind her spending. She could have asked Captain Jarn Theffig for some extra coin, but she didn't want to appear weak and needy. She never wanted to appear weak and needy.

Astil was nearly finished eating when she heard the door open. Instinctively, she looked up but immediately looked away again, not wanting to catch anyone's eye. She heard two male voices, and then the sound of the door closing. She glanced quickly at the newcomers out of the corner of her eye and saw two well-dressed young men, no more than twenty years of age, gazing around the dining room. One, of medium height and well built, had dark hair and a short, dark beard. The other, taller and thinner, had ginger hair, a scraggly tuft of a beard sprouting like an unruly weed from a round chin, and long arms that gave him a gangling appearance. She looked down and continued eating.

The young men took the table in the center of the room. Astil focused on her soup, but she could feel their eyes on her. The young men ordered wine and began to talk and laugh boisterously. After a few minutes, she heard chairs scraping against the flagstone floor and footsteps approaching.

"Good evening, my lady," the dark-haired young man said to her. "My name is Millardo Fippin, and this is my good friend Gorno Hambree."

Astil clenched her teeth. The last thing she needed tonight was two young men on the prowl bothering her. "Irmie Avril," she said, without looking at either of them.

"A lovely name," Millardo replied, a practiced smile wreathing his face.

Astil had to resist the urge to roll her eyes. Instead, she forced a smile and said, "Thank you," before turning back to her soup.

"May we join you?" Gorno asked. "It seems a shame that a beautiful woman should dine alone."

"I think not," Astil said. "My husband should be along any moment. Sir Kessel Avril, a knight of Brythyn."

She knew they didn't believe her but hoped she had deterred them anyway. That hope was in vain.

"All the more reason we should join you," Millardo said. "When good Sir Kessel arrives, Gorno and I will stand you both to the house's finest wine. And I know this house's finest, because it's from my own vineyards."

"Your father's vineyards, you mean, eh?" Gorno said, and they both laughed.

"Sir Kessel won't like it if he sees me in the company of two strange young men," Astil said.

Millardo waved away her concerns with a backward flick of his hand. By now, all three of them knew a game was being played. Without invitation, the two young men sat down, Millardo across from Astil, Gorno to her right. Astil finished her soup and bread and started on her beef, ignoring them despite their attempts to engage her in conversation. When they ordered more wine for themselves, they ordered a goblet for her as well. When it arrived, she ignored that, too.

The serving maid came to take away her empty bowl and plate and asked if she wanted anything else.

"Another goblet of the spiced, if you please," Astil said, staring at the maid, who was eyeing the goblet already in front of her. The desire to make a statement to the two young rakes outweighed the need to watch her coin.

"But we've already bought you a goblet of wine," Millardo said, the hurt look on his face too obvious to be genuine. "It isn't courteous to refuse wine bought for you out of kindness and friendship."

"It isn't courteous to sit down without being invited," Astil said. She was tired of the game and wished only to rid herself of these insufferable youths who had the impudence to lecture her about courtesy.

"You should have invited us," Millardo said. "We're harmless enough."

"I doubt that," Astil replied.

"Quite harmless," said Gorno. "Innocent as lambs."

"And yet you won't run away."

"Aye, we are persistent," Millardo said with a bright smile.

"Your persistence grows tiresome."

"If you're tired, you should hire a room and rest."

"I have a room."

"Have you?" said Gorno. "Have you, indeed?"

"I just said so, did I not?"

Millardo glanced around the room, and then said to Astil in a voice that was barely above a whisper, "If it's coin you want, we have plenty."

Astil was about to throw her wine in his face, when a thought occurred. She felt a smile spread across her face, saw the two young men misread her expression and smile back knowingly. That prompted her to laugh. The two fools, still misjudging the situation, laughed with her.

"You say you have coin?" Astil asked.

The young men nodded. "More than enough, I should think," Millardo said.

"Well, then, I believe I'll retire to my room. It's on the third floor, next to last one on the left. But it wouldn't do to follow me up, would it?"

"No," Millardo said. "There's a back stairway leading up from the kitchen."

"We're on good terms with the cook and serving wenches," Gorno said. He jerked a thumb toward Millardo. "On account of his father's wine trade. A few coppers will buy their silence."

"How very lovely," said Astil. "Before I retire to my room, I should like to see some of that coin you mentioned. And I'm not meaning coppers, if you please."

Millardo nodded and produced a fat leather coin purse from under his tunic. He loosened the string that held it closed and shook out some silver coins, which he placed on the table. Astil took them and said, "That should do," before shooting Gorno a questioning glance.

"Uh, he'll be paying for both," the young man whispered.

Millardo rolled his eyes, took an equal number of silver coins from his purse, and handed them to Astil.

"One at a time," she said, standing up. She looked at Millardo. "You first. Give me ten minutes." She looked at Gorno. "Give us an hour before you come up—understand?"

Gorno licked his lips and nodded eagerly. "Third floor, next to last room on the left."

Astil left the table and headed for the stairs. She strode quickly to her room and entered, leaving it dark but with the door open a few inches to give her a bit of light from the torches illuminating the hallway. A wedge of moonlight flowed in through the room's lone window and spilled onto the floor. She got her rope from her saddlebag and set it on the bed, loaded her crossbow, and placed it next to the rope. She strapped on her special belt with its daggers and spin knives. Then she waited. Before long, she heard footsteps in the hallway, but there were too many. Both young men had come at the same time.

"Damn them," Astil muttered, and she closed and locked the door. A moment later, she heard a soft rapping.

"I'm here," Millardo said in a low voice.

"I told your friend to come after an hour," Astil said.

"He says he wants to watch."

"Five more silvers. Slide them under the door."

Astil heard the sound of a coin purse jingling and imagined Millardo bending down to slide the coins under the door. When the first coin appeared, she yanked open the door and saw the young man bent low, just as she had figured. She delivered a kick to his waiting jaw and heard it crack. She saw his companion's eyes go wide before she sent her left fist into his throat. She followed with a blow from her right fist, which broke his nose. He cried out, and she felt his flailing hands clutch at her. She spun away before he could get a grip, wrapped an arm around his throat, and squeezed. When she felt him lose consciousness, she heaved him into the room, where he crumpled to the floor. She heard Millardo moan and looked down at him sprawled on the floor, his broken jaw already swelling up. She kicked him in the ribs and told him to be quiet. Then she dragged him into the room and closed the door.

She took their daggers and searched them for other weapons, found none. Then she picked up her crossbow and aimed it at Millardo's left eye. "You," she said. "Face down on the floor, clasp your hands behind your back, and cross your ankles." When the young man hesitated, she approached him and made ready to deliver another kick. He quickly complied with her command, still whimpering, and Astil tied his feet together and then bound his wrists behind him. She cut another short length of rope and tied one end to the rope binding his hands. "Bend your legs," she commanded. He did, and she tied the loose end of the rope to the one binding his ankles, forcing his legs to stay bent. "There, that should do." She tore two strips from his tunic and balled one up before pinching his nose closed. He opened his mouth to breathe, and she stuffed the balled-up cloth into it. She used the other strip to secure the gag, knotting it tightly behind his head. She went to Gorno, who was still out, and secured him in the same way.

She dragged them into a corner of the room and left them on their sides, then went to the door, opened it a crack, and glanced down the hallway. There was no one about. She closed and locked the door and returned to the young men. Millardo's chin was the size and shape of a mush melon and the color of the sky at twilight. He tried to grunt something through his gag, and Astil saw a drop of drool slide down his ruined chin. She picked up her crossbow and aimed it at him. "Quiet or I'll put a bolt into your ear and see if it comes out through the other one."

He flinched and squeezed his eyes shut, shaking his head from side to side. She went to him and slid a hand under his tunic, feeling around for his coin purse. "Do you like that?" she asked. "Because that, my young friend, is all the touching you're likely to feel tonight, unless I decide to break a few more bones in your once-pretty face."

Astil found his coin purse and shook it over the bed, watching the coins drop. She counted them aloud and then turned back to Millardo. His eyes looked like those of a deer surrounded by a howling pack of mountain blaygers.

She heard a moan and saw Gorno's eyes flutter open. He, too, strained to speak against his gag, but only muffled grunts and groans issued forth. She looked from one to the other, shaking her head. "What shall I do with you, then? Kill you quickly? Torture you first? Or break all your bones, pluck out your eyes, and cut out your tongues to keep you quiet?" She produced a dagger and held it in front of her. The young men went perfectly still, but their eyes reflected terror. She threw it and watched it embed itself into the wall above Gorno's head. The two young men began whimpering again, and tears streaked Millardo's broken face.

Astil pulled her dagger from the wall above Gorno and then slid a high-backed wooden chair in front of them and sat down. "I'm going to rest now. When I wake up, I expect to find you exactly as you are. If I don't, I'll cut your throats. Do you understand?"

Millardo and Gorno both nodded.

Astil counted up Millardo's coins and then put them back in his purse, which she put into one of her saddlebags. She went to the door, opened it, and peered out. There was no one about. A few coins were scattered on the floor where Millardo had dropped them, and she picked them up before closing the door and locking it. She tore two more strips of cloth from Millardo's tunic and used them to blindfold both men. Then she undressed, got into bed, and fell asleep.

Chapter 21

Jarn went to the door of Lady Grenling's suite, on the third floor of the Mang, and nodded at the two Vothan Riders standing guard. They stepped aside, and he knocked on the door and entered. Lady Grenling, still wearing her black dress, emerged from an inner room and gave Jarn a warm smile. The outer chamber was small but comfortable, with two cushioned chairs facing one another in the middle of the room. An oak sideboard stood along one wall, and candles in sconces on the walls provided sufficient illumination. A low oak table between the two cushioned chairs held an unlighted candle, a crystal salt dish, and a goblet of water.

"I was hoping I would see you tonight," Lady Grenling said.

"I'm sorry it's so late," Jarn said. "Was your meal satisfactory?"

"Yes, thank you," Lady Grenling replied, and she sat on one of the cushioned chairs. Jarn took the chair opposite. "When will we be leaving for Rynland?"

"We'll discuss that later," Jarn replied. "First I want to apprise you of the latest tidings in the investigation of your daughter's abduction."

Lady Grenling nodded. "Go on."

"We have a witness who saw Sir Longboke in Skunnik eight days ago. I intend to find out why he was here only a few days before your diplomatic mission left Mystell. You wouldn't know anything about that, would you?"

Jarn saw her eyes go wide for just an instant, but she quickly regained control. "No. But Skunnik and Mystell

186

are not far from one another, and Brythyn and Acrin have long had warm relations. Brythyners often visit here."

"You don't find it curious?"

"No, not at all. Who was it saw Sir Longboke?"

"A local man," Jarn said, not yet ready to divulge details. "I also plan to question Willim Gilpin again. I still believe he was involved in Talsie's disappearance."

"But you talked to him before, and he denied it."

Jarn suppressed a smile and wondered if she would realize her mistake. "I suspect others are involved as well," he said.

"What others?"

Jarn waited a moment and then reached into his tunic and produced the saffite ring Lady Grenling had given to Astil. "Do you remember this?"

"Of course," Lady Grenling replied. "Talsie's ring."

"Talsie's? Not according to Astil. She told me the ring belongs to you."

"Did she?"

"Yes. I would know the truth of the matter, if you please."

Lady Grenling took a breath and then said, "Yes, the ring is mine."

"Why did you tell Astil—and me—that it was Talsie's?"

Lady Grenling looked down and heaved a great sigh. When she looked up again, a tear was rolling down her cheek. Jarn wondered if she had ever been a stage player.

"I … I made a mistake, Captain. I did not trust your sorceress, and so I was afraid to give her anything of Talsie's. I feared she might use it to cast a spell on my daughter or gain possession of her will. That woman frightens me."

Jarn gazed at her but said nothing.

"I want you to find Talsie, Captain. Not that sorceress."

"After I take you to Rynland?"

Lady Grenling flashed a wide smile and nodded. "You will find her, I know you will. And you'll bring her to me in Rynland, won't you please, Captain? And I'll pay you handsomely for all your troubles. Perhaps, when all this is past, you will even visit us in Rynland from time to time, though you must never tell anyone our whereabouts."

"You have it all planned."

She nodded. "And we'll leave tomorrow, as you promised."

"I made no such promise."

"To Rynland we must be bound, Captain."

Jarn shook his head and stood up.

Lady Grenling rose and went to the sideboard, which held a lighted taper in a holder. She picked up the taper and used it to light the large candle on the low oak table between the chairs. It glowed brightly, waving and dancing, although there was no breeze. She took a pinch of salt from the salt dish and threw it into the candle flame. It hissed and flickered, and sparks of blue and green jumped from it.

"What are you doing?" Jarn asked.

Lady Grenling picked up the water goblet and poured water in a circle around the candle. Then she closed her eyes and said in a low voice, "To Rynland we'll be bound."

"No, I'm sorry …"

The candle flame shot up with a hiss that sounded as if it might have come from an angry viper. Jarn stared at

188

it, drawn by the colors that flared inside the orange fire. He suddenly felt the weight of his responsibilities and anxieties, as if a great burden lay heavy on his shoulders. His eyes ached, and he felt his eyelids drooping, but he couldn't look away from the candle flame, which waved slowly, creating a pattern that looked like a slithering snake made of fire. He heard Lady Grenling speaking, in a dark voice that sounded far away.

"Where shall we two go next morrow? Away from here, away from sorrow. We'll leave before the sun is risen, leave this place, this surly prison. Thence to Rynland we'll be bound, in secret, lest we two be found."

***

Jarn didn't remember leaving Lady Grenling's quarters. He didn't even remember arriving in his own quarters, but now that he was there, he was eager to sleep. He badly needed rest, and he would have to rise early to prepare for the trip to Rynland.

He heard a knock and went to the door to open it. Bleuek and Liora were standing there, smiling. Jarn frowned at them.

"Braga thinks Sir Longboke may be close to breaking," Bleuek said. "He believes that if you talk to him, he may come clean."

Jarn squeezed his eyes closed and ran his fingers through his hair. "Sir Longboke?"

Bleuek nodded. "Aye. Braga has been pressing him."

Jarn closed his eyes and tried to think about what Bleuek was telling him. "Braga is with Sir Longboke?"

"Aye. We should go now, put the pressure on."

189

For some reason, Jarn could not make sense of what Bleuek was saying. "Go where?"

Bleuek and Liora shared a quick glance, and then Liora stepped into the room and put her hand on Jarn's chest, gently pushing him backwards.

"Don't do that, Liora," Jarn said.

"How much wine have you had tonight?" Liora asked.

Jarn frowned at her. "None since we had our supper. Why?"

"Because you're acting like a man who's had too much wine or not enough sleep."

Jarn nodded. "You're right, I need sleep. If you two will leave, I can get some."

"Did you not hear what Bleuek just told you? Sir Longboke may be close to breaking. Braga thinks he'll confess if you talk to him."

Jarn stared at her, the words she had spoken seeming to bounce around inside his dull head. "I don't understand."

Liora took Jarn's arm and led him to a wooden chair in a corner of the room. "Sit."

Jarn sat.

Liora looked at Bleuek. "Come in and close the door."

"No, Bleuek, do not come in," Jarn said. "Liora, get out. I need sleep."

Bleuek looked from Jarn to Liora, and then stepped into the room and quietly closed the door behind him.

Jarn glared at Bleuek and got to his feet. Liora pushed him back into the chair. Then she knelt down and peered into his eyes. He flinched when she put her thumb on one of his eyelids and pushed it up.

"What are you doing?" Jarn protested.

"What are *you* doing?" Liora replied.

"I'm going to bed."

"What about Sir Longboke?"

"He can wait until I get back from …"

"Get back from where?"

"Never mind."

Liora shrugged, smiled, and let go of Jarn's eyelid. Still smiling, she stood up and delivered a hard slap to Jarn's face. It knocked him off the chair and sent him sprawling.

"Good gods," Bleuek said. "What's going on?"

Jarn curled up on the floor, torn between wanting to sleep right there and a strong desire to get up and throw the two intruders out of his quarters.

"I think someone put a spell on him," Liora said. "Look at his eyes."

Jarn got to his knees and stared at Liora, trying to understand what she had just said.

"What do we do?" Bleuek asked.

Jarn sank back to the floor and closed his eyes, half listening to the conversation, half dropping off to sleep.

"It must have been Lady Grenling," Liora said. "You and Braga go to her quarters and bring her here. Before you go, put some soft candle wax in your ears. Take a gag and use it on her. Don't let her speak. Tie her hands behind her back, and don't let her touch anything. Then bring her here, even if you have to knock her out and drag her."

Jarn slowly rose to his feet. He glared at Liora but was too tired to yell at her. "Get out," he said. "I need sleep. I have … I have something to do tomorrow."

Liora went to a low table, picked up a pitcher of water, and filled a large pewter goblet. She turned around, approached Jarn, and threw the water in his face.

Jarn felt himself tottering, but Bleuek caught him before he fell.

"Stay on your feet," Liora said to him.

"I need sleep," Jarn muttered.

Liora took his arm and led him in a march around the room. "Sleep is the last thing you need, Captain."

Chapter 22

For the second night in a row, Kurff left his quarters in the Beldur Palace after dark to trek south through the city, only this time he wore his uniform. He crossed Faire Street and entered Sonto Street, glancing at the neighborhood inns and taverns. Their windows glowed with a soft light, drawing revelers, gamblers, and high-priced whores along with knights, traveling merchants, and officers from nearby castles and manors. The neighborhood, the prosperous northern ward known as the Basket, was always lively that time of night, especially the blocks near the Beldur Palace, the Mang, and the Palace of the High Hext. Kurff stopped and glanced back toward the Beldur. It looked elegant under the abundant torchlight illuminating it, and he knew the Palace of the High Hext would be even more lavishly illumined. Even the somber Mang always looked less drab at night.

Kurff continued on his way, crossing Tuffin Street. The door of the Seven Trees Inn opened just as he strode by, and the sound of laughter and chatter mingling with the rattle and tinkle of plates and knives spilled into the street. He glanced through the door and saw a roaring hearth fire and the bright faces of men and women crowding the inn's long tables. A tankard of ale would have gone down nicely just then, but Kurff kept walking. He nodded to a pair of Yellowshirts on patrol and spotted two mounted Vothan Riders crossing Sonto Street a block away. They ignored him. He knew that the Riders, not wanting to give offense to Acrinites still unhappy about the Vothan Renewal, would try to remain as unobtrusive as possible. How long such deference to Acrinite

193

sensibilities would hold, no one knew, but the Voths, lacking the numbers to high-handedly impose their will, were wise to show some consideration to the recently defeated but much more plentiful Acrinites.

A few blocks on, the streets were quieter, the inns and taverns fewer and smaller and less grand than those in the Basket. The streets were darker, too, and not as many Acrinite Guards patrolled the area. Down in the Bolt, where Kurff was headed, no Yellowshirts or Vothan Riders were likely to be present at all. The Bolt had its own rough system of order, and the authorities, including the Voths, seemed mostly content not to meddle in it.

Kurff picked up his pace, and entered the Bolt twenty minutes later. The note he had read and then burned mentioned a building he was familiar with, although he had never been inside. It was not far from the Posthole Inn, although the mazelike character of that part of the Bolt made their proximity less than obvious. Kurff wondered if the Posthole would have any customers. He doubted it. Over the last year, Kurff had seen few customers there. Mostly, he just saw the proprietor, Maekel Gindee, and sometimes his helper, Hussert. Kurff smiled. There was a piece of work. He still found it difficult to believe that Maekel trusted him.

The Bolt, in its own peculiar way, was as lively as the Basket, only Kurff knew he wouldn't find many knights or manorial officials or well-dressed merchants, though he would see plenty of gamblers, whores, and cutpurses. Not many Bolters would challenge an armed Yellowshirt—unless they were thoroughly drunk and surrounded by friends—but Kurff remained on his guard.

He heard much the same laughter and chatter and clatter that he had heard in the Basket, only here in the

Bolt the noise seemed to have a hard edge, ringing more of desperation and need than of warmth and merriment.

An alehouse door opened, and two drunks stumbled out, just in front of Kurff. One of them lost his footing and fell on his face in the street. Kurff stopped and looked down at the man, and then turned to his companion, who was staring back at him.

"Evening, sir," the man said to Kurff as his friend slowly rose to his feet. "Nice night, eh?"

"See that you two stay out of trouble," Kurff growled, and then he continued on his way.

A half block on, he looked over his shoulder. The two men were gone.

The building Kurff was heading toward was in the heart of the Bolt, where narrow streets often turned one way for a block and then turned again, sometimes twisting back on themselves. Some streets were only a block long, others little more than alleys. Some crossed narrow streams over rickety wooden bridges, others dropped suddenly to pass under wobbly footbridges. Kurff found the alley he was looking for, walked a block, and then turned left into another alley. A half block on, he turned right, entered another alley, and saw a small, narrow, and obviously unoccupied structure. A sign on its wall announced, in small, faded gray letters, "Krindoll Brewery."

Kurff stopped and slowly turned around, looking and listening. The night was quiet, and he heard and saw nothing save a few chirping insects. He glanced up and saw a half moon surrounded by a profusion of stars. He looked around again, all his senses alert, and tried to determine the location of the Posthole Inn in relation to where he was. Finally, he headed down a narrow passageway between the brewery and an abandoned stable and came to a small yard overgrown with weeds and scrub brush. The back door, covered in weeds nearly up to the door handle, was locked, but Kurff had no trouble springing the lock. He pulled open the door and stepped inside.

A musty aroma of stale ale greeted Kurff when he stepped inside. He put the candle he had brought into a small brass holder and used a flint to light it. Holding the candle at arm's length, he glanced around the room. A brick fireplace took up half of the wall to his left. A large cask stood in front of it. An iron kettle sat on the floor next to the cask, and a half dozen smaller casks lined the opposite wall. Bronze pails and woven baskets were scattered on the floor amid bits of grain. A rake and a straw broom leaned against a corner.

Kurff took a couple of steps forward, peering into the gloom. An arched doorway led to another room. He passed through and looked around. Save for a small square table in the middle of the room, it was empty. A stairway led to the second floor, and Kurff climbed it and explored two more rooms. They were empty as well, but a door in one of the rooms opened to a narrow stairway that led to an attic. He climbed it and looked around. There were two dormer windows, one in front, the other in back. Kurff went to the front dormer and looked out, but it was so encrusted with dirt he could barely see through it.

He stepped back and swept the candle around, peering intently. A little gleam of metal caught his eye. He crouched down and saw a small door handle attached to what appeared to be a low door. He opened it and thrust the candle inside. It looked like some kind of storage space, empty. Cool air moved inside the space.

Kurff got on his knees and crawled inside, the candle out in front of him, its flame flickering. But the storage space held no secret passages, no hidden doorways, no magic entrances, just a rotted timber that let in air from the outside. Kurff swore under his breath and then crawled backwards out of the space. He went downstairs and returned to the room he had first entered, wondering if someone had set him a trap.

He made another inspection of the room he had first entered, and then stepped into the front room. This time he noticed an old heavy rug under the small square table. He shoved the table aside and then bent down and grabbed an edge of the rug with both hands. He lifted it and threw it back, revealing a trapdoor in the floor. A rusty iron ring was attached to it. Kurff grasped the ring and pulled. The door creaked on its hinges. Kurff opened it all the way and thrust the candle through the opening. An iron ladder led down to a lower level. Kurff blew out the candle and put it and the holder into a pocket of his cloak. Then he dropped his legs through the opening, felt for the ladder with his feet, and began to descend into the darkness.

He counted nineteen rungs before he came to a hard floor. He retrieved his candle, candleholder, and flint from a pocket of his cloak and put the candle in the holder. He lit it with the flint and held it out, peering into the gloom. The basement, which appeared to be empty, was larger than the building above.

Kurff began to explore, and soon found a steep wooden stairway that led down to a lower level. He descended, counting fourteen steps. The new room, smaller than the first, had another stairway going down. Kurff descended its thirteen steps.

The third basement had no stairway leading down. Still holding the candle, which had burned halfway down, Kurff leaned back against a wall to get his breath. He looked around. The side of the room away from the stairs had an arched opening into another room. Kurff walked to the opening, stepped through, and came to what looked like a ten-foot-high, ten-foot-wide tunnel lined with dun-colored bricks. He squared his shoulders and began to walk.

Kurff followed the tunnel to a room the size of a minor lord's banquet hall, which seemed to have been carved out of bedrock. It smelled like a pile of cold, wet stones. He stopped and listened, heard nothing. He found a torch and lit it with the candle flame, then looked around, turning in a complete circle as he did. Trestle tables and long wooden benches were stored against the right-hand wall. In the middle of the wall to his left was an arched entryway, and Kurff headed for it, slowly drawing his sword as he went. He entered a room nearly as large as the first one. It appeared to be soldiers' quarters, with rows of narrow bunks. A door on the far wall led to another, smaller, room divided into four sections. It looked to Kurff like officers' quarters. He returned to the first room and passed through another doorway, which led to a kitchen. Beyond the kitchen was a pantry, store rooms, and a small but well-stocked armory, all unoccupied. There were no more tunnels. He had come to the end of the line. He headed back the way he had come.

With his torch providing more light than the candle had, Kurff quickly found his way back to where he had started, in the sub-subbasement below the Krindoll Brewery. When he climbed to the middle basement, he noticed a door he had not seen before. He hesitated a moment and then quietly opened the door and thrust the torch through. There was another tunnel. Kurff entered, closing the door behind him. This tunnel had a dirt floor and a wood ceiling and rough timbers shoring up the walls. It smelled like a forest after a rain, and the air inside was cool and damp. Kurff took a breath and began walking.

He came to another basement, but a mundane one, no barracks, no armories, no officers' quarters, just a narrow set of wooden stairs leading up to a closed door. The basement smelled of ale and wine and rat droppings. Wooden casks lined one wall, big barrels for ale, smaller ones for wine. Wheels of cheese lay on a huge oak table, and slabs of salt beef hung from hooks attached to chains suspended from ceiling rafters. The sight of food reminded Kurff how hungry he was. He was thinking about cutting off a hunk of cheese for himself when the door at the top of the stairs opened and a wedge of light poured down from above. Kurff froze. Keeping his eyes on the stairway, he started to back up, heading back the way he had come, into the shadows. Maekel appeared at the top of the stairs and began descending.

Still walking backward, treading as quietly and carefully as he could, Kurff kicked a metal pail, which clattered and rolled. He reached for his sword, but when Maekel raised the crossbow he was carrying, he froze again.

"Evening, Kurff," Maekel said when he stepped onto the floor. "Go ahead, draw your sword, but drop it in front of you, if you please."

As Kurff unsheathed his sword, he tried to calculate the likelihood of launching a successful attack. He figured he could probably duck Maekel's shot and run him through before he could reload, but the sound of more footsteps on the wooden stairs gave him momentary pause. Hussert appeared a moment later, a crossbow in his hand, a mindless grin on his flat face. Kurff sighed and dropped his sword in front of him.

"The dagger as well," Maekel said, and Kurff drew out the blade and dropped it next to the sword.

Hussert grinned like a mindless fool. "Hoy, Kurff. What's doin'?"

Chapter 23

Jarn was sitting on a chair, his head slumped forward and his fingertips rubbing his brow. Liora had walked him around the room too many times to count and then walked him up and down the hallway outside his quarters, until Braga and Bleuek returned with Lady Grenling. The lady had a gag in her mouth, and her hands were tied behind her back. When she saw Jarn, she looked at him with pleading eyes. He stared back at her, his mouth slightly agape, but said nothing.

Liora pointed to a wooden chair in a corner of the room. "Put her there."

Braga escorted Lady Grenling to the chair and told her to sit. She sat.

"Braga and Bleuek, a word outside, if you please," Liora said. The three stepped into the corridor, and Liora whispered something to the other two. When they came back into the room, Liora approached Lady Grenling and glared at her. "I know you put a spell on Captain Jarn. You'll remove it now, or I'll remove your head."

Lady Grenling shook her head and then shrugged. Liora struck her across the face. Jarn leaped up from his chair and lurched toward them, but Braga set himself between Jarn and the two women. Jarn stopped, glaring at the big man.

"Sit down, Captain, if you please," Braga said evenly.

Jarn put a hand to his forehead and shook his head. "What's going on, Braga? I don't understand."

"That woman put a spell on you," Braga said.

"A spell?"

"Aye."

201

Liora drew her sword and put the tip under Lady Grenling's chin. "And now she's going to take the spell away." She crouched down and stared into Lady Grenling's eyes. "Aren't you?"

Lady Grenling glared back at Liora and shook her head. Liora turned to Braga. "You and Bleuek fetch Willim Gilpin and bring him here. Shackled and manacled."

Jarn closed his eyes and let his mind go blank, but he opened them and looked up when the door opened. He saw Willim Gilpin, his hands tied behind his back, standing just outside the door, with Bleuek on one side and Braga on the other. Braga gave Willim a shove, and he lurched into the room, barely keeping his feet. When the young man spotted Lady Grenling sitting in the back corner, his eyes went wide. Bleuek fetched another chair from Jarn's sleeping chamber and set it down facing the lady. Braga shoved Willim into it, and the young man stared at Lady Grenling across a distance of eight feet.

Liora turned to Willim. "We know about you and Lady Grenling, so don't bother to deny it. We also know that she put a spell on Captain Jarn, but so far she has refused to undo it. I will give her ten seconds to reconsider." Liora approached Willim and put a finger on his neck where a blood vessel throbbed. "If she continues to refuse, I'm going to cut you just here and watch you bleed your young life all over Captain Jarn's floor."

"No," Willim said, rising from his chair. "You can't."

Braga, who was standing behind Willim, put his huge hands on the young man's shoulders and pushed him back down. When Willim made to speak again, Braga cuffed him across the face and knocked him from the chair. Braga and Bleuek picked him up and set him on the chair

202

again, and this time Braga kept his hands on Willim's shoulders.

"You might also be interested to know that your lady planned to go away with Captain Jarn and leave you behind."

Lady Grenling shook her head violently and began to make loud noises, trying to speak through her gag.

Liora turned to her. "What's it to be my lady? Will you take away the spell, or do you prefer to watch your young man bleed to death?"

Lady Grenling shook her head.

"Karysondra, no," Willim shouted at Lady Grenling. "They'll kill me."

Lady Grenling looked at him, heaved a long sigh, and shrugged.

Liora unsheathed her dagger. "I hope you enjoy his screams," she said before turning toward Willim.

"No!" Willim shouted in a high-pitched voice. "Please!"

As Liora approached Willim, her dagger gleaming under the torchlight, Braga raised a hand, as if to stop her. "I've just had a thought, Captain," he said to Liora. "Let us not be in a rush to kill the young man. Let me cut off one of his hands instead. When the lady hears his screams, she might think again about breaking the spell she wove over Captain Jarn. If she doesn't I'll cut off his other hand."

Liora seemed to consider Braga's proposition.

"Shall I fetch an axe?" Bleuek asked. "In case we need to chop off his feet?"

Willim broke free and tried to run, but Bleuek, quick as a cat, cut him off and tackled him to the floor. As

203

Willim sobbed, Braga and Bleuek picked him up again and slammed him back into the chair.

"Please," Willim said, his voice breaking. "Please don't hurt me. I'll tell you everything. I'll tell it all."

Lady Grenling stood up suddenly, her face red, her eyes wild, her head shaking from side to side. She glared at Willim, trying again to talk through her gag, but it was all grunts and groans and deep-throated growls. Liora pushed her back into the chair and held her fast. "Bleuek, you know what to do," she said.

Bleuek came over and pinched Lady Grenling's nostrils until she turned blue and lost consciousness.

"No!" Willim shouted.

Jarn sprang up from his chair, but Liora pointed her sword at his chest, and he stopped short. "Sit and don't get up again, Captain. I know this witch has beguiled you, but she'll put an end to it, or I'll put an end to her."

Jarn staggered backward, and then spun halfway around, reaching for his chair. He missed, and wound up on the floor, his eyes closed, his breathing punctuated by moans.

"He's unwell," Braga said. "He may be—"

"I know," Liora said, interrupting. She turned to Willim. "You'll tell us the truth, and then you'll persuade the lady to take away the spell. If you don't, I'll let Braga dismantle you one limb at a time."

Braga helped Jarn into his chair again, where he sat quietly, breathing deeply, listening and watching. Liora, still holding her dagger, was looking at Willim Gilpin. "Tell your tale, tell it true, and tell it all," she said to the young man.

Willim nodded, swallowed once, and began. "Lady Grenling it was hatched the plot, although it seemed to come together slowly, over time, little hints and nods and offhand suggestions, mostly from her. Four of us were in on it, Talsie, Lady Grenling, Sir Longboke, and me. We meant to get far away from Brythyn, away from Lord Grenling, as far as we could."

"Just a moment," Liora said. "There's a rumor that you're a suitor to Talsie Grenling, but we now know it's her mother your black heart beats for. Is Talsie aware of that?"

"Yes, she's aware. She doesn't care." He glanced at Lady Grenling, only eight feet away. "Talsie doesn't want me. Her mother does."

"What about Sir Longboke? Why was he invited into your little plot?"

Willim gave a short laugh. "He's in love with Talsie. He's besotted with her, the poor fool."

"Does Talsie love him?"

Willim snorted and shook his head. "Talsie loves Talsie."

"Go on, then," Liora said. "Tell us about the plan."

"We had to wait until arrangements were made for Lord Grenling's recent journey to Skunnik to negotiate treaties with the Voths. Talsie and Lady Grenling were to accompany him, Talsie so she could marry that fat swine Lord Keddro. We decided that on the way here from Mystell, Talsie would complain about the ceremonial bother that attends high and mighty lords arriving in Skunnik and ask permission to enter the city separately, through a lesser-used gate. Lady Grenling was to ask Longboke to accompany her."

"And what if Lord Grenling was opposed?"

Willim shrugged. "He wasn't. If he had been, Talsie would have had a fainting spell or a good long weep, and he'd have yielded just to be rid of her."

Liora nodded. "Go on."

"Talsie and Longboke were supposed to ride directly to Minnik, where I was waiting at an inn. Once they arrived, I was supposed to ride to Skunnik, go to the Stone Bridge Inn, and wait for Lady Grenling, who was supposed to get away whenever she could. Talsie and Longboke were to proceed to Corticoe, a village in Wyndor near the Shaffroth. Lady Grenling and I would ride to Wyndor and meet Talsie and Longboke at an inn in Corticoe. In Wyndor, we would hire a boat and sail east on the Shaffroth all the way to Rynland, where we would start our new lives."

"But Talsie and Sir Longboke never arrived in Minnik," Liora said. "So you rode to Skunnik."

Willim nodded and then pointed at Bleuek. "He and the witch-girl captured me. You know the rest."

"Not all," Liora said. "If Sir Longboke knew Talsie did not return his feelings, why would he agree to such a plan as you've described?"

Willim shrugged. "Ask Sir Longboke."

Braga, still standing behind Willim, grabbed a handful of the young man's fine brown hair and picked him up by it. "She's asking you, villain."

"I don't know," Willim said in a desperate voice. "Perhaps he thought he could win her over."

Braga dropped him back into the chair.

"Your plan went awry," Liora said. "What happened?"

Willim shook his head. "I don't know the answer to that, either. But I know Sir Longboke was half mad at the notion of being in close quarters with Talsie for weeks or months and then most likely being spurned by her. There's no telling what a madman might do."

Liora frowned. "You believe Sir Longboke is responsible for Talsie's disappearance?"

He shrugged. "Who else?"

Jarn stood up and stretched. "I think it's time to remove the lady's gag and hear what she has to say. I don't believe she has the strength to try any more spells."

Lady Grenling stared at him, her eyes wide in surprise.

Liora went to her and removed the gag. "It seems we don't need you to undo Captain Jarn's spell after all."

Chapter 24

Aarla awakened, fully alert. The cool night air carried something she could feel but not name, a whisper of insubstantial energy that had seemed to call to her in her sleep. She stared up at the half moon and then closed her eyes and concentrated. Sometimes she knew things. Other times, she knew there was something she needed to know.

She rose and made her way from the clearing in the woods to the nearby stream, dipped her face in it and drank. She returned to the clearing and saddled Cutter. "Sorry, boy, we must be off," she told him. "We'll take it slow and careful."

Aarla walked Cutter slowly along the trail that led to the road, listening to the night. She heard an owl hoot and gazed up, saw the bird's silhouette atop a tall tree. In the next instant, it was gone, and she imagined it diving toward some doomed mouse scurrying innocently along the ground.

She came to the road and stopped, looked left and right. All was quiet and dark, the only light from the moon and stars. She looked up, wishing the moon was full but thankful that the sky was untroubled by clouds. "We'll go slow," she said again to her horse, and then she mounted up and headed toward the city.

She rode Cutter as quickly as she dared through the moonlit night, unsure where she was going but trusting her peculiar gift to lead her. She was only a mile from Skunnik when she came to another road, narrower than the main one, which split off to the left. Without thought, consideration, or doubt, she took the new road, slowing Cutter from an easy canter to a walk, looking around at the dark woods, sometimes glancing up to see a fragment of moon or a cluster of stars between the high treetops.

The path divided again, and once more she took the lesser way, little more than a trail, which soon began to rise gradually. The going was slow, but Aarla wouldn't risk her horse by a too-hasty dash in the dark. The trail leveled off again, and she soon came to a clearing, where she stopped and looked around. She heard only a soft breeze rustling through the trees of the forest and the distant buzz of insects.

Aarla spurred Cutter and they moved on, still at a walk, until the trail began to descend, even more gradually than it had climbed. The trail leveled off again, and ten minutes later Aarla emerged from the forest and entered a rock-strewn field. The sound of a river flowing nearby broke the silence, and Aarla saw moonlight glinting off what she knew must be the Ondamin River, a tributary of the Shaffroth. Aarla headed for it. When she reached the river, she proceeded along its north bank, still not sure what she was looking for.

After ten more minutes, Aarla came to a shallow ditch. She dismounted and approached it. She looked toward the city, which loomed in the distance on higher ground, and then toward the river. The ditch looked to be part of a drainage system, taking storm water from Skunnik and emptying it into the Ondamin. She peered along the length of the ditch toward the city, but the channel soon dissolved into darkness.

She mounted up again, returned to the edge of the woods, and dismounted. This time she did not hobble Cutter. "I'll be back," she whispered to the horse. "If not, you know what to do."

She stroked his head and then headed on foot back to the ditch.

The bottom of the storm ditch was soft and slightly damp, and Aarla felt small bits of earth clinging to her boots as she strode along it toward the city. As she walked, the ditch began to climb gradually, but the ground on either side rose at a slightly greater angle, so the ditch appeared to become deeper even as it rose. Soon, the sides of the ditch were taller than she was, and before long the earthen floor and walls had changed to brick. And then the ditch became a tunnel and she was inside, the stars and moon gone.

Aarla stopped and lit one of the candles she had brought. The small flame provided just enough illumination for her to see where she was going and avoid loose bricks or treacherous holes that might trip the unwary.

She started walking again, sensed the tunnel still rising, still gradually. It curved slightly to the left, so slightly it was barely noticeable. She knew she was now under Skunnik's outlying streets, a hodgepodge of narrow lanes and twisting alleys that surrounded the city's central grid. The floor was slightly bowl-shaped, and Aarla imagined what it might be like during a long, intense rainstorm. Water would roar through the narrow channel and take with it everything in its path until it reached the river.

She picked up her pace. The blackness ahead seemed to melt and turn to a dark gray. She must by now be within the city's central grid, where grate-covered inlets on the paved streets captured rainwater, which flowed down upright pipes to the main outflow channel. Perhaps a trace of moonlight had slipped through one of the inlets, relieving the darkness.

Aarla came to a stairway made of stone steps, along the right wall. It led to a balcony eight feet above the floor. She climbed to the balcony and walked along it, ducking her head to avoid the ceiling. After a few minutes, she stopped. She closed her eyes. She turned around and began to retrace her steps. She stopped and closed her eyes again. She opened her eyes and put her hands on the cool brick wall. She took a few steps and came to a narrow opening in the wall. She thrust her candle through the opening and peered in. She slid through sideways, keeping the candle ahead of her. The opening widened into a four-foot wide tunnel, six feet high, made of stone.

As she walked, the tunnel began to descend slightly, and Aarla felt her heartbeat increase, heard a vague whisper inside her mind. She switched the candle from her right hand to her left, and unsheathed her dagger. She also had a short sword, a gift from Bleuek, and she knew how to use it.

Five minutes later, Aarla rounded a bend and came to a large room. The floor sloped downward to the left, and at the bottom of the slope, a hundred feet away, lay another tunnel entrance. She stopped and peered at it for a long moment, and then walked down the sloping floor and approached the new opening. When she reached it, she stepped through, into another tunnel. She closed her eyes and cocked her head, listening. Her eyes snapped open, and once again she began to walk.

Aarla heard voices. She blew out her candle, pressed herself against the wall, and crouched. Maintaining contact with the wall, she crept ahead through the darkness. Around a bend, in the far distance, a square of gray appeared high up, interrupting the blackness of the tunnel. It was an opening to the outside, at street level, and it allowed the dim light from the moon and stars to filter in. Aarla heard a creaking sound, and then something obscured the gray square. She crouched lower and crept forward again, stopped when the voices became distinct. A large mass was rising toward the gray square, hoisted by what she now recognized was a Drazelite windlass, a machine she had seen once before during construction of a castle in Telna. It was hauling up a platform on which sat another kind of machine she also had seen before, a medium-sized stone thrower. She took a few steps backward and leaned against the wall, still listening, trying to determine how many men were ahead of her. As for what they were doing there, she had no doubt.

Aarla didn't know how long she had before the artillery crew would return to the tunnel. They had left behind in the chamber some large rocks and a pile of cloth-covered clay pots—which she suspected held charmfire—possibly for use on another day, but maybe to be retrieved and hauled up to the stone thrower within the next few minutes.

Charmfire—she had seen it before and well knew its danger. The street mage she had traveled with used it in some of his illusions, but only in small quantities, and he also had a substance that could counteract it. The clay pots that the rebels were using were large enough to burn down a house if one exploded on its roof, and though she knew how to make the nullifier, she lacked both the proper ingredients and the time. But if she could ignite one of those pots without letting the burning substance come close to her, she could cut off the rebels' retreat through the tunnel and force them back aboveground, where Vothan Riders would cut them down or capture them.

Aarla held out her candle and took a couple of steps away from the wall, looking around for a loose brick. She spotted a broken one, just over half the size of a whole one. She looked back toward where the men were setting up the stone thrower and then made a dash for the brick, snatched it up, and returned to the wall. She would have to creep up to one of the large clay pots, set its cloth covering aflame, and then retreat to a safe distance before hurling the brick at it, breaking the pot and loosing the charmfire. She would have to get far enough away to stay safe but not so far as to hinder her aim. And she had to do the job before the artillerymen ceased their operation and made their escape through the tunnel.

She crouched down and approached the nearest pot, smelled the pitch and tallow that soaked its cloth covering. Despite the coolness of the underground tunnel, she felt warm, and a sheen of sweat covered her brow. She looked up to where the artillerymen were finishing their preparations, heard the sound of the stone thrower being winched back to make ready for firing. She looked at the cloth-covered clay pot in front of her and slowly moved the candle toward it.

Chapter 25

Jarn and Liora sat across from Sir Longboke in one of the interviewing rooms. The knight looked distraught and bedraggled, as if he hadn't slept in days. Jarn thought he also looked as if he wanted to unburden himself.

"We know about your little conspiracy," Jarn said. "But we would hear the tale from you. Take care you tell us the truth."

Sir Longboke nodded and told his tale. It was much the same as Willim Gilpin's testimony. When he was finished, Jarn asked him the question Liora had asked Willim. "If Talsie did not return your feelings for her, why did you take part in this reckless scheme?"

"I wanted to help her," Sir Longboke replied. "It didn't matter that she … that she did not return my feelings, as you say. All that mattered to me was giving her a chance to be happy and content. She deserves as much."

"Perhaps you believed she might learn to love you," Liora said, remembering what Willim had said not long before.

Sir Longboke shrugged and gave her a wan smile. "I maintained a glimmer of hope, true, but in my heart I knew better."

"Your tale matches Willim's and fits the known facts," Jarn said. "Lady Grenling, though she would not yet confirm it, did not refute it. But there is still one question, and a rather important one—where is Talsie?"

Sir Longboke looked down and shook his head. "I don't know," he whispered in a hoarse voice.

"Do you still maintain you were rendered unconscious by some dark sorcery?"

Sir Longboke nodded. "Yes."

"Perhaps you hid her away somewhere," Liora said. "Perhaps you'll have your way with her yet."

Sir Longboke stood up so quickly that his chair flew backwards and skidded across the floor, slamming into the wall behind him. Jarn and Liora both sprang to their feet and drew their swords. The knight glared at them, and for a moment Jarn thought he might launch himself at one of them, hoping for a sword thrust that would end his misery for all time. Instead, he took a breath, picked up his chair, and sat back down. "Everything I told you is true," he said. "We were sitting in that clearing, just off the road, I on my boulder and Talsie on the downed tree, refreshing ourselves before the final jaunt to Minnik, where Willim was supposed to be waiting. That's the last I remember before waking up and finding Talsie gone."

"Then where is she?" Jarn muttered, half to himself. He was suddenly tired of the case, tired of these stupid, petty conspirators, tired of the Lords Grenling and Keddro, tired of Skunnik, tired of the entire Acrinite Territory. He thought about Maiya the singer and the pleasant few hours he had spent in her company, a short but welcome respite from lovesick knights, treacherous ladies, and arrogant lords. He thought about the life she led and wondered if such a vagabond existence would suit him. It had suited his ancient ancestors, and something of their roving ways still lived inside every Voth, most especially the Vothan Riders. But duty made an even stronger pull, and Jarn rejected the foolish notion of running away. As he did, something flicked at the edge of his consciousness, and he tried to grab it.

215

"Captain?" Liora said.

Jarn came out of his reverie and looked at her, gave her a crooked grin and a little shrug. He was about to respond, when he heard the first boulder strike the south wall of the Mang.

***

"So, Kurff, looking to get some information you might not otherwise get?" Maekel asked. He was grinning, but there was menace behind it.

"Aye," Kurff said. "I'm always looking to get information."

"You should take care where you look. Snooping around in the wrong place can get a man killed."

"Aiding rebels can get a man killed as well," Kurff said.

"Careful, Kurff. You're in no position to make accusations."

"Do you deny it?"

"Deny aiding rebels? No, I don't deny it. I'm proud of it."

"That's good to know," Kurff said.

Maekel sneered. "You can act brave, Kurff, but not long ago we were discussing what would happen if the Acrinites ever rose up and threw off the Voths, do you remember?"

Kurff nodded. "I remember. We figured the mutineers would level charges of collaboration against any Yellowshirts who stayed behind and then hang the lot of us."

Maekel raised his crossbow higher and aimed it at Kurff's chest. "Except for any collaborators who managed

216

to get themselves killed through their own heedless meddling before the mutineers, as you call them, get a chance to hang them."

"Who do you report to, Maekel?" Kurff asked, trying to decide which way to duck when the bolt came for him. "You're not clever enough to be high-placed leader, not even of rebel filth."

"Shut your hole, Kurff," Maekel said.

"How many rebels are under some kind of spell, Maekel? How many are thralls? What about you, are you a mere thrall to some Acrinite lord or ulder, or maybe a Gurgeonite prince?"

Hussert frowned and aimed his crossbow at Kurff. "Hoy, Kurff, that's no way to talk." Hussert turned to Maekel. "Can I do it, Maekel? Can I kill him?"

Maekel snorted a short laugh. "You may. Your reward for being a loyal servant. Aim for the middle of his chest."

Hussert grinned like a dull child, and glimmers of saliva appeared at the corners of his mouth. "I want to use my sword."

Maekel roared with laughter. "Do you indeed? Have you ever used your little sword to kill a man?"

Hussert's eyes went wide, and he shook his head. "No," he said. Still grinning, he drew his shortsword.

Kurff tensed and bent his knees, shifting his weight forward, ready to move, ready to fight with only his fists if he got the chance.

The door at the top of the stairs opened. Kurff glanced up and saw a figure silhouetted against the soft yellow light coming from the Posthole Inn's kitchen. "Don't kill him," a voice called down. Kurff thought the voice sounded familiar, but he couldn't quite place it. "Not yet. Bring him up. I would talk to this one."

Hussert muttered something under his breath and then sheathed his sword. Kurff let out the breath he'd been holding.

"Upstairs," Maekel said, gesturing toward the steps. "And don't try anything you might regret."

"I won't," Kurff said, meaning it.

***

Jarn felt the building shake when the first stone hit the south wall. Startled, he and Liora looked at one another, but it was Sir Longboke who spoke first.

"It sounds like you're under attack," the knight said.

Jarn glared at him. "You stay here." He got up and opened the door, telling the guard to make sure Sir Longboke didn't leave the room. Then he and Liora left the Rats Nest and ran up the stairs to the Mang's ground level, where other Riders were gathering.

"One-armed stone thrower," Jarn heard someone say, just before another stone smashed into the south wall. He and Liora followed the crowd up a wide stone staircase to the top floor of the four-story building, and then up a narrow wooden stairway that led to the roof, where they ran to the south side of the building. Jarn saw the next stone as it flew toward the wall, and he flinched in spite of himself as it crashed into the building not far below him and just to his left. Pieces of the Mang's wall were raining down from where the stone had struck it.

Three more shots hit the wall and took chunks out of it, though the Mang, as sturdy a structure as Jarn had ever seen, showed no signs of major damage. Jarn also realized that the stones were smaller than the ones he had seen launched from siege engines during past battles. Judging by the rate of firing, only one thrower was engaged, and it must have been a fairly small one. It couldn't be very far away, which meant that, unless the men firing it could make themselves invisible, they would soon be captured or killed.

The trajectory of the next shot was higher than those of the previous ones, and the stone seemed to be burning. It fell short of the building, landing on the grassy expanse between the front of the Mang proper and the south curtain wall, fifty yards away. A bloom of fire erupted from the point of impact, spreading across the grass like the remnant of a wave spreading over a beach, until it was thirty feet in diameter. A blazing dome, half as tall as a man and nearly as bright as the sun, hung suspended for another moment, looking like an enormous burning mushroom cap, crackling and sizzling and filling the air with an acrid, unnatural smell. Flaming streamers of blue and green and red shot out of it, rising twenty feet into the air, twisting like the worms of corkscrews and reminding Jarn of the candle flame Lady Grenling had used to put a spell on him.

"Charmfire!" someone yelled.

Another shot hit near the first, and another mushroom of fire ignited and lit up the yard in front of the Mang. A squadron of mounted Vothan Riders appeared from the west side of the building, heading toward the main gate, at the south end of the grounds.

"Don't go near it," a man shouted down to them. "Don't let the fire touch you."

The gate swung open, and the Riders raced through, two by two, and galloped down Zayet Street. Another shot passed over their heads and landed in the lawn, spreading more charmfire.

The grass where the shots hit was still burning, and Jarn knew it would keep burning until there was nothing left for the fire to consume. If charmfire hit a man, he was doomed to the same fate, and pouring water on it only spread it and would not put it out.

Down in the yard, a party of men carrying buckets filled with dirt appeared and cautiously approached the fires. "Don't let it touch you," the man who had called down to the Riders repeated. On the wall-walk of the south curtain wall, guards were gathering to watch the party of Riders advancing down Zayet Street toward the presumed location of the stone thrower.

Liora turned to Jarn. "Damned rebels."

Jarn had nearly forgotten she was there. He looked at her and nodded.

Another pot of charmfire hit the yard, spreading its eerie flames and peculiar odor.

"We should go back inside," Liora said.

Jarn nodded, but he was reluctant to leave. He looked at the guards on the wall-walk and then scanned all around. Whatever thought had been knocking on the door of his mind earlier was trying to get his attention again, but still he could not pluck it out. He looked at the wall-walk. There were no guards on the north, east, and west sides of the curtain wall. He felt his insides drop, as if he'd been snatched from the ground by a swooping dragon and hoisted a thousand feet into the air within the space of two seconds.

"Feint," he murmured, half to himself.

"What?" Liora asked.

"Feint," he repeated.

She frowned. "You feel faint? It's probably a remnant from that spell."

Jarn shook his head. "Misdirection," he said, staring to the north. In the next instant, dozens of grappling hooks flew above the top of the north curtain wall, dropped over, and held fast. "North wall," Jarn screamed, but even as he began running, more grappling hooks were flying over the east and west sides of the wall.

Jarn and Liora and the others who had been watching from the roof, took off running, descending the narrow stairway back into the Mang as quickly as possible and racing for the wide stone steps that would take them to the ground floor. By the time Jarn and Liora arrived outside, a company of Riders was deploying behind archer's screens in the north yard, loosing arrows from longbows and bolts from crossbows. Up on the wall-walk, men who had gathered to watch the action to the south had returned to the round towers that rose from the curtain wall at regular intervals and locked their sturdy oak doors on the side facing the rebels. The men in the towers climbed to the upper level where they could fire bolts from loopholes and small square windows. Some of the rebels had run down the stone steps that led down in places from the wall-walk, but they were quickly dispatched by the first company of Riders to deploy in the yard. Other rebels stayed up on the walk, crouching and firing and reloading and falling when they were hit.

The Riders began calling out for the rebels to yield. Instead, some ran toward the defensive towers and were quickly cut down, and others launched themselves from the forty-foot-high wall-walk and died or were grievously injured when they hit the ground.

And then the battle was over. Nearly a hundred rebels had taken part, and most were dead. Riders took the few survivors to the physician's room, where the healers would try to save them. The defenders atop the outer wall were reinforced, and companies of Riders rode out to patrol the area around the Mang. Officers rode to the Beldur Palace and the Palace of the High Hext to inform the Acrinite leaders of what had taken place. All that remained was the return of the Riders who had gone after the rebels who had manned the one-armed stone thrower.

***

Aarla heard shouting from above. Expecting to see the platform begin to descend, she looked up. Instead, she saw men hurriedly sliding beams into openings just below street level, horizontally, as if they were arranging putlogs to support a hoarding atop a castle's curtain wall. Moments later, darkness fell again, as the men shoved sections of street pavement on top of the beams they had placed.

Aarla stepped back, away from the charmfire pot. She waited, listening, thought she heard the sounds of horses and shouting from above. The noise soon faded. She took one last look at the clay pot, and then turned to walk back the way she had come. That's when she saw three men standing there, two of them aiming loaded crossbows at her, the other one just smiling.

***

Kurff was tied to a wooden chair in the dust-covered, windowless storage room behind the Posthole Inn. The room was actually a small stone barn that was connected to the back of the inn by an enclosed passageway of rough timbers that ran from the barn to the inn's back door. Dirty kitchen utensils were piled on a bench in one corner, and stale loaves of bread and a moldy wheel of cheese were heaped on a small table along a wall. Wooden trenchers, pewter plates and tankards, and spoons in various sizes partly filled a wooden crate. The only light came from a flickering candle on a heavy oak table in the middle of the room. Maekel was sitting on the opposite side of the table, staring at him, and Hussert was leaning against a wall, grinning like a fool, his crossbow in his hand. The man who had called down to the basement to tell Maekel not to kill Kurff—yet—was standing in the shadows a few feet behind the proprietor, the hood of his dark brown cloak still covering his head and obscuring his face. Kurff had visions of the High Hext or his holy minions come back to seek revenge against Yellowshirts who had remained behind after the Vothan Renewal. The thought made him shiver. Truth be told, he never had much use for the High Hext or his priests, and he had been happy to see the backs of them, even if it took the hated Voths to drive them out.

"Who's your friend?" Kurff asked Maekel. If he was going to die, he wanted to satisfy his curiosity first. And attack his new enemies in the only way that was left to him.

"Shut your hole," Maekel snapped.

"Is he your chief? Is he the leader of your rebel friends?"

Maekel stood up and glared at Kurff. "I told you to shut it."

"Do you wait on him? Serve him his tea?"

Maekel skirted around the table and quickly approached Kurff, violence in his eyes.

"Get his meals for him?" Kurff said, grinning. "Wipe his—"

Maekel struck Kurff with the back of his hand, drawing blood from the Yellowshirt's lip and nearly upending the chair he was tied to.

"Enough," said the man in the brown cloak. "Don't let the rogue provoke you."

Again, the voice sounded familiar, but Kurff still couldn't place it. "Who are you?" he asked. "A Gurgeonite? You don't sound like a Gurgeonite, but you have the stench of the Gurgeon about you."

Maekel hit Kurff again, but Kurff rolled with it as best he could and laughed.

"Enough, I said!" the brown-cloaked man shouted at Maekel. "You're letting this scoundrel make a fool of you."

"Who are you?" Kurff asked again. "And why have these villains seized me? I've done nothing wrong."

"You were digging about where you had no business being," the man said.

"I'm an Acrinite Guardsman. It's my business to be anywhere in the Acrinite Realm."

"You mean the Greater Vothan Realm, don't you?"

Kurff shrugged. "The Acrinite Territory then."

"As long as your Vothan masters give you their leave," Maekel said. "Isn't that right?"

To that Kurff made no reply.

"What's wrong, Kurff?" Maekel said. "You ashamed to be a Voth-loving traitor to your country?"

224

"I'm no traitor. I fought the Voths, and plenty of other enemies as well, while you were busy stealing sheep and trying to turn your sisters to whoredom."

Maekel struck Kurff another blow across the face, this time opening a cut in his upper lip and drawing more blood. "And for all your fighting, the Voths took over our country anyway."

Kurff spit blood onto the sawdust-covered plank floor. "It wasn't our country," he murmured. "Or have you forgotten that awkward fact?"

"The Acrinites have lived here for a thousand years," the hooded man said. "We've made our homes here. Our livelihoods are here, and our ancestors lived here and called this place home. Who are you to say it isn't our country?"

"What you say is true enough," Kurff said. "Yet it was all based on a lie. There's no honor in it."

"And did your father and his fathers before him know about the lie?"

"No," Kurff admitted. "Most didn't know. But some did. The High Hext and his minions knew."

"Take care when speaking of the High Hext," the cloaked man said.

"Bugger the High Hext, and bugger you as well."

Maekel hit Kurff again, this time with his closed fist. The cloaked man said nothing. Maekel kept punching.

"Can I hit him, too?" Hussert asked. He had been leaning against a corner of the room, silent until then.

Maekel, breathing heavily, glared at him.

"That will be enough hitting, for now," the cloaked man said.

Maekel bent toward Kurff until he was an inch from his bruised and bloodied face. "Your stinking Voth friends came in and took what was ours."

"Reclaimed what was theirs," Kurff said. "You can cut it up, season it, and cook it any way you like, but the land was theirs, and the Acrinites stole it before the Voths took it back."

"Spoken like a true traitor," Maekel said, backing away from Kurff.

"I'm no traitor. But I'm not afraid of the truth."

The cloaked man stepped closer to Kurff, but his face was still obscured by the hood. "And where were our ancient ancestors supposed to make their home?" he asked.

"Around Lake Poltek," Kurff replied.

"A narrow strip of land around a huge lake," the man said. "Hardly a prize for such as we."

"It's good land," Kurff said. "And there are fertile islands in the lake."

"Ah, yes, our ancestors could have been fisher folk and gull hunters and collected pretty shells and smooth stones."

Kurff shrugged. "Mayhap. But they would not have dishonored themselves and their children."

"The man is a stinking traitor," Maekel yelled. "Let me kill him now."

Hussert, who was still leaning against a corner of the room, took a step forward and looked at Maekel. "You promised I could kill him."

"I changed my mind," Maekel said.

"Quiet, both of you," the hooded man said. "When the time comes, I'll decide who kills him. I may want to do it myself."

Chapter 26

The large meeting room in the Rats Nest was crowded but quiet, only an occasional chair scraping across the stone floor or a sharp cough breaking the heavy silence. An air of anxious anticipation pervaded the room. Commander Lahgoh sat at the head of the table, looking stern, almost angry, as he listened to various reports concerning the events of the previous evening. On the wall behind him, the slab of slate still held the chalked names of those involved in the Talsie Grenling matter, which Jarn had written there two days before—*Talsie Grenling, Lord Grenling, Lady Grenling, Sir Longboke, Willim Gilpin, Lord Keddro, Nevvin, Astil.* It seemed like two months ago.

But this meeting was not about the Talsie Grenling case. It was about a company of vaunted Vothan Riders who had left their positions and allowed nearly a hundred armed rebels to scale the walls of the Mang and invade the grounds. Jarn wouldn't want to be in their boots right now.

He stifled a yawn and tried to focus his attention on the Rider addressing the chamber, a saddlemaster named Chesk, who had led the pursuit of the rebels who had manned the stone thrower. Jarn's eyes burned from lack of sleep, and his head had nodded more than once, but he knew sleep would have to wait until Commander Lahgoh had heard everyone's account. He glanced up at the meeting room's high windows. The night sky was slowly growing lighter as daybreak approached, the stars dimming and finally disappearing against the first blush of dawn. Another day had arrived, and he was still no closer to finding Talsie Grenling.

Commander Lahgoh had already heard from the officers in charge of the men on the wall-walk who had left their posts. They would be lucky to keep their rank. The Acrinite rebels had been on a suicide mission, and an ultimately ineffective one at that, but the breach in discipline was distressing just the same. And the news that rebels had penetrated the grounds of the Vothan Riders' headquarters, even if only for a short time, might embolden other Acrinites to take similar action against the hated Voths.

Chesk was concluding his report. "We still don't know where the rebel artillerymen entered the city and how they deployed the stone-thrower without being noticed."

Lahgoh raised an eyebrow. "Perhaps they were," he said. "Noticed, I mean."

Saddlemaster Chesk made no reply to that, but Jarn understood the implication—it was possible that some Acrinites had, indeed, seen the rebels bring their thrower into the city but decided not to inform the Voths. Two of the artillerymen were in custody, and they might eventually decide to come clean, though Jarn had his doubts. Two others had died fighting the Vothan Riders who had pursued them.

The outer door opened, and Jarn turned toward it. Bleuek entered the room, his face pale, his hair disheveled.

"Saddlemaster Bleuek," Lahgoh said. "What is it?"

"It's Cutter," Bleuek replied. "Aarla's horse. He's here. He's come back without her."

***

Kurff was awakened by footsteps sounding from the passageway that connected the small barn to the Posthole Inn proper. The blood had dried around his mouth, but the blood that had dripped from his nose felt sticky. He wrinkled his nose, but it didn't help. The small space between his nose and upper lip felt as if a leech fresh out of the river was clinging to it. He tried to put it out of his mind. His face hurt from the beating Maekel had inflicted on it, but his teeth and bones seemed to be intact, and though his nose hurt, it didn't hurt enough to be broken. He thanked the gods he was still alive and then focused on the approaching footsteps.

There were too many for three people. "In there," he heard Maekel say. He looked at the entrance to the passageway and saw the young witch-girl, Aarla, being shoved along by Hussert. Her hands were bound behind her, but she didn't appear to be hurt. He caught her eye and thought she gave him the slightest of nods, although he couldn't be sure. The expression on her face, impassive as usual, didn't change, didn't even register surprise at seeing him.

"This one was found skulking about the storm drains," Maekel said to Kurff as Hussert pushed Aarla into a straight-backed wooden chair and tied her to it. "What do you know about it?"

Kurff laughed. "All these rebel adventures of yours have fuddled your brain, Maekel. Why would I know anything about the wee witch's skulking?"

"Because you were doing the same. The two of you are clearly in league."

Kurff laughed harder, felt a gob of not-quite-dried blood tickling his nose. "You're clearly a fool."

"You'll answer me, or I'll have your head."

"If you want to know why she was skulking about the storm drains, why don't you ask her."

"I have done. She won't talk."

"Good for her."

Maekel drew his dagger. "It won't be good for her if I cut off an ear or perhaps a finger or two."

"And when her father finds out, he'll turn you into a spider."

Maekel frowned. "What do you mean?"

"My father is a virrling," Aarla said.

Maekel glared at her. "And I'm the king of the Wandremes."

"The Wandremes don't have a king," Aarla told him.

"You're a lying wench."

"And you're a lackwit fool," Kurff said. "A flea has more brains."

Maekel approached Kurff, holding his dagger in front of him. There were more footsteps from the passageway, and a moment later the cloaked man stepped into the room, his face still obscured by the cloak's hood. He was carrying a loaded crossbow.

"Step back, Maekel," the man said. "Sheath your knife."

Maekel stopped, glared at Kurff, and then took a step back. Hussert, still leaning against the wall, snickered.

"These two were plotting something," Maekel said. "We need to find out what it was."

"Leave it be," the hooded man said. "It makes no matter."

"Let me beat it out of him," Hussert said, stepping away from the wall and approaching Kurff. He stopped and looked at Aarla. "Or her."

The cloaked man brandished his crossbow. "Never mind. It's time to make an end of the traitor among us."

Kurff tensed, every sense focused on the man in the brown cloak. His mouth went dry, and he felt his heart hammering in his chest. "Before you kill me, tell me who you are," he managed to rasp. "Show yourself."

The cloaked man raised his crossbow.

"Wait, I can do it," Hussert said, stepping closer to Kurff. "I can make him talk."

"Stay your tongue," Maekel said to him.

"I'll tell you about our scheme," Aarla said. "I'll tell you everything. But only if you don't kill him."

"You'll tell us anyway," the hooded man replied.

"Show yourself," Kurff said, forcing himself to hold his voice steady. "I don't believe you're a rebel leader. You might maybe could lead a herd of swine to slaughter, but not rebels or anyone else who can lay claim to being a man."

Hussert ran up to Kurff and slapped him hard across the face. "I'll make him talk. Let me. Then kill him."

"Step away from him," the hooded man commanded.

"He'll talk, I swear I can make him," Hussert said, nearly pleading.

"Step away, I said."

Hussert hesitated a moment and then stepped aside. Lord Keddro raised the crossbow and took aim.

Kurff, his jaws clenched so tightly that his teeth felt as if they might crack, squeezed his eyes closed and waited.

"You'll pay for this," Aarla said. "All of you. The Voths will find you."

The hooded man moved his arm to the right and fired. The bolt hit Hussert in the chest. He cried out in pain and fell backward, writhing and moaning. After a moment he lay still.

The hooded man looked at Kurff. "As I said, it was time to put an end to the traitor among us."

Kurff, sweating and trembling, glared at the man. "You bastard."

"Other traitors will come to similar ends," the man said, and then he turned and disappeared through the passageway.

***

By the time dawn broke, Astil was miles from Winnik, riding east on the road to Stannik, a fair-sized town on the Kott River, another tributary of the Shaffroth. Early-morning sunlight spilled over a wide meadow glistening with dew, and in the near distance rows of cabbage, greenleef, and other vegetables stretched to the horizon like ranks of green-cloaked soldiers on the march. She passed a stone farmhouse, a large wooden barn, and a kepple orchard. The rustic setting made her long for the boundless charms of a large city.

She had left the Dragon's Tooth Inn early, before sunrise, rousing the inn's young stablehand from sleep and slipping him a small silver coin for his trouble. As for Millardo and Gorno, she had left the two where they were, tied up tight, bruised and bloodied, but still breathing. She reckoned that once they were finally freed, they would most likely worry more about their wounded pride than about their scrapes and bruises. Scrapes and bruises would heal more quickly. They would probably concoct some sham story that did not include a woman getting the drop on them. The notion brought a smile to Astil's face, and she imagined the two scoundrels explaining their battered state—and the loss of Millardo's silver—to the young man's wealthy father.

The smile did not last long. Astil felt uneasy. Worse yet, she didn't know why. She thought about Aarla, her sometime adversary, who had tracked her down just days before, and not for the first time. It was irksome. Astil was the master tracker, the best in the known world, and it vexed her that a mysterious young waif, little more than a child, could know her whereabouts—and perhaps other things about her as well—whenever she turned her thoughts to the task.

Astil told herself she shouldn't feel troubled. Her talent was far better than Aarla's strange gift of sometimes "knowing" things. What was the good of a random thought coming unbidden into one's mind? And yet Astil, too, now that she thought about it, had sometimes experienced such knowing. The occurrences had always seemed more annoying than useful, and she generally ignored them. Perhaps she should have taken them more seriously.

Perhaps Aarla, too, possessed more gifts than she admitted or even realized. If her father was a virrling, which Aarla had claimed and Astil had no reason to doubt, then the meddlesome imp might be more powerful than anyone knew. Even Aarla herself might not be aware of the extent of her own powers.

Astil had warned Captain Jarn not to send the little witch after her, at the risk of scuttling their deal, but the

Vothan Rider would do whatever he thought necessary to find Talsie Grenling and also to show the Riders in the best light. Astil had no particular quarrel with Jarn, and expected him to keep his word and return her gold. She might even devise some additional plans of her own concerning the captain, who was, she had to confess, a fine figure of a man, even if he was too noble for his own good.

She put the thought out of her mind. Perhaps she would return to it, perhaps not, but for now she had to focus on her immediate task. Yet she could not shake her disquiet. What if Aarla was following her?

Astil tried to think logically. If Aarla were nearby when Astil found Talsie Grenling, what matter? The waif would report back to Captain Jarn that Astil had lived up to their agreement, and Astil would get her gold. Nor would it matter if Astil decided to break the agreement and abandon the search for Talsie. She would lose her gold and return to her status as a wanted criminal, but that was no worse than before. In fact, it was better, because she would have her freedom. She could dye her hair and disappear in Rynland or Telna or the Hirple Realm, or sail across the sea to the Hundred Isles and begin again. A woman of her talents and determination could make her way anywhere in the known world.

But why was she even thinking about the troublesome waif? There was no logical reason for Aarla to be following her. Why did she continue to intrude on Astil's thoughts? A notion flashed through Astil's mind, unbidden, and she shook her head as if to throw it off. There was some connection between her and the waif, and Astil didn't know whether she should try to discover what it was or put distance between herself and Aarla and erase

234

the waif from her mind and memory, if she could. *If she could.*

Astil growled to herself, gritted her teeth, and spurred her horse to a canter, determined to make Stannik by midday. She passed another farm and soon spied woodland in the near distance. It was midmorning, which meant that by the time she reached the other side of the woods, she would be only an hour from Stannik. There she would take a midday meal and reconsider her plans.

When Astil reached the woods, she reined to a halt and looked back the way she had come, as if she expected to see someone behind her. The road was empty, the morning still quiet, only birdsong and insect chatter disturbing the silence.

"You're going mad, Astil," she muttered to herself, and then she turned around again, spurred her horse, and entered the woods.

Chapter 27

"Someone should send word to Yellig," Jarn said. He was sitting at the round table in the alcove of his inner office with Bleuek, Braga, Liora, and Commander Lahgoh. They were discussing Aarla' disappearance and what to do about searching for her.

"Nobody can find Yellig's woods," Lahgoh said. "Except Aarla. Or another virrling, perhaps."

"Line Commander Lahgoh is right," Bleuek said. "We need to find Aarla ourselves. If Yellig finds out she's gone missing ... well, he won't take it well. I request leave to search for her. I'll go by myself if need be."

No one spoke for a moment, but everyone knew what everyone else was thinking—given the state of the Talsie Grenling investigation, Jarn would be hard pressed to spare anyone to search for Aarla.

Liora finally broke the silence. "Let Bleuek and me have a day or two to look for Aarla. You can spare us for that long."

Jarn nodded. "Very well. Sir Tarris is due to report back today. I'll ask him to assist you as well."

"Kurff might be of some use, too," Lahgoh said. "He knows the city better than any of us."

Jarn nodded and turned Bleuek. "Go to the Beldur and fetch him. When Sir Tarris arrives, I'll have him report to Liora."

Liora stood up. "I'll see to the horses and start thinking about a plan."

"I'll help you," Braga said, and then he, Bleuek, and Liora excused themselves and left the office.

After they were gone, Lahgoh turned to Jarn. "I know you haven't slept, but I need to ask—how goes the Talsie Grenling investigation?"

"Not well," Jarn said. "Although we managed to uncover a farfetched conspiracy hatched by her mother and involving Talsie, Sir Longboke, and Willim Gilpin, we're no closer to actually finding her."

Lahgoh frowned. "A conspiracy?"

Jarn nodded and told the commander about the plan the four schemers had hatched to get away from Lord Grenling.

"Press Sir Longboke," Lahgoh said. "There may be more in that quarter to be gleaned."

"I will. But I don't believe he's guilty."

"Someone is. Unless the girl scarpered."

Jarn nodded. "Or was seized by a dragon and taken to his mountain lair."

"If she did bolt, where would she go?"

"That, Commander, is the question of the hour."

Lahgoh stood up. "Think about an answer. Don't be afraid to follow a hunch."

"Besides Astil, hunches are all I have," Jarn said, standing up.

Outside, someone rapped loudly on the door to the office.

"Enter," Lahgoh called out.

A solemn-faced young man wearing a pink tunic and a dark-blue jacket cut from fine cloth entered the room and glanced at Jarn before turning to Lahgoh. Jarn recognized him as Mander Ribinsin, an assistant to the Vothan diplomat Respero Nelgard, who was negotiating the treaty between Vothan and Brythyn with Lord

Grenling. "Minister Respero wants to see you and Captain Jarn," he announced.

"When?" Lahgoh asked.

"Now."

"What's it about?" Jarn asked.

"He'll tell you," the young man replied.

Lahgoh muttered something under his breath, but they followed Mander to the southwest corner of the Mang, a section of the building that housed ministers, justiciars, diplomats, deputies, and various other functionaries from Vothan. Jarn rarely had reason to visit that section of the building, and he noticed that the hallways were wider and the ceilings higher than in the far less embellished section of the Mang that the Vothan Riders occupied. Even the doors and doorframes looked more elegant. A few small paintings in the Vothan style decorated the walls, which seemed to have been freshly painted. Apparently the Vothan diplomats and other officials were settling in nicely. Jarn was determined not to and longed for the day he would be reassigned back to Vothan.

They climbed a spiral staircase to the top floor and walked down a wide corridor that was illuminated by torches set in ornate sconces on the wall. Mander stopped halfway down the hallway, opened a door, and gestured for Jarn and Lahgoh to step inside. They entered an elegant antechamber large enough to serve as a banquet room or even a small ballroom. A series of tall, narrow windows, typical of the Mang, let plenty of sunlight into the room, which was appointed with polished tables, heavy cabinets, and tall bookcases, all in a matching style and made of the same dark wood. The room also boasted a small inn's worth of plush chairs and sofas covered in a blue and gold fabric that looked soft enough to drop an egg onto without breaking it.

Mander led them through the anteroom and into another, smaller chamber, narrow and windowless and furnished with a long oval table and more than a dozen chairs, suggesting a meeting room. Mander opened a door at the far end of that room, and they entered Minister Respero's inner office, which was larger than the meeting room but only half as large as the antechamber.

Minister Respero was staring out a window when they entered. Mander cleared his throat and announced their arrival. "Line Commander Lahgoh and Captain Jarn are here, Minister."

Respero turned around and nodded. His dark-gray, finely cut wool cloak and butter-colored silk tunic would not have looked out of place on a Brythyn lord or a Telnan noble.

"Thank you, Mander," he said to his assistant, who nodded and left the room.

After Mander left, Minister Respero gestured Jarn and Lahgoh toward a round table near a window. Jarn and Lahgoh took seats, and Respero went to a sideboard and fetched a bottle of Vothan strong red and three polished silver goblets. He set the goblets on the table and filled them before sitting down. The three men took drinks, and then Respero began.

"I'll come straight to the reason I asked to see you two. There's a rumor that you have Lady Grenling in custody. I trust it's only a rumor."

"No, it's true," Jarn replied.

"Lady Grenling is married to a Brythyner diplomat," Respero said sharply. "Diplomatic courtesy is usually extended to wives."

"Usually, yes," Jarn said. "But the lady tried to put a spell on me. Under Vothan law, that makes her a criminal. She also left her husband's household."

Respero stared at him as if he had just sprouted a tail. "The lady is a spellcaster?"

Jarn nodded. "We also uncovered a scheme concocted by Lady Grenling and three others, including Talsie Grenling, to flee from Lord Grenling and go into hiding. We have two of the other schemers in custody as well. One is a young friend of Talsie's with whom Lady Grenling is having an unlawful romance. Talsie, sadly, is still missing."

Respero shook his head as if he could not believe what he was hearing. "This matter does not bode well for my negotiations with Lord Grenling. How do you propose to resolve it?"

"If we return Lady Grenling to her husband, he may do her harm. If we let her go, we'll have released a criminal."

Respero leaned back against his chair and furrowed his brow. Then he picked up his goblet and took a long drink. "This situation will require a great deal of delicacy," he murmured. "Please do not proceed with any disposition of Lady Grenling until I have a chance to think it through and talk to you again. But do make sure she's comfortable. I don't want her treated like a prisoner, even if she is guilty of a crime."

"We've made sure the lady is quite comfortable," Lahgoh said.

"Good," Respero said. "As I'm sure you two are aware, Vothan is on the brink of taking its rightful place in the known world. Now that we've recovered the land that was always our birthright and also exposed the

240

Acrinite deception that denied it to us for so long, we stand as equals among the realms."

"We'll drink to that," Lahgoh said, and the three drank from their goblets.

Respero refilled the goblets and then turned to Jarn. "Tell me, Captain, apart from this sad business with Lady Grenling, how is your investigation proceeding? Surely you have some leads, some clues, some ideas."

"Leads have gone nowhere, clues are nonexistent, and we're all out of ideas," Jarn said. "We will question Lady Grenling again, as well as the two others we have in custody, but we don't expect much from that quarter."

Respero frowned at Jarn. Jarn met his gaze without blinking.

"Are you telling me, Captain Jarn, that after five days the only progress you've made in your investigation is the seizing of the wife of the diplomat sent here from Brythyn to negotiate an important treaty with Vothan?"

"I'm afraid that's so, Minister," Jarn replied.

Respero looked at Lahgoh. "What have you to say, Line Commander?"

"Captain Jarn and his team have worked tirelessly to pursue every path. They will continue to do so until they find Talsie Grenling."

"Lord Grenling—my negotiating partner—wants his daughter back, and he will hold the Voths responsible for the lack of progress. Meanwhile, an important treaty, as well as my reputation, are hostage to this unfortunate situation."

"Astil may yet find the girl," Jarn said.

"The sorceress you engaged."

Jarn and Lahgoh both nodded.

"The finest tracker in the known world," Jarn said.

"I don't like sorcery."

"Nor do I," Jarn said. "But we're pursuing all avenues in our search for Talsie."

"Do you trust this Astil?"

Jarn hesitated a moment before replying. "I believe she'll try to do what she agreed to."

"But do you trust her?"

"Not entirely. But we're holding a large amount of gold that belongs to her—gained honestly, by the way."

"It's a sad day when Vothan Riders have to depend on sorcery," Respero said, making no attempt to hide the distaste he clearly felt.

"Sorcery may also have been at work in Talsie's abduction," Jarn said. "The knight who was with her when she was taken says he was felled by dark magic. When he awoke, the girl was gone, or so he claims."

"It's also possible that the girl doesn't want to be found," Lahgoh said. "She may have scarpered."

Respero frowned. "Are you saying the girl put a spell on this Brythyner knight so that she could disappear?"

"No, no, of course not," Lahgoh said. "We're just recounting all the possibilities, considering every imaginable twist." He turned to Jarn. "Isn't that right, Captain?"

But Jarn was staring through the window as if he was looking at a castle sprouting from a cloud.

"Captain?" Lahgoh repeated.

Jarn turned from the window and gave Lahgoh a brief, blank stare, and then turned to Respero and nodded, as if to himself. "Yes, that's right, Minister, we're recounting the possibilities. Considering the twists. Pursuing all avenues. All avenues."

Chapter 28

Kurff stared at Hussert's body, which lay less than six feet away, his dead eyes open and staring. Blood from his wound was pooled under him, and the bolt was still embedded in his chest. Kurff's hands were still tied behind his back, but he clenched his fists and strained against the rope binding his wrists, which succeeded only in chafing them. He felt as if he should apologize to Hussert, but he was not one for futile or sentimental gestures. Better to think about vengeance, although given the current state of affairs, that thought was almost as futile as apologizing to a dead man.

Kurff looked at Aarla, who had been tied to a wooden chair a few feet away, her hands still bound behind her back. She was eyeing him intently, which Kurff found unnerving.

"Why did they kill him?" she asked.

"He was working for me," Kurff replied. "They must have found out."

"Working for you how?"

"I suspected that Maekel was a rebel. Hussert was spying on him for me."

Aarla continued to stare at him, but Kurff detected a slight frown on her usually impassive face.

"Does Captain Jarn know?"

Kurff shook his head. "No, no one else knows. I took up the task on my own." Kurff nodded toward Hussert's body. "The only other man who knew was him."

"Who was he?"

"He used to work in the kitchen of the Beldur Palace, before the Voths took over. We used to talk about things.

He wanted something more than kitchen work, wanted to make his mark in some way."

"What will they do with us?" Aarla asked.

Kurff shrugged. "We'll probably end up like him."

"Why haven't they done it yet?"

"They'll probably torture me for information. You they'll most likely hold for ransom."

"We need to get out of here," Aarla said.

Kurff gave a short laugh. "How do you propose we do that?"

Aarla gave a jerk, and her chair moved an inch. She tried again, and the chair moved another inch. "Try to turn your chair around. If we get back to back, I may be able to untie the knot on the rope binding your hands together."

"And I may sprout wings and fly away."

"I used to travel with a street conjurer," Aarla said. "Among our tricks were escapes from ropes and chains and locked vaults. My hands and fingers are strong, like steel springs."

"We're not performing street tricks," Kurff muttered, but he pressed his feet against the floor and wrenched the chair to the left, trying not to grunt. The chair moved. He did it again. Aarla moved her chair another inch, then Kurff did. They alternated, falling into a rhythm, each small shove by one seeming to spur the next shove by the other. Even their breathing settled into a regular pace. By the time they maneuvered the chairs back to back, Kurff was perspiring and breathing heavily. Aarla remained calm and hadn't broken a sweat.

"You all right, lass?" he whispered to Aarla, trying not to sound winded.

"All right," she replied. "My hands are tied at the wrists, but I can move my fingers. I'll try to untie your knot."

"Have at it," Kurff said.

The chairs were simple ladderbacks, with plenty of space between the three cross-rails that made up the backs. Kurff leaned forward slightly and moved his wrists to the space between the seat and the lowest rail. The knot was between his wrists and his back, so he twisted his wrists to move the knot where she could get to it. A moment later he felt her fingers.

A half hour later, she stopped. Kurff's wrists were still bound tight.

"Shall I try to untie your knot?" Kurff asked, envisioning his meaty hands and stubby fingers trying to do what she had failed to.

She made no reply.

"I say, shall I try your knot?" Kurff asked again.

"Did your friend carry a blade?" she asked.

"Aye, a boot knife."

"I didn't see them take it."

"Nor did I."

Aarla began moving her chair again, this time toward Hussert's body. Kurff wrenched his chair around an inch at a time so he could see her. Sweat pooled on his forehead and ran into his eyes. He blinked and shook his head, swore softly.

"Which boot?" she asked.

"Right boot, I think. How will you reach it?"

She planted her feet firmly on the floor and thrust herself backward. The chair tipped over and landed on its back, Aarla with it. Pushing with her feet, she slowly maneuvered the chair close to Hussert's right boot. She

245

crossed one leg over the other and tried to turn the chair onto its side. Kurff eyed the door to the passageway, but all was quiet.

She finally moved the chair to where she wanted it and reached through the back of it and into the top of Hussert's right boot.

"Anything?" Kurff asked, once again glancing toward the door.

"I can't reach far enough in," she said. "We need to get his boot off."

"Desecrating the dead," Kurff muttered.

"Trying to save the living," she replied. "He won't care."

"You're a deal tougher than you look, girl."

"Aye, I am that."

Kurff sighed and then maneuvered his chair close to Hussert. When he thought he was in the position he wanted, he tipped the chair sideways, nearly on top of Hussert's right leg.

"I'll hold his leg, you try to pull the boot off," Aarla said. She maneuvered into position, using one leg of the chair and her body weight to hold Hussert's leg hard against the floor. "Ready."

Kurff wriggled closer, stuck his bound hands through the back of the chair, and felt Hussert's boot. He grabbed the toe and pulled, but his hands slipped off. He tried again with the same result. He tried a third time with no more success. "Damn," he muttered. His clothes were damp and the dried blood on his face was becoming sticky from perspiration.

"Try again," she said.

"I need to change position. I need to hold the heel of his boot to have any chance of pulling it off."

246

"Can you do it?"

"I think so," he replied. Then, in a low voice that was not much more than a whisper, he said, "Sorry, lad."

With an effort that left him nearly out of breath, Kurff positioned his chair on top of Hussert's body, the back of it now nearly parallel with the floor. He looked up at the ceiling, saw the cobwebs that festooned the corners, and breathed deeply a few times. He reached back again, trying to gain purchase on his dead friend's boot heel. "I think I have it," he said. "Hold tight." He leaned forward and tried to pull, felt the boot start to come off. He pulled again, felt it move another half inch. He repositioned himself and pulled again. This time the boot moved a couple of inches. One more attempt and the boot slipped off.

Kurff waited while Aarla used her feet to push herself into position, then he tried to hold the boot where she might reach it. They were back to back again, sideways on the floor. He felt her scrabbling with her hands inside the boot.

"I feel a handle," she said. She grunted as she strained to stretch her bound hands as far as possible through the back of her chair. "I have it."

She pushed her legs to move away, and Kurff saw the end of the knife handle in her fingertips. "Get a good grip, if you can."

"Ready," she said.

Kurff struggled to get into position back to back with Aarla and pressed the rope binding his hands against the knife edge. He moved his bound hands back and forth as far as he could, hoping he wouldn't slip and cut himself.

"It's working," he said. "I can feel it." He stopped for a moment to rest his aching wrists.

"I hear something," Aarla whispered.

A moment later, Kurff heard footsteps sounding in the passageway.

***

Jarn entered the Shieldstone Inn, one of the many hostelries in the Shield that catered to performers as well as the wanderers who sometimes followed certain popular minstrel troupes from town to town. Like most inns and taverns in the Shield, it was small and clean and cozy and possessed its own unique character. The high-backed wooden chairs in the common room were painted red, and the same color was prominent among the room's decorations, which included paintings of sunsets and sunrises as well as still lifes of shiny kepples, a painting of a river cog with red sails, and a portrait of a golden-haired woman in a long red dress. That one caught Jarn's eye. The woman's pose was casual rather than formal, with one arm draped nonchalantly over the back of the chair on which she sat, and her head cocked just the slightest bit. Her half smile and knowing eyes suggested cool anticipation, but there was warmth there as well, perhaps even heat.

Jarn turned away from the painting and walked to the bar. The barkeep, a young man with wary eyes and straight black hair that would have fallen to his shoulders were it not pulled back and tied, nodded at Jarn, neither smiling nor frowning. It was a common response from Acrinites to members of the Vothan Riders.

"What can I get for you, Captain?"

"The troupe that was staying here the night before last, two men and two women, can you tell me if they're still here?"

"Aye, they are, but they'll be leaving today, so they tell me."

"I need to speak to the woman named Maiya, if you please."

The barkeep hesitated a moment and then said, "I'll go up and tell her you're here."

Jarn went to an empty table and sat down on a red chair to wait. He eyed the painting of the woman in the red dress, still captivated by her eyes and smile. He turned when he heard footsteps on the stairs and saw the barkeep coming down.

"She'll be here in a trice," the young man said.

Jarn nodded. "I'll have two goblets of your finest wine, if you please. Nothing too sweet."

The barkeep went behind the bar and filled two goblets, came around again and set them on Jarn's table before returning to the bar. Jarn took a sip and decided it would do. He glanced again at the painting and then heard someone coming down the stairs. He looked and saw Maiya. She smiled, and he forgot about the woman in the red dress.

Jarn stood up and pulled out a chair for Maiya. "Thank you for seeing me."

"It's my pleasure, Captain," she said and sat down.

Jarn sat down across from her. "I ordered some wine. Sloken mellowine, I think."

She took a sip. "Excellent," she pronounced.

"I want to ask you about the Gliffring Festival."

249

Her smile widened. "Do you mean to go? It's a fine treat for those of us who love music and dance and a bit of theater."

"I do, but it won't be the music and dancing I'm after—not this time, anyway."

Still smiling, she raised an eyebrow, reminding Jarn for just a moment of the woman in the red dress. "I take it your constabulary duties must interfere with your pleasure."

Jarn nodded. "Sadly, yes. But with a bit of luck, I may return to the festival before it's over."

"Well, then, I wish you a bit of luck and more. But what would you know about the festival?"

"How long does it go on?"

"As long as people are willing to perform, and as long as other people are willing to watch. But that's usually around two weeks. Some groups stay the whole time, others for only a few days."

"I presume it takes place on the Gliffring fairgrounds in Sloken."

She nodded. "Toward the front is an area that's like a big, shallow bowl. The better-known troupes perform on a stage that's set up at one end. Others perform here and there throughout the grounds. There's a place outside for food vendors to cook as well as places for people to pitch tents or park wagons."

"Do you talk to your fellow performers?"

"Oh, yes. Friendships are renewed, new friends are found, new romances are kindled, sometimes old ones are rekindled. Sometimes old feuds are revived as well."

"So, it isn't all harmony and fellow feeling."

"No, but then what is?"

"Tell me something, amid all these friendships and romances and occasional feuds, do folks ever switch from one troupe to another?"

She nodded. "Yes, sometimes. Now and then a troupe will disband for one reason or another, but a member might want to continue performing. Such a one may try to join another group."

"What about would-be performers, folk who might be new to the game? It would seem Gliffring might be just the place for them to try to jump in."

"Oh, yes, that's true. Gliffring is where many make their start. Even more try and fail."

"And what do those who fail do?"

Maiya shrugged. "Go back home to the life they hoped to escape."

There was a pause in the conversation then, but a comfortable one. They sipped their wine and glanced around or looked at one another. "You look as if you want to ask me something else," she said at length.

"I wondered what you would have done if you weren't singing with your little troupe."

"It doesn't bear thinking about," she said.

"I thought you might say something like that."

They finished their wine.

"I must go," Jarn said. "Thank you for speaking with me."

They stood up.

"Perhaps we'll speak again in Gliffring," Maiya said. "After you've attended to your business."

"Perhaps we will," he said.

**

251

The footsteps in the passageway stopped.

"What's this?" the man named Maekel shouted. A moment later, Aarla felt the rope binding Kurff's wrists break. At nearly the same moment, she heard the twang of a crossbow firing, and then a shout of pain from Kurff. She pushed her feet against the floor and heaved herself away from Kurff as he grabbed the rope binding him to the chair and slithered under it, finally freed. But the bolt from Maekel's crossbow had gone clean through Kurff's chest just below his left shoulder, and blood streamed from the wound.

Maekel drew his sword. Kurff picked up the chair and held it in front of him, the legs pointed at Maekel. He took a few steps sideways to put Hussert's body between them. Aarla, still holding Hussert's knife behind her, and still on her side, used her feet again to push herself into a position where she could observe what was happening. Maekel shot her a quick glance and then returned his gaze to Kurff.

"How long do you think you can hold that chair, Kurff?" Maekel said.

"Long as I need to," Kurff replied.

"That's a nasty wound I gave you."

"I've had worse."

Maekel stepped to his right. "You could bleed to death from a wound like that."

Kurff stepped to his right, keeping Hussert's body between himself and Maekel. "You're a bad shot, Maekel. If you want to play at being a rebel, you'll have to practice."

"That chair getting heavy yet?" Maekel asked, and he made a feint with his sword.

Kurff didn't flinch, and a moment later he took a quick step forward and thrust the chair toward Maekel, who backed up a step. Kurff, now only a couple of feet from Hussert's body, held his ground but didn't advance. Maekel sidestepped again and flicked the tip of his sword toward Kurff, who moved sideways to keep himself directly opposite his opponent.

Aarla shifted position again, her eyes focused on Maekel.

"That's a good, sturdy chair," Maekel said, moving sideways again. "Solid oak, it is. Cost me a deal of coin."

Kurff said nothing. The chair he held sank an inch or two. It dropped again, more this time, and two of its legs touched the floor.

Maekel sprang forward, his sword pointed at Kurff. Kurff lifted the chair and swung it awkwardly, nearly losing his grip on it. Maekel laughed and retreated.

Kurff set the chair down on two legs again and wiped his brow. "If you want to fight, give me my sword."

"He wants his sword, does he?" Maekel said.

Kurff, breathing heavily, backed up a step and set the chair down for a moment. He pressed his right hand against his wound, then wiped it on his shirt before picking up the chair again. He held it closer to his body than he had before, and it was barely off the ground.

"Bash his head in," Aarla called out to Kurff.

Maekel glared at her. "The little bitch speaks. I'll deal with you soon as I'm finished with him."

"Coward," she said.

"I'll enjoy cutting your throat," Maekel told her.

"Bash his head in, Master Kurff," Aarla said again.

But Kurff was leaning on the back of the chair, swaying slightly from side to side. Maekel turned his gaze from Aarla and started toward Kurff. Kurff backed up, dragging the chair with him. He moved behind Aarla and waited.

"Oh, very pretty," Maekel said. "Very pretty indeed. Using the girl as a shield. And she calls me the coward. The great Yellowshirt warrior hiding behind a mere girl to protect himself. You disgust me." He stepped over Hussert's body and advanced.

Kurff groaned and bent forward in a crouch. Aarla felt him take the knife from her hand. Maekel was within a sword's length of her position when Aarla looked at the doorway, opened her eyes wide, and screamed, "Oh, no!"

Maekel's eyes went wide with surprise, and he began to turn toward the doorway. At that moment, Kurff rose up suddenly and launched himself at Maekel. Maekel turned back toward Kurff again, but it was too late. Kurff plunged the knife into the tavern keeper's chest.

Maekel cried out, and his sword dropped to the floor. The expression on his face was one of surprise and horror. Kurff pulled the knife out of his chest and stepped back.

"Kurff, you rotten traitor," Maekel rasped, and he staggered back before swaying and dropping to his knees. A moment later he fell sideways to the floor and lay still.

Kurff cut the ropes binding Aarla's wrists and then the one holding her to the chair.

"Stay here," she whispered as soon as she was freed, and then she went to the passageway and peered down it. She saw no one and quietly made her way to the back room of the Posthole Inn. No one was there. She examined the canisters of herbs and spices sitting on shelves along one wall and found what she was looking for. She grabbed a canister and returned through the passageway to the small stone barn. Kurff was sitting on the chair he had wielded, his head drooped forward, his right hand pressed against his wound. He looked up when she came through the doorway.

"We have to leave," he said.

"Not just yet," Aarla said. She approached Kurff and set the canister on the floor. Then she took his shirt collar in both hands and gave a sudden tug. The shirt ripped along the shoulder seam, exposing the wound.

"So, you do have strong hands," Kurff murmured.

She nodded and then picked up the canister, took off the lid, and poured a coarse red powder on the wound. A moment later it was no longer bleeding.

"Ground spike pepper," she said. "Good for stopping bleeding. Also excellent in venison stew."

"You learn that from your father the virrling?"

Aarla shook her head. "My father would have used a spell to stop the bleeding. I learned the trick from the street mage I used to travel with."

"May the gods bless your street mage, wherever he is," Kurff said.

"We can leave now," Aarla replied.

Chapter 29

After speaking with Maiya, Jarn returned to the Rats Nest, where he was surprised to see Aarla, who was sitting at the meeting table next to Bleuek. Kurff was sitting there as well, bare-chested, and Liora was wrapping a long linen bandage around his chest and left shoulder. Braga and Grion were looking on, and Jarn wondered what new horrors had been visited upon the Talsie Grenling case.

He looked at Aarla. "You look as if you have a story to tell."

"I do, Captain," Aarla said.

Jarn nodded and then looked at Kurff. "You look as if you've a story to tell as well."

"I do," Kurff said. "My story and the lass's story have much in common."

"There's a statement I never expected to hear," Jarn said.

Aarla and Kurff filled him on their adventures underground and in the stone barn attached to the Posthole Inn.

"Commander Lahgoh has been informed," Grion told Jarn after the tales had been told. "He's sent some Riders to retrieve the bodies."

"Let me make sure I understand all this clearly," Jarn said to Kurff. "You've been spying on the proprietor of the Posthole Inn, who you suspected of being a rebel. Your confederate, a man named Hussert, now dead, left you a note with certain information, which led you to an underground rebel facility and then to the basement of the Posthole, where you were captured. Aarla, also taken

256

prisoner after venturing underground, was detained with you, but the two of you managed to free yourselves and kill the Posthole's proprietor, a rebel named Maekel. But the man who seemed to be Maekel's superior never revealed himself and is still at large."

Kurff, his wound treated and bandaged, was putting on a fresh tunic that someone had found for him. He winced as he stretched out his left arm, but he gritted his teeth and made no complaint. "That's right, Captain. I led Maekel to believe that I might be sympathetic to the rebel cause, hoping to glean news that way. All I managed to do was get Hussert killed, for which I'm sorry."

"You should go back to the Beldur and get some rest," Jarn said. "You and I will talk again."

Kurff nodded and stood up.

Braga and Grion stood up as well. "We'll go with you," Grion said. "To the Beldur."

Kurff snorted. "You going to tuck me into bed?"

"If you like," Braga said. "I'll even warm some milk for you."

"Save the milk for your cats," Kurff said. "If you're going to wait on me, you'll warm me up a goblet of spicewine instead."

Liora stood up. "I'll accompany you as well. I want to make sure your wound doesn't begin bleeding again."

Kurff raised an eyebrow and then made a slight bow in her direction. "Thank you, Captain. Your presence will be a vast improvement over this lot," he said, gesturing toward Braga and Grion.

"The insolence of these Yellowshirts," Braga said, shaking his head.

The four headed for the door.

"One other thing," Jarn called after them. The four stopped and turned to him. "Kurff, I thank you for your help. I—we—appreciate your courage. And your honor." He considered apologizing for suspecting the man of being a rebel but decided it wasn't the right time.

Kurff nodded to Jarn, and then he and his three escorts made their exit.

Moments after they left, Line Commander Lahgoh and Minister Respero entered the meeting room.

Bleuek and Aarla stood up.

"We'll be off as well," Bleuek said.

Jarn looked at Aarla. "Stay at the Mang tonight."

She frowned at him.

"Just this once," Jarn said. "Please."

Aarla shrugged and nodded, and then she and Bleuek turned toward the door and left the Rats Nest, leaving Jarn alone with Lahgoh and Respero.

"We have news to tell you," Lahgoh said to Jarn. "We'll go to your chamber."

A minute later, they were sitting at the round table in the alcove of Jarn's office, goblets of strong red in front of them. Jarn looked at Lahgoh expectantly, but Respero spoke first.

"Lord Grenling wants your search for his daughter called off," the minister said. "He complained about Vothan incompetence and stupidity, and he plans to have his own searchers take over the job."

"And you, of course, told him that he and his searchers could go bugger themselves if they thought we would agree to his insolence—in a much more diplomatic way, no doubt."

"I told him no such thing," Respero replied. "As of now, you are no longer tasked with finding Talsie

258

Grenling. For us, the case is closed. Lord Grenling has put Sir Tarris in charge of the new investigation."

Jarn didn't know whether to be delighted or outraged. "We shouldn't let Brythyners push us around," he muttered.

"They aren't," Respero said. "Anyway, Grenling has a point."

Jarn considered telling him and Lahgoh his latest thoughts about the now-aborted investigation but decided, for now, not to. For the time being, he would keep his new theory to himself.

"If you were to discover any clues, or even, perhaps, find the young woman, you are to inform the Brythyners," Lahgoh said. "But you're not to take any action yourself."

"Meanwhile, the treaty negotiations with Brythyn are temporarily suspended until Grenling decides to resume them," Respero said. "If he ever does."

"You should take some time off," Lahgoh said to Jarn. "Visit Rualgar for a few days, if you like."

"Perhaps I will," Jarn said. "I may want to talk to Lady Grenling one more time, if there's no objection."

"You had better hurry," Lahgoh said. "We're releasing her as a gesture of good will toward Brythyn. She'll be rejoining Lord Grenling."

Jarn frowned. "She didn't object?"

"Oh, no, she said she was eager to return to normal, and she also expressed every confidence that her own people would find her daughter."

"What of Sir Longboke and Willim Gilpin? Surely you won't let Grenling take Sir Longboke. The man threatened to have him tortured."

"Longboke stays here, for now, in custody," Respero said. "But eventually we'll have to turn him over to the

Brythyners. Willim Gilpin will be released to return to Brythyn or do whatever he pleases."

"I doubt he'll be returning to Brythyn," Jarn said. He stood up. "I'll go to Lady Grenling now. Thank you for your news."

Lahgoh and Respero stood up.

"And you'll take some time away?" Respero said. "To restore yourself, relax a bit?"

Jarn nodded. "By tonight, I'll be in another realm, drinking wine and listening to minstrels."

***

"I would like to ask you a question or two, if you don't mind," Jarn said to Lady Grenling. They were in the front room of her suite in the Mang, sitting across from one another on blue upholstered chairs. Late afternoon sunlight streamed in through the windows, casting the room in a soft glow. The light suited Lady Grenling, Jarn thought, softening her face, which bore a sad expression.

"Would you care for some tea, Captain, or some wine?" Lady Grenling asked.

Jarn shook his head. "No, thank you. I'll only trouble you for a few minutes, then I'll be off."

"It's no trouble, Captain. I've always enjoyed your company."

"And I yours—except once."

She heaved a sigh and looked genuinely remorseful. "If it's about the spell, Captain, I'm sorry. I felt I had no other choice. Anyway, it didn't work, not well enough, anyway."

Jarn didn't know whether to believe her. She seemed sincere, but he knew her skill at playing roles was equal to

260

that of any stage player. "Voths tend to be unreceptive to spells," he said. "If you hadn't caught me at a weak moment, it wouldn't have worked at all. I'm at fault as much as you are. I accept your apology."

"I'm glad. I assume you have been told that my diplomatic courtesy has been restored to me and that I will be returning with Lord Grenling to Brythyn."

Jarn nodded. "I wish you good fortune."

"Thank you." She hesitated a moment and then said, "Has there been any news about …"

"I and my people have been removed from the investigation of your daughter's disappearance. Your own people are assuming responsibility for the case. Sir Tarris is in charge."

Lady Grenling nodded. "I see. Well then, what questions do you have for me?"

"You used a candle and water and salt in your attempt to spell me. Are such things always necessary?"

"No, not always. There are different ways to cast spells."

"You also used words, a kind of rhyme. Are such words always needed?"

"Yes, as far as I know."

"Tell me, Lady Grenling, does Talsie have any spellcasting abilities?"

She hesitated a moment before replying. "I don't know."

"What do you believe?"

"I've suspected that she does, though I've never witnessed it."

"Did you base your suspicions on the notion that such skills run in families—like singing or a talent for playing the lute?"

Lady Grenling nodded. "Why do you ask, Captain?"

"I merely wondered and wanted to satisfy my curiosity. Now that the Voths are out of the investigation, it no longer matters." He stood up. "I'll take my leave now. All the best to you, Lady Grenling."

She stood up and extended her hand. "Perhaps we'll see one another again sometime."

He took her hand for a moment. It felt cooler than he remembered. "Perhaps we will," he said, hoping it wasn't true.

Chapter 30

Astil sat at a table in a back corner of the Candlewick Inn, a tidy, brightly lit establishment a couple of blocks from Gliffring's town square, where she could look through one of the large front windows and watch people coming and going on Delver Street, the main avenue through the town. Because of the festival, all the inns were full or their rooms spoken for, so Astil had to bribe the innkeeper to get a room there. Her room looked out onto the street and allowed a perfect view of the inn across the way, which was called the Laughing Lute. Getting a room with that view had boosted the price of the bribe. She had paid for the room and the bribe with Millardo's silver, which had brought a smile to her face.

She still had a half tankard of ale and part of a half-loaf of dark bread in front of her, but the wedge of cheese and the kepple slices she had ordered were gone. She twisted off a chunk of the crusty bread, put it in her mouth, and chewed, swallowing it down with a gulp of ale. Men occasionally entered the dining room, often in groups of two or three or four, and they always glanced around the dining room and always noticed the dark-haired woman sitting by herself in the back. Some of them nodded at her or smiled, but, getting no response, they quickly looked away, sometimes with a shrug, sometimes with a brief muttering under the breath. So far, no one had approached. If any decided to, she would show them her dagger and reward them with what she called her ice smile, a practiced look that had sent chills down the spines of more than one fearless knight.

She drained her tankard and placed it back on the table. She felt for the scarf around her neck—Talsie's scarf—and wrapped her right hand around it, not too tight, and then closed her eyes. A moment later, she smiled. *I know where you are, Talsie*, she thought. Then she frowned. The picture of Talsie that filled her mind was replaced by a picture of Aarla. Yet this time, she did not feel as if Aarla was following her. Why then did thoughts of the waif keep intruding?

Perhaps one day she should try to make an ally of the little witch. But the girl was as upright as the damned Vothan Riders, maybe more so. And yet, she had lived by her wits for years before meeting the Riders, so how upright could she really be? The two had more in common that either one of them would probably care to admit.

Too many more of these troublesome thoughts would drive Astil mad. She closed her eyes for a moment and thought about Talsie, pictured her again in her mind. She heard the sound of horses cantering and cartwheels rolling and glanced through the front window. Men on horseback rode by, carts and farm wagons as well, taking sheep or eggs or milk to the market. Red-robed freykons walked past, heading to the village querl, and carpenters and masons and other workers ambled toward taverns for a midday meal or back to their work. Food vendors strolled about calling out, "Meat pies" or "Roasted chicken legs" or "Kepples and pears for sale." Mingling among these familiar sorts were hordes of visiting minstrels, jugglers, dancers, and players, all come to town for the festival.

Astil finished her ale and stood up. Now that she was in Gliffring during the town's famed festival, it was time to enjoy some music, and she knew just the troupe she wanted most to hear.

***

Jarn reached Gliffring in the late afternoon and tried, without success, to get a room at an inn. He gave up after the sixth attempt, but persuaded the innkeeper of the Three-Eyed Mountain to let him stable his horse in the inn's stable and also rent a corner of the tack room to sleep that evening. It cost him nearly all the coin he had brought, but he had enough left over for a quick meal of lamb stew and a tankard of ale. As soon as he was finished, he headed for the fairgrounds, a quarter mile away.

The grounds were vast and green. A large stage had been constructed at one end, and beyond the stage lay a farm field, now covered with tents, that was even larger than the fairgrounds. Most of the performing groups would have a chance at the big stage, usually for only an hour or two during the two weeks of the fair, but there were other, casual venues along the edges of the grounds, where groups set up and tried to attract an audience. Sometimes singers would stroll through the grounds, singing and beckoning people to come and listen to their troupe. All during the festival, performing groups would come, sometimes for only a day or two, and then leave, making space for the next newcomers. When not on the main stage, most groups would take their turns at the informal places, hoping people would stop for a while and listen, maybe even toss a coin or two into the baskets they set out. Sellers of food and wine were gathered in the southwest corner of the grounds, sometimes venturing through the crowd with carts or barrows, calling out their offerings. Now and then Jarn caught the aroma of roasted meat or a freshly baked fruit pie as he strode through the crowd. He found himself scanning for cutpurses and chided himself for his constabulary zeal. The people in the crowd, where young and old mingled, seemed peaceable and relaxed, looking for nothing more than a night or two of entertainment, or perhaps a bit of romance. Here, for a couple of weeks, apprentices, milkmaids, and farm hands mingled easily with wealthy merchants, highborn ladies, and members of various royal courts.

Jarn wondered if he would see Maiya and her troupe, but he feared he might be a day ahead of them. No matter. His reason for attending the festival was not for his own pleasure, though he would surely like to hear—and talk to—Maiya again.

The air was beginning to turn cool but remained pleasant, the sun still shining brightly in a clear blue sky. As Jarn made his way through the crowded grounds, he ignored the jugglers and street mages and players and focused on the troupes of minstrels. It was the height of the festival, and there were dozens performing, each with a small audience. He stopped at one troupe and looked at the woman who was singing. She had a good, clear voice, well-trained but perhaps a bit too rehearsed, at least to Jarn's ear.

He left and found another group of minstrels, this one with two women singers. Neither was as good as the first, Jarn thought, but he was no expert. After a few minutes, he continued on his way, past a group of acrobats, a troupe of drummers, and a pair of stage players whose bawdy play was drawing loud laughs and more than a few gasps from their audience.

He stopped at none of those, proceeding slowly through the crowd, until he came across a group that reminded him of Maiya's, with two men playing instruments and two women singing.

He called up a mental image of Talsie Grenling, wishing he had brought the portrait of Talsie that Lady Grenling had given him. No matter. The two women singers were both older than Talsie and both had dark hair. Jarn waited until their song was finished, then he applauded for what he thought was an appropriate amount of time, and turned to walk away. And came face to face with Astil.

He stopped and stared at her. She looked as surprised as he felt, but her expression quickly turned to one of self-satisfaction.

"Astil," Jarn said.

She nodded. "Captain Jarn. I hope you didn't follow me here. You promised you wouldn't."

"I didn't," Jarn replied. "Though I'm glad to know that your gift did not fail you. You've found Talsie, I presume."

Astil nodded. "She's here in Gliffring. How did you catch on?"

"Someone I was speaking with mentioned that musical gifts often pass from parent to child, sometimes down through many generations. Other such gifts do as well, including spellcasting."

"You've lost me, Captain. Let us have this discussion over tankards of ale or wine, and you can clear it up." She pointed to a tavern with a sign depicting a blue cloud

267

against a pink sky. "The Blue Cloud will do nicely. My treat."

"I don't want to lose Talsie."

Astil gave him a sly smile. "Ah, but you haven't quite found her yet, have you?"

Jarn stared at her. "But she is here in Gliffring, is she not?"

Still smiling, Astil nodded and then headed toward the Blue Cloud. Jarn followed, glancing around at the milling crowd as he walked.

Inside the tavern, which was crowded, they found a small table near the front of the room and ordered two tankards of ale. Astil, true to her word, paid for them. "You were saying, Captain," she said after they had sampled their ales.

"Lady Grenling tried, and temporarily succeeded, in putting a spell on me," Jarn said.

Astil stared at him. "The lady is a spellcaster?"

Jarn nodded. "I believe her daughter is one as well. It's another of the gifts that pass down through generations."

"Ah, yes, I think I see what you're getting at. You believe that Talsie had her mother's gift and used it to put a spell on that knight—Sir Longboke."

Jarn nodded.

"To what end?"

"To get away. To become lost and stay lost."

"Yes, but why?"

"That's what I plan to ask the young lady—as soon as you tell me precisely where in Gliffring I'll find her."

"I'll do better than that," Astil said. "I'll take you to her. And later, after we've returned to Skunnik, you will return my gold to me. Isn't that right, Captain?"

Jarn raised the tankard to his lips, tilted his back, and took a long drink of ale. When he set the tankard back on the table, Astil was staring at him with raised eyebrows and an expectant smile.

Jarn shook his head and laughed. "Yes, Astil, that is right. I will return your gold to you."

A bright smile wreathed Astil's face. She downed her ale and called for two more.

Before they had finished their second rounds, Astil looked toward the staircase that led to the guest rooms and smiled.

Jarn looked in that direction and saw a pretty young woman with short dark hair descending the stairs.

Astil called out to her, "You there, young mistress who's so good with a song."

The young woman stopped and turned to her. "You heard me sing."

"Yes, with those minstrels from Rynland—the Restless Rovers, I think you call yourselves."

"I'm not one of them," the young woman said. She gave a little laugh. "Not yet, anyway. They were only trying me out."

"They're fools if they don't take you on."

The young woman smiled. "Thank you. I'll tell them you said so."

"My name is Astil. This is Jarn."

"I'm pleased to know you. I am Tayrana. But I should be getting back to the fairgrounds. There may be other troupes willing to give me a trial."

"Let us stand you to an ale or some mellowine first," Astil said. "There is something we would discuss with you."

"Are you members of a minstrel troupe?"

269

"I'm afraid not," Jarn said.

The young woman's smile vanished. "I should go," she said.

Astil stood up. Jarn stood up as well.

"We can talk in the back room or outside," Astil said. "There's a small commons less than two blocks away. It will only take a moment, Talsie."

The color drained from the young woman's face, and Jarn, thinking she might faint, made ready to catch her.

"What do you want?" Talsie Grenling whispered.

"Only to talk to you," Astil said.

"We've been looking for you," Jarn said. "We need to speak with you."

Tears welled in Talsie's eyes, and her face seemed to crumple, like a flower wilting under a desert sun. She looked around, as if searching for help, but there was no help at hand. Her shoulders slumped. She heaved a heavy sigh and gave a barely perceptible nod. "The commons, then," she murmured and headed toward the door.

Astil and Jarn followed Talsie out of the tavern, Jarn hoping she wouldn't run and cause an unpleasant scene. She didn't. They entered a street still bustling with people, some heading for the fairgrounds, others looking for a tavern where they could enjoy a tankard of ale or a goblet of Telnan mellowine before returning to the fair.

The three headed east, Astil and Talsie walking side by side, Jarn a couple of paces behind them, his eyes on Talsie. After walking two blocks, they entered the commons, a small, grassy rectangle dotted with pink and yellow wildflowers. Astil pointed to the far corner, where a low wooden bench, unoccupied, waited. "There."

The grass swished as they walked past a group of six people who were perched on the ground around a blue blanket. Spread across it were two wicker baskets of bread and cheese and shiny red kepples, three plump wineskins, a lute, two horns, and a pipe. Jarn thought about Maiya and wondered if he would see her at the festival. He knew it was unlikely and once again focused his attention on Talsie.

When they reached the bench, Astil and Talsie sat down. Jarn remained standing, watching the young woman who had been the object of his investigation. She was staring down at the ground in front of her, her face a mask of despair. Jarn had spent days trying to figure out how to find her, but now that he had succeeded, he felt no sense of triumph. He glanced at Astil. She gazed back at him evenly. He wondered what she was thinking. Probably about her gold.

Talsie looked up at Jarn, the expression on her face changing suddenly from dejection to fierceness. "What do you want with me?"

"I'm a captain in the Vothan Riders," Jarn said. "I have constabulary duties in what is now the Acrinite Territory. When you disappeared, everyone assumed you had been abducted. It was my duty to investigate."

"I wasn't abducted."

"No, you weren't," Jarn said. "But you made certain everyone would believe you had been. Why?"

"I'd rather not say."

"Sir Longboke is in custody, accused of a crime that never took place."

Talsie closed her eyes and furrowed her brow. "He's innocent, clearly."

"Clearly," Jarn said. "And when you come back with me to Skunnik, you can prove it."

"I'm not going back with you."

271

"We shall see," Jarn said. "Why did you carry out this trickery?"

Talsie hesitated a moment and then glared at Jarn. "To get away, if you must know. Now that I've succeeded, I'll not return. If you want to take me back, you'll have to kill me first and take back my dead body."

"Captain Jarn is a man of honor," Astil said. "He would never kill an innocent young woman." She turned to Jarn and raised an eyebrow. "Would you, Captain?"

"No, of course not," Jarn said. He looked at Talsie. "You said you wanted to get away—what did you mean?"

"I wanted to get away from my father." Talsie glanced down at the ground for a moment and then back at Jarn. "And my mother."

"A common wish among children, especially those with strict parents," Jarn said. "But you're no longer a child."

"My desire is no mere childish fancy. My father doesn't want me and never did. He wanted a son, and my mother can no longer bear children. He also decided to marry me off to Lord Keddro, against my most fervent wishes. As for my mother, she is … unwell in her mind. I feel sorry for her, but she seems to prefer it that way."

"She told me you and she were close, that you confided in her."

Talsie gave a brief, mirthless laugh. "And so she may believe, but I assure you it is not true."

"Lady Grenling was in custody, too," Jarn said. "So was Willim Gilpin."

Talsie looked surprised. "Why?"

"Your mother tried to put a spell on me."

Talsie seemed about to speak, but apparently thought better of it and made no reply. She avoided Jarn's gaze

272

and stared past him at the group of minstrels in the middle of the commons who were still enjoying their brief break from performing.

"Have you nothing to say about your mother's spellcasting gift?" Jarn asked.

Talsie, still looking past Jarn, shook her head.

Jarn decided to change direction. "During our investigation of your supposed abduction, we discovered the scheme that you and your mother hatched with Willim and Sir Longboke. The one you betrayed."

"I had to," Talsie said. "I needed to get away—from all of them."

"Why?" Jarn asked.

Tears streamed from Talsie's eyes and she shook her head slowly.

"Best to tell the whole story," Astil said, her voice as gentle as Jarn had ever heard it.

Talsie gazed into the distance again for a moment and then turned to Jarn. "Once the Voths took control of Acrin, I suspected that my upcoming marriage to Lord Keddro would be called off. The thought of such a happy outcome, of course, came as a relief to me. I could hardly wait for the official word to come. When a letter from Lord Keddro arrived by a messenger, I went into my father's private chamber one day when he was gone and found the letter. It was locked in his desk, but I had no trouble solving the lock and finding the letter."

"Ah, a kindred heart," Astil said, smiling. "If I ever need an apprentice …"

Jarn frowned at her and then turned back to Talsie. "And did this letter confirm your suspicions about canceling the wedding?"

273

"Oh, yes," Talsie said. "But not for the reason I suspected."

"Which was?"

"With the demise of Acrin as a sovereign realm, the marriage would no longer signify a bond between equals. That was part of it, but there was another, much more important reason."

"Go on," Jarn said.

"The letter also confirmed that Lord Keddro is a leader of the Acrinite rebels, and thus it would not have been wise to allow me to reside in his castle."

Jarn stared at her openmouthed. "Lord Keddro is a rebel leader?"

Talsie nodded. "And my father is helping him. If the High Hext should return to power and restore Acrin to its former glory, both will be amply rewarded."

"The High Hext won't be returning to power," Jarn said. "And if what you say about Lord Keddro is true, we'll deal with him appropriately. I don't suppose you have the letter, do you?"

Talsie shook her head. "No. But after I read it, my father became wary, as if he suspected that I knew what was in it. Perhaps I did not put the letter back just the way I found it. Whatever the reason, he became suspicious. And I'm reasonably certain that he meant to do away with me."

"Do away with you how?"

Talsie shrugged. "I don't know. He and Lord Keddro would have arranged something clever."

Astil frowned. "Are you telling us that you believe your father was planning to kill you?"

Talsie nodded. "He cares nothing about me. He cares only about power. Power and gold."

274

"Gold, of course, does have its peculiar charms," Astil murmured, half to herself.

"So, in fear for your life, you went to your mother to concoct a scheme to get away, all the while planning to betray the others," Jarn said.

"My mother was just as eager to leave. She often spoke about it, and she was ... she was having ..."

"We know about her romance with Willim Gilpin," Jarn said.

Astil gaped at Jarn. "Truly?"

Jarn nodded.

"I told my mother that I knew about their affair, knowing she would tell Willim," Talsie said. "I figured that once they realized someone else knew, they might be more inclined to follow through on my mother's strong desire to be free of my father."

"How did you involve Sir Longboke?"

Talsie looked down. "He's devoted to me."

"So you decided to take advantage of that."

Talsie nodded. "Yes." She looked at Jarn. "But you'll set him free, will you not?"

Jarn shrugged. "Your father believes he's guilty of a crime."

"You know better."

"Your father does not."

"Why should that matter?"

"Because if I tell Lord Grenling that I have proof that Sir Longboke is innocent, he, Lord Grenling, will want to see the proof."

"And I'm the proof," Talsie said in a soft voice.

Jarn nodded.

"I'm not going back," Talsie said. "You'll have to find another way."

275

"Is Longboke still in Vothan custody?" Astil asked Jarn. "Or has he been removed to Brythyn?"

"Still at the Mang," Jarn said.

Astil flashed a smile. "Then the solution is simple. I'll rescue him from his imprisonment, and he'll be free to go on his way."

Jarn frowned at her. "You'll do no such thing."

"Have you a better idea?"

"Yes," Jarn said.

"I won't let you take Talsie back with you," Astil said.

"How will you stop me?"

"You don't want to find out."

"You won't get your gold."

Astil shrugged. "Some things are more important than gold."

Jarn gaped at her, hardly believing what he had just heard. He waited, as if she might give him a wink or flash a grin, signaling that she had been japing. Instead, she met his gaze with an expression that bespoke unwavering determination.

"Very well," he said at length, still staring at Astil. "I'll return to Skunnik and have word sent to Lord Grenling that Talsie is alive and well in Gliffring and looking to join a troupe of minstrels. He'll send his own men to look for her." Jarn decided, at least for now, not to mention that the Voths had been removed from the investigation and Lord Grenling's men were already searching for Talsie.

"We seem to be at an impasse," Astil said with a cold smile. "How exciting."

No one spoke for a few moments. Jarn heard the group of minstrels behind him laugh, no doubt at some clever jape one of them had made. A bird began singing somewhere above them, and another bird answered with its own song. Jarn felt the warm sun on his neck, closed his eyes for a moment, and breathed in the pleasant afternoon air. He felt lightheaded and thought he heard music in the distance.

Jarn opened his eyes and looked at Astil, who gazed back at him without blinking. Her face wore an expression he couldn't read, but he thought he detected equal measures of quiet defiance and hopeful anticipation. He turned to Talsie. He had made his decision.

Chapter 31

DAY 7

Jarn was sitting in Lahgoh's private chamber in the Mang, watching as his commander lit another candle before going to the sideboard to pour two tankards of Vothan strong red from a pewter pitcher. Lahgoh handed a tankard to Jarn and then sat down behind his desk. They both took long drinks, followed by another. Lahgoh was smiling, but he was eyeing Jarn as if the captain had walked in with mud on his tunic.

"How did you enjoy your time off?" Lahgoh asked.

"Very well, thank you. I enjoyed some music at the Gliffring Festival."

"Excellent. Tell me about it."

"I will," Jarn said. "But I'm hoping you'll fill me in on developments here first."

"Of course. Aarla has left Skunnik to spend some time with her father, much to Saddlemaster Bleuek's regret. Kurff is at the Beldur Palace, still recovering from his wound. Lady Grenling has returned to Brythyn with Lord Grenling, and I also released Willim Gilpin. Lord Grenling demanded that I release Sir Longboke to his custody, but I declined."

"He's still here at the Mang?"

Lahgoh nodded.

"We can let him go," Jarn said.

Lahgoh leaned forward and eyed Jarn. "Why should we let him go?"

"In Gliffring, I ran into Astil. The two of us had a nice conversation with Talsie Grenling."

278

Lahgoh's eyes went wide. "You found her?"

"Yes. Astil found her first. I've returned her gold to her."

"Is Talsie well?"

"Yes, quite well."

"Where have you put her? I would like to speak with her before you return her to her family."

"I didn't bring her back," Jarn said. "She's fleeing from her family. I decided to let her. She won't be going back to Brythyn."

Lahgoh narrowed his eyes at Jarn. "Best tell me the whole story, Captain."

"Talsie learned that Lord Keddro is a rebel leader, and that her father is aiding him. She had reason to believe that Lord Grenling suspected that she knew, and she was afraid he might do her harm, even do away with her."

Lahgoh was staring at Jarn as if he had just grown another head. "Lord Keddro a rebel leader?"

"So Talsie told me."

"Had she proof?"

"She told me that she read a letter from Lord Keddro that was meant for Lord Grenling's eyes only. The proof is in the letter, which, alas, she did not have when I spoke with her."

"Do you believe her? Do you believe such a mad tale of intrigue?"

Jarn nodded.

Lahgoh eyed him. "I've always known you to be sensible, Jarn, and to have keen instincts in such matters. But this tale stretches the boundaries of credibility."

"If we can manage to keep a close watch on Lord Keddro without him suspecting, we'll find out if what Talsie told me is true."

"Where is Talsie now?"

Jarn shrugged. "Probably still in Gliffring. Or anywhere."

"I see," Lahgoh murmured. He heaved a sigh and then got up to fetch the pitcher of wine. He refilled both tankards.

"What will we do about Lord Keddro?" Jarn asked after they had both taken long gulps of wine.

"We have no proof of his guilt, so we can't seize him," Lahgoh replied. "But I'll consider your suggestion that we watch him closely."

"We might consider sending a few spies to Brythyn as well, to keep eyes on Lord Grenling."

"Perhaps," Lahgoh replied. "But we can't spread ourselves too thin. Besides, Brythyn is a sovereign realm. Perhaps I should talk to Respero about these matters."

Jarn shrugged. "Perhaps. Or perhaps not."

"Tell me, Jarn, how did you manage to find her?"

"It was something Respero said, plus a few other thoughts that had been rolling around in my head, banging against one another but not adding up to anything until Respero made his comment."

"What comment?

"About Talsie putting a spell on Longboke. He was right, that's how it happened, how she made her escape. She's a spellcaster, like her mother. She placed a spell on Longboke with her singing voice, and then ran, from her father, from her mother, and from the little group of schemers led by her mother. She cut her hair short, dyed it

280

dark, and headed for Gliffring, hoping to join a minstrel troupe."

"Did she? Join a minstrel troupe, I mean?"

"By now, probably so. The girl has the gift of song, though her father tried to squelch it."

"You realize that this puts an end to the treaty with Brythyn."

"I thought that was already finished. Anyway, some things are more important than treaties."

Lahgoh sighed and then picked up the pitcher of wine. "Another?"

Jarn shook his head and stood up. "I'm off to the Millstone Tavern. Our friend Astil has promised to stand me to a round or two of ale. Care to join us?"

Lahgoh raised an eyebrow and shook his head. "I think not, but thanks just the same. Let me know tomorrow how you fared with Astil—assuming you survive the encounter."

"I'll do that," Jarn said before heading for the door.

THE END

THE END

www.ingramcontent.com/pod-product-compliance
Lightning Source LLC
Chambersburg PA
CBHW011458170626
46814CB00008B/2948